MERCY KILLING

*Death's not so simple
when there's money involved...*

When affluent New Yorker Joyce Hauptman
dies suddenly, the investigator suspects something other than natural causes. Joyce's
husband, Charles, stands to inherit her wealth
and is the obvious suspect, but Detective
Lenny Shaw quickly discovers that things
aren't what they seem. As Charles maintains
his innocence, and the influence of his powerful father-in-law intrudes, Lenny is hurled
towards a conclusion that is as shocking as it
is violent.

*Stephen Solomita titles available from
Severn House Large Print*

Monkey in the Middle
Cracker Bling

MERCY KILLING

Stephen Solomita

Severn House Large Print
London & New York

This first large print edition published 2011
in Great Britain and the USA by
SEVERN HOUSE PUBLISHERS LTD of
9-15 High Street, Sutton, Surrey, SM1 1DF.
First world regular print edition published 2009 by
Severn House Publishers Ltd., London and New York.

British Library Cataloguing in Publication Data

Solomita, Stephen.
  Mercy killing.
  1. Police--New York (State)--New York--Fiction.
  2. Chronically ill--Death--Fiction. 3. Detective and
  mystery stories. 4. Large type books.
  I. Title
  813.5'4-dc22

  ISBN-13: 978-0-7278-7954-7

Severn House Publishers support The Forest Stewardship Council
[FSC], the leading international forest certification organisation. All
our titles that are printed on Greenpeace-approved FSC-certified
paper carry the FSC logo.

MIX
Paper from
responsible sources
FSC® C018575
www.fsc.org

Printed and bound in Great Britain by the
MPG Books Group, Bodmin, Cornwall.

One

As crime scenes go, this one is deliberately understated. A cruiser parked in the driveway, lights off, the engine shut down, a morgue wagon with two attendants inside parked behind the cruiser. The morgue wagon's headlights are off, but the engine's running and the interior light casts a dim glow over the passengers. One of the attendants is asleep with his arms folded across the steering wheel and his head resting in his hands – no surprise as it's four o'clock in the morning. The other is reading a tabloid newspaper which he holds a few inches from his eyes.

There are two cars parked at the curb on either side of the driveway. The first, a Toyota Prius belonging to the office of the Medical Examiner, is empty. The second, a Ford Crown Victoria, is occupied by my boss, Detective-Lieutenant Carl Morelli. He's sitting behind the wheel, smoking a cigarette.

And that's it. No yellow tape, no crime scene van, no crime scene cops in paper jumpsuits, no paramedics, no reporters.

But the scene's incongruous anyway. Jamaica Estates is one of the most affluent neighborhoods in the New York borough of Queens and the three-story colonial to my right, with its slate

5

roof and fluted chimneys, is suitably impressive. It's the house my mother's dreamed about all her life.

I get out of the car, instinctively hunching my shoulders against the cold. It's only October 7, but the temperature is in the low forties and there's enough wind to clatter through the branches of a red oak at the edge of the property. I glance up as the moon ducks behind a cloud, emerges a few seconds later only to vanish again, the clouds flowing across the sky like breakers over a troubled sea.

'You should thank your lucky stars,' Morelli declares when I get into his car. He's got the heater going and the interior's warm enough to be comforting.

'For what?'

'That you're not gonna be workin' in some alley littered with needles and crack vials, freezin' your ass off.'

The truth being the truth – not to mention the obvious being the obvious – I acknowledge Morelli's pronouncement with a simple nod. I don't like Morelli, not at all. Somewhere along the line, he assumed the cops under his command were plotting against him. Maybe he was born suspicious, I have no way to know. But I do know that he second-guesses every move his detectives make, as I know that two of my fellow detectives have turned snitch and that I commonly discover my case files out of place, or the documents within those files out of sequence.

I don't take this personally because Lieutenant

Morelli's an equal-opportunity snoop, but I'm sure about the files because I have a great memory, a definite plus for working detectives.

Morelli tosses the remains of his smoke onto a flagstone path. 'So, whatta ya know, Shaw?'

'About this case?'

'Yeah.'

'Nothing. Me and Lowenstein spent most of the tour looking for Angel Morales.'

'You find him?'

'We were close before you called me out here.'

Morelli narrows his eyes, an attempt to intimidate. He thinks I'm cracking wise and he's right. But I don't react. 'This guy, Hauptman,' he says, 'had a sick wife. I'm talkin' about FUBAR, Shaw, as in fucked up beyond all repair. She had a stroke five years back and she's been helpless ever since. Now she's dead and the death investigator's suspicious. He thinks she mighta been poisoned.'

There was a time when a forensic pathologist from the Medical Examiner's office attended every suspicious death in New York. No more. Doctors are too expensive. Now the city uses death investigators the way lawyers use paralegals.

'You're figuring what, boss, a mercy killing?'

'Maybe.' Morelli leans toward me, his breath reeking of tobacco. 'Or maybe Charles Hauptman got tired of payin' the nurses, or changin' his wife's shitty diapers. Or maybe there's a high-end insurance policy out there. From what the nurse says, Hauptman was in charge of his wife's care for six hours a day. He did every-

7

thing the nurses did, including deliver food and meds through a tube that went into his wife's stomach. If you can deliver food and meds through a tube, you can deliver a poison. Who's to know?'

'What's her name?' I ask. 'The wife?'

The question takes Morelli by surprise. His mouth narrows and his eyes flick up to the roof liner above his head. Morelli's a big-time Catholic, especially when it comes to abortion. He once told me he'd vote for Osama bin Laden before he'd vote for a politician who supported baby-killers. Sitting next to him while he fumbles for a name, I'm certain that mercy killers fare no better on his list of offenses against the heavenly order.

'I don't know,' he finally says. 'I don't remember her name. What difference does it make? Murder is murder.'

'Is that what the DI said, that we're lookin' at a homicide?'

'No, only that he's *very* suspicious.' Morelli wags a finger in my direction. 'But I know what happened here. I can smell it. And what I want you to do is get a confession.'

'Whether he did it or not?'

'Look, Shaw...' Morelli stops with his mouth still open, the annoyed look on his face slowly dissolving. 'Do me a favor,' he says. 'I was a homicide detective for ten years and I worked hundreds of cases, so don't mistake me for some bureaucrat who spent his career behind a desk. My gut's tellin' me the guy's dirty and I want you to work him over while he's still vulnerable.

8

And forget the boo-hoo routine. Check your sympathy at the door and do your fucking job.'

I know I should keep my big mouth shut, that Morelli won't be dissuaded, but I can't resist the obvious. 'If the wife was poisoned, the ME's gonna find traces of the poison in her blood or her tissues. So what's the point of subjecting the husband to an interrogation before the autopsy? Suppose the DI's wrong and the poor slob's innocent?'

Morelli stares into my eyes for a moment. Another attempt to scare me, but I don't look away. Finally, he decides to ignore my comment altogether.

'I kept everything low key because I don't want Hauptman to think he's a suspect. Routine, routine, routine. That's what I told him and that's how I want you to start your play. No reason to read him his rights, just a few questions, so sorry. You got that, Shaw?'

'Sure thing, boss.'

Morelli shakes his head. 'Sometimes,' he tells me, 'I swear I think I'm cursed.'

Hauptman's living room is bigger than my one-bedroom apartment in Long Island City. The furnishings are old, heavy and comfortable, and the oil paintings on the wall, mostly landscapes, are vaguely familiar. Above the fireplace, a full-figure portrait of a man in a striped business suit hangs by itself. The man wears a straw hat, a skimmer, and he carries a thin walking stick. A gold watch chain, heavy and substantial, crosses his vest. The family patriarch, no doubt, he looks directly at me, his eyes the color of slate, the Vandyke covering his chin sharp as a spear point.

Mounted on the frame, a plaque reveals the subject's name, Otto T. Baum, and a date: 1916.

The room is empty except for the death investigator, a Sikh named Amar Singh. Amar's perched on one end of a long couch. At my approach, he taps his blue turban and glances at his watch.

'I do not work for the police department, Leonard,' he informs me. 'I am working for the medical examiner.'

I assume he's complaining about the wait, but as I didn't cause the delay, I don't feel especially remorseful. I nod at the coffee cup on the table.

'There any more of that, Amar?'

'In the kitchen.' He points to a door twenty feet away. 'Through the dining room.'

Cup in hand, Singh follows me to the kitchen where I find a middle-aged woman and a uniformed cop. Obviously a nurse, the woman wears a white blouse, white pants and white running shoes. The cop I know fairly well. His name is Carter and what he's doing, without being too obvious about it, is keeping an eye on the nurse.

The nurse is seated before a small table, hovering over a cup and saucer. I smell bourbon in the cup, bourbon on her breath, and it's obvious that she's been crying.

I offer my hand. 'Detective Shaw. I'm sorry for your loss.'

For a long moment, she examines my face, just

10

drunk enough, apparently, to stare without apology. I favor her with a fatherly expression. Having passed my fortieth birthday a year ago, I can now do fatherly and get away with it, even though I've never been a father and hope never to become one.

'Shirley Borders.' She lays her palm against mine without gripping my fingers. 'You'll have to forgive me. I'm not doin' so good.'

'You were close to the deceased?'

'The way you say that? Deceased? Like Joyce was some kind of thing, instead of a human being.'

I toss Officer Carter a hard look, wondering if maybe he, too, has been helping himself to the bourbon. He offers a lopsided smile in return, pretty much confirming my suspicions.

'Sorry, Nurse Borders, I didn't mean to offend you. Were you close to Mrs Hauptman?'

'I've been taking care of Joyce since she came out of the hospital five years ago. Naturally, I've bonded to her. That always happens. But I can't speak for Joyce. She was too damaged for me to know what she was thinking.'

'Was she in a vegetative state?'

'What do you know about vegetative states? You a doctor, maybe a neurologist?'

I ignore the confrontational tone, though I'm well on the way to concluding that rapport is off the table. 'My Aunt Margaret,' I tell her, 'she had an allergic reaction to shellfish and stopped breathing for about six minutes. Her diagnosis is permanent vegetative state.'

Somewhere in her fifties, if not her early

11

sixties, the nurse is a heavy-set black woman with braided hair which she's pulled into a bun. Her thick arms are folded over her chest and her chin has a defiant tilt. Though she isn't laughing at the moment, the corners of her eyes are marked by deep laugh lines.

'Sometimes Joyce was there and sometimes she wasn't. But she was breathing on her own. She wasn't on a ventilator.'

Singh raises a corrective finger. 'The deceased did not breathe through her nose or her mouth. She breathed through a tracheotomy.' He turns in my direction, yet somehow fails to perceive how annoyed I am at the interruption. 'That means through a tube in her throat.'

'Did she speak?' I ask the nurse.

'No, she didn't. But she could sometimes signal yes or no with eye blinks.'

'Sometimes?'

'Yeah.' Nurse Borders lifts her cup and drinks. 'Sometimes.'

'So, what was her life like, when she was aware?'

'You bein' sarcastic?'

I pour myself a cup of coffee, using Officer Carter's mug, which smells of booze as I knew it would. There's an open carton of milk by the refrigerator and I add a few drops, deciding, as I watch the coffee lighten, that I've had enough bullshit for one night. I cross the room and take a seat across from Nurse Borders.

'Listen up, nurse, because I'm not gonna repeat myself. I have a few questions for you, a few questions that I expect you to answer. You

12

can answer them here or you can answer them at the precinct. It's up to you.'

Nurse Borders stares at me in a hopeless attempt to prove that she isn't intimidated. But I'm not bluffing and she knows it.

'Charles,' she finally says, 'he loved that woman. He was devoted to her. As I hope to stand before my Lord, detective, I've been a nurse for thirty-five years and I never met anybody like him.' Shirley Borders shakes her head. 'Among the nurses, we had this little joke. Like what was wrong with us that we couldn't find a man who'd do for us like Charles did for Joyce? Ya know, he could've dumped her in a nursing home, visited every other Sunday. He could've divorced her and found himself a trophy wife. But he didn't. He brought her home, he cared for her.'

She begins to cry, the tears running down her cheeks to collect on her chin, but she doesn't look away. 'At night, before he went to sleep, he used to come into her room and kiss her on the forehead. "Love ya, honey." That's what he told her, whether she was awake or asleep. "Love ya, honey." You know what my husband does when he gets into bed? He rolls onto his side and farts.'

I let that sit for a minute, then ask, 'Except for the stroke, how was Mrs Hauptman's general health?'

Nurse Borders releases a sigh that goes on and on. 'Joyce had her problems, Lord knows. She had urinary-tract infections, three or four. That's common when patients have an indwelling catheter. And she had two pneumonias that I recall. One about a week after she came out of the hospital, another maybe eight months ago. But the seizures were the worst of it.'

'How often did they come?'

'Two or three times a month. You could tell they hurt her real bad. Sometimes, she'd cry afterwards. That was awful hard on Charles, awful hard, because there was nothin' he could do.'

'No medications?'

'We tried everything from Neurontin to Dilantin to Valium, but...'

Her voice drops away and I let the silence build. Though my bullshit radar is on full alert, I'm sensing defiance, not deception. Nurse Borders is pissed, possibly with Amar Singh who already questioned her. Beyond that, she's telling a story that she believes.

'What about recently?' I finally ask. 'Any recent changes?'

Her eyes drop to her hands. 'Nothin' special.'

Amar Singh chooses this moment to intervene. 'The rash and the gastroenteritis, what about them? Are they not recently occurring?'

'Joyce was on ampicillin for an infected tooth, as I already told you.' The nurse's tone is sharper now and she's staring at Amar. 'Whenever she was on antibiotics, especially ampicillin, she developed a fungal rash and gastroenteritis, and this time was no exception. We were treating the rash with Lotrisone and the diarrhea with Kaopectate. If you don't believe me, all you have to do is check her meds. They're on a shelf

14

in the armoire.'

Nurse Borders turns to me. 'All homecare nurses make notes at the end of every shift. If you read mine, you'll see that the rash and the diarrhea began two days after we started Joyce on ampicillin. Go back a little further, you'll see that Joyce was treated for the same condition about five months ago with the same result. Now my man over here...' She pauses long enough to jerk a thumb in Singh's direction. 'My man here isn't a doctor and he isn't a cop, either. He's a wannabe out to make trouble for decent folk. So, if he's got your ear, you might wanna take a step back.'

I look up at Officer Carter. He's leaning against the wall, punching a text message into his cellphone. 'You get Nurse Borders' address and phone number?' I ask him.

'Yeah.'

'What about the other nurses?'

'Got them, too.'

'Good man.' I turn back to Nurse Borders. 'You can leave.'

'Can I get my things from Joyce's room?'

'What things?'

'I have a stethoscope and a blood-pressure cuff.'

I slide my chair back and stand up. The kitchen is huge, with a granite-topped island and a breakfast nook large enough to accommodate a table and six chairs. 'Did the Hauptmans have children?'

'Uh-uh.'

'You know why?'

The nurse laughs. 'Charles is a very formal man. Very proper. I would no more ask him a personal question than I'd ask a stranger.'

'What about other relatives, brothers and sisters?'

'Charles has a brother, Terence. He calls pretty often – I know because I answer the phone when Charles goes out – but he never came to visit, not while I was around.'

'Were there any visitors at all?'

'Joyce's father visited every couple of weeks. He's some kind of big shot with the city.' She pauses long enough to draw a breath. 'Now, can I get my stuff?'

'No, you can't, you'll have to come back after the autopsy.'

'Does that mean you think Charles had something to do with...'

'What I think is none of your business.'

But Shirley's not going quietly. She polishes off the last drop of her fortified coffee, then lets me have it. 'Tell me somethin', detective. Did they drain out every drop of human sympathy before they gave you that badge? Charles Hauptman is hurtin' bad. I mean real, real bad. And what are you gonna do? You're gonna drag his wife down to the morgue and cut her into pieces. And why? Because some damn fool whispered nonsense in your ear?'

But Shirley's got it all wrong. If a death investigator orders an autopsy, that autopsy is performed. The medical examiner doesn't work for the police department or for the district attorney. He's a bureaucracy unto himself. But I

16

don't bother to explain the facts of life. What's the point?

'Officer Carter will escort you to your car, nurse.' I hand her my business card. 'And I expect you to make yourself available if I need you in the future.'

Like any good detective, I lie at the drop of a hat. I lie about evidence I don't have, witnesses and surveillance cameras that don't exist, snitches who never dropped that dime. But I wasn't lying when I told Nurse Borders about my Aunt Margaret, the one in a permanent vegetative state. I'd been to see her at the Cabrini Nursing Home in lower Manhattan only a few weeks before, when I provided moral support to my mother. So I'm not surprised by anything I find in Joyce Hauptman's first-floor room, including Joyce Hauptman. There's the equipment, the compressor, the feeding pump, the IV pump, the hospital bed with its crank handle, an oxygen concentrator on wheels. And there's Joyce herself, with her legs pulled so far up they rest against her chest like the blades of a folding knife. Her feet are arched, the toes bending toward the heels, and her toes are folded, one over the other. I can't see her left hand, but her right is little more than a claw, while her mouth is twisted into a grimace that might be easily mistaken for agonized. She could be anywhere from forty to seventy years old.

Talk about misnomers. You hear vegetative state and you imagine Sleeping Beauty in her bed, resting comfortably. I mean, vegetables are immobile, right? A pile of tomatoes in a super-market doesn't move, a peach on a tree just hangs there. OK, maybe the peach sways a bit when the wind's up, but it doesn't move on its own. Human beings in a vegetative state, on the other hand, go through regular cycles, asleep and awake, and when they're awake they commonly experience involuntary contractions as the damaged neurons in their brains fire randomly. Over time – and what do they have except time? – they fold in on themselves, as if withdrawing still further from the world.

I think the obvious thoughts: this is a blessing, nobody should have to live this way, no family should have to deal with injuries on this scale. Amar stands next to the bed, holding the blanket. He's revealed Joyce's back and wasted buttocks. The rash Nurse Borders spoke about is evident. Joyce's skin is bright red, even in death.

'You have a time of death?' I ask.

'According to Nurse Borders, the victim's breathing became labored in the early evening and she stopped breathing altogether at eleven-thirty. This is consistent with the lividity, rigor and body temperature I observed when I arrived at one o'clock.'

'Her breathing was labored, but nobody called 911?'

'There was a Do Not Resuscitate order in place. Even if paramedics were called in, they could do nothing.'

'Then how was the state notified?'

'Oh, yes, excuse me for being imprecise. Charles Hauptman did call 911. But not until he

18

was sure that his wife had expired.'

I stand at the foot of the bed for another moment. Nurse Borders was right, Amar Singh is an amateur sleuth. And she was also right in pointing out that he's not a cop or a doctor.

'Could the nurse be right, Amar? About the rash and the diarrhea?'

'Borders is not a registered nurse, she's an LPN. One year of training, Lenny, this is all she has.'

I shake my head. I asked Amar a direct question, which he chose not to answer, a sure sign of evasion. I rephrase the question: 'Could Joyce Hauptman's rash and her diarrhea have been caused by the antibiotic she was taking? What was it again?'

Amar tugs at his beard, his expression grim. 'Ampicillin.'

'Right. So, if I were to go online now and type ampicillin and side effects into a search engine, would rash and diarrhea come up?'

'Yes,' he admits, 'most certainly.' Then his lips part in a triumphant smile. 'But there is this, too, which Nurse Borders forgot to mention. Come, look closely at the victim's arm.'

In full rigor, Joyce's very thin arm refuses to move when Amar tugs her elbow. 'Here, along the forearm, you see these lesions?'

A series of tiny red bumps, perhaps two dozen, are scattered over Joyce's forearm. They seem vaguely familiar, but I can't put my finger on where I've seen them before.

'They look like pimples.'

'They are not. They are erythematous papules,

indicative of poisoning by arsenic or one of its many derivatives.'

Dutifully, I take a closer look. Then I remember. Not all that long ago, I developed a rash on my right hip. The dermatologist I saw didn't call the red bumps erythematous papules. He told me I had psoriasis and the treatment he prescribed, a steroid cream, took care of the problem.

'I want you to do something for me, Amar. I want you to put yourself in Charles Hauptman's shoes, just for a minute, and I want you to assume that his wife died of natural causes. You've put everything you have into keeping her alive. You've been grieving for so long it seems like your natural state. You're so drained you feel halfway to dead yourself. Now this detective walks into your life, this detective who thinks you killed your wife, and proceeds to launch an all-out assault on your psychological well-being, fragile though it is. How would you feel?'

To his credit, Amar lowers his head. He's now unable to meet my eyes. But he doesn't answer and I have to prod him into speaking.

'How would you feel, Amar?'

'I hear what you are saying.'

'Good, because I have another question. Is there any other condition that can produce these lesions? Besides poisoning?'

His head drops another inch, but he isn't backing down. 'Yes, several,' he admits. 'But you must be seeing the other side of this coin. Hauptman is familiar with the side effects of antibiotics. He's seen them with his own eyes. If he researched poisons online he would quickly discover that arsenic poisoning...'

I know where his argument's going and I wave the rest of his answer away. There's nothing to be gained by continuing the discussion. Singh has jumped from *could have* and *might have* to *probably did*. I've made the same jump many times with the usual suspects, the husbands, parents and boyfriends. I made the jump, then put them in a small room and kicked the psychological crap out of them for as long as they were willing to take it. Hoping all the while to elicit a damaging admission or two, even if they didn't confess.

Amar's cellphone rings and I watch him reach into his pocket. 'My wife,' he explains. But it's not his wife. I know this when his eyebrows fly up to his hairline and he begins to splutter. He carries the cellphone out of the room, leaving me alone with Joyce Hauptman.

I cover Joyce's body, pulling the sheet up to her neck, then take a quick look around. On the upper shelves of an armoire, I find Joyce's prescription drugs, including the Lotrisone and Kaopectate mentioned by Nurse Borders. The drawers of the armoire contain medical supplies, as do the drawers of a double dresser and the room's single closet. There are diapers by the dozen, boxes of waterproof Chux, urinary catheters and catheter-care kits, bottles of saline and sterile water, feeding bags and urine-collection bags, lemon glycerin mouth swabs and a dozen

21

boxes of powder-free latex gloves. Joyce's toiletries are neatly arranged on top of the dresser, skin creams, deodorant, shampoo, baby powder, soap, disposable washcloths. I don't find anything out of place, certainly no convenient bottle of arsenic, not even a can of bug spray.

I'm just shutting the closet door when Amar returns. His full lips are compressed and his normally round eyes are narrowed to mere slits.

'There will be no autopsy at this time,' he announces. 'My immediate supervisor was not senior enough to inform me. I have to be called by Deputy Director Gold.'

'Did he give you a reason?'

'He is a she, Jennifer Gold.'

'I stand corrected.'

'Please do not have a joke with me.' Amar's accent thickens, as it always does when he's pissed off. 'My judgment has been called into question by one of the mayor's appointed. This woman, she is a...' He searches for the right word, then says, 'She is a political hacker.'

'Hack,' I correct.

'She has never in her life been going to a crime scene. Never once. But now she is telling me there is no real evidence of a homicide. She is saying allow the police to investigate, always later the autopsy may be performed.'

'Why, Amar? What was her excuse?'

'Religion. She is claiming that the Hauptmans are observant Jews and their religion forbids autopsy. This is bullshit, Leonard, and you are knowing it.'

Singh is wrong. Jewish law forbids any cutting

22

of a dead body, except when the law of the land demands it. In this particular case, the law of the land, as defined by Deputy Director Gold, has chosen not to act. Personally, I can't fault her. There's no hard evidence that a crime has been committed.

'What I will do,' Singh threatens, 'is write my report in such a way as to bring shame on this politician. I will make my suspicions clear.'

I smile and say, 'Get 'em,' but I know Amar's threat is an empty one. Death inspectors are not civil servants and they have no union. They serve at the whim of the medical examiner. When the screws are put to Amar Singh, father of four, he'll write the report his bosses want to read.

Two

Amar Singh leaves a few minutes after Officer Carter returns. I escort Amar to the door, but I'm already thinking about what to do next. Morelli's instructions are not off the table because someone reached into the ME's office to prevent an autopsy. The ME has no authority over the NYPD. If the bosses at 1 Police Plaza demand an autopsy, Joyce Hauptman will simply be exhumed. Jewish law also forbids cremation.

'So, detective,' Carter says, 'what's next?'

'You anxious to go back out on patrol?'

'Fuck, no.' He displays a bag of donuts. 'I got enough ammo here to hold me for the rest of my tour.'

'Well, you're gonna have to postpone the feast. For now, I want you to go upstairs and join your partner. Make sure Hauptman remains in his room. I'm gonna creep the house.'

Carter doesn't ask me if this search is legal because he knows it's not. Still, he's reluctant to abandon his meal. Tough shit. At this point, the police are still officially sympathetic and I can't have him disrespect Hauptman's grief by slobbering away on a jelly donut.

I wait until Carter's on the stairs, then return to Joyce Hauptman's room and look down at her covered body. With her legs against her chest, her head bent down into her shoulder and her arms pinned tight to her sides, she might be a carton ready for shipping. The undertaker will have to straighten her limbs to get her into a coffin and I doubt he can do it without breaking bones. Jewish law requires burial with twenty-four hours if at all possible, and Joyce will still be in rigor mortis, her limbs frozen.

I take another look around the room, my eyes finally settling on a red hairbrush lying between tubes of skin cream on the dresser. The brush hasn't been cleaned recently and there are dozens of gray hairs caught up in the bristles. I'm tempted to stuff a few of them into my shirt pocket, but I don't have a search warrant and the hair would be inadmissible in a court of law. There's no point.

Although I don't have time for a thorough

24

search, what strikes me, as I make my way to a small office on the side of the house opposite Joyce Hauptman's sick room, is the absence of anything recognizably Jewish, from the art on the walls to the knick-knacks on the bookcase. And there are no specifically Jewish books, either, no history of the Jewish people or of Israel, not a single biography of a Jewish leader, no study of American-Yiddish culture. Growing up, my best buddy was a Jewish kid name Morty Tannenbaum. His mother once told me the surest evidence of a Jewish household was a mezuzah, a small cylinder containing a Hebrew prayer, tacked to the outside of the door frame. But there's no mezuzah on Charles Hauptman's door frame.

My search of the office, though rushed, is fruitful. I discover a clearly marked folder in the top drawer of a wooden file cabinet: INSURANCE POLICIES. There are four policies in the folder, two for Charles and two for Joyce. The total payoff on Joyce's policies is $720,000, with Charles the beneficiary.

The policies provide a clear motive for murder. If Charles Hauptman were ever to be charged with killing his wife, they'd be evidence at trial. But the policies were purchased in 1991 and 1992, long before Joyce Hauptman's stroke, and they aren't out of line, given the Hauptmans' affluence. It would be more unusual if there were no policies at all.

I replace the file and take another: WILLS. The Hauptmans have reciprocal wills. The surviving spouse gets everything. Again, so what? The wills are perfectly appropriate, especially for a childless couple.

I take a quick turn through the basement, descending a steep flight of wooden stairs. To my left, a small room contains the water heater, the furnace and a sump pump in the corner. To my right, a much larger room is crammed with boxes. There's also a pingpong table in the center of the room, but the table, a pair of paddles and the sagging net are covered with dust.

At the far end of the house, in a tool room, I discover a shelf bearing two boxes of rat poison. I get excited, but only for a moment. The active ingredient in this particular brand is warfarin, an anti-coagulant. I don't know exactly what warfarin is, but I do know an anti-coagulant would cause massive internal bleeding, which was not the case with Joyce Hauptman. Back in uniform, I'd responded to a 911 call of a woman in distress. The woman had been injecting herself with Heparin, a blood thinner prescribed by her doctor to prevent blood clots. Heparin is always injected beneath the skin, but she'd pushed it into a vein in her forearm, her reasons made clear in a brief suicide note. She was dead by the time I arrived, her skin so pale she might have been an albino.

Three

You get one chance to *make* a first impression
and one chance to *take* a first impression. One
chance before the questions begin and the guard
is raised, before the first punch is thrown, the
first blow struck. One chance to measure your
quarry, to devise a strategy to fit the individual.
Instinctively, I prolong this opportunity as long
as I can, pausing in the doorway to examine the
man I intend to rake over the coals. At this point,
I'm not worried about questions like guilt or
innocence. Nor do I feel the slightest pity for the
victim's husband. I am, as Nurse Borders accused, without a drop of human sympathy.

Just as well, because Charles Hauptman's devastated by what he's been through. His eyes are
dark hollows that might have been gouged from
the unyielding bone and his hollow cheeks press
against the line of his teeth. His mouth is slack
and slightly open, his lower lip drooping, his
head bowed in defeat. He does look up when
I come into the room, but only for a moment,
his indifference that of a man who no longer
wonders what life has in store, a man without
horizons. But he's younger than I expected, in
his mid-forties, a short man, slight of build, with
a comb-over that fails to conceal his nearly bald

27

scalp. Though his eyes are fixed on the gray carpet, he twists the wedding ring on his left hand, spinning it first one way, then the other, over and over again.

I take another step onto the tightly woven carpet and let my eyes sweep across Hauptman's enormous bedroom. The room is large enough to accommodate a queen-sized sleigh bed, a triple dresser, an armoire, two nightstands and a pair of upholstered loveseats on either side of a glass table. There's a treadmill in one corner, its running surface folded up, and a small writing desk beneath a window, and a whole lot of empty space. Mounted on the wall above the bed, a painted screen depicts two cranes on a beach. The birds are obviously courting. They dance with their wings outstretched, their necks intertwined, over undulating sand dunes.

Two enormous paintings grace the walls, one between the two windows, the other behind the loveseat where Charles Hauptman now sits. Obviously the work of a single artist, the paintings are at least three feet high and six feet across. Each depicts a quiet sea veiled by what I assume to be morning mist. The mist is a rosy pink that reflects in the calm waters to lend the scene a romantic and gentle aura. But there are flies in this ointment. In the upper right of the painting hung between the windows, a pair of warships, an aircraft carrier and a smaller ship bristling with cannon, rest side by side. Dwarfed by the surrounding ocean, the ships appear to be a great distance away.

The second painting repeats the ironic theme,

a peaceful sea transformed by early light, a pair of oil tankers crossing at the horizon, their smokestacks trailing a line of soot that extends to the frame. The oil tankers are large enough in the picture to be instantly noticed, at least by me, but again, they're dwarfed by the surrounding sea and sky.

At the bottom right, in crimson letters, I find the artist's name and a date: E. Morville, '95.

I'm impressed – the whole room speaks of money and taste – but not so impressed that I overlook the absence of any recognizably Jewish object, or the fact that Charles Hauptman is neither wearing a yarmulke nor reciting Kaddish, the prayer for the dead. I nod to Carter and his partner and they leave the room, drawn to the bag of donuts in the kitchen like flies to a corpse.

Hauptman looks up as I approach. 'I'm Detective Shaw,' I say before offering the usual bromide. 'I'm sorry for your loss.'

I extend my hand and Hauptman takes it. Though his hand is soft, his grip is surprisingly firm, and I sense an inner resolve, perhaps the resolve that got him through the years after his wife's stroke. He motions me to a chair on the other side of the coffee table and I accept with a nod, my eye drawn to an overflowing ashtray, a pack of cigarettes and a monogrammed lighter. I point to the cigarettes.

'You mind?' I ask. 'I stopped smoking years ago, in August of 2000 to be exact, but I still have an occasional craving.'

Hauptman nods and I light up. The first lungful has me reeling, but then I settle down, the nicotine receptors in my brain screaming with glee. You bad boy, where have you been?

In no hurry, I lean back to enjoy my smoke. Hauptman's legs are crossed at the knees and he's leaning forward as though coddling an upset stomach. The posture is closed and appears defensive, but I'm too experienced to draw any conclusions. Hauptman could be a guilty man drawing down into the fortress of himself. Or he might be a man in pain guarding against further emotional assault. Or maybe he commonly adopts this posture, maybe he's defensive by nature.

I take another hit on the cigarette, a little voice in my head insisting that all my troubles, physical and mental, can be traced back to the day I abandoned nicotine.

'How are you doing, Mr Hauptman? Are you all right?'

'How am I doing? Now there's an interesting question.' His thin voice is pitched low and he continues to fiddle with his wedding ring. He does not look up. 'I feel about the same as I did before Joyce...' He stops long enough to swallow hard. 'I was in the room, you know. I watched Joyce take her last breath.'

I nod as gravely as I can manage. 'It must have been very difficult.'

'Actually, I didn't feel much of anything. Or at least anything beyond exhaustion.' He swipes at his mouth with the back of his right hand. 'I'm not saying I haven't had my ups and downs over the years. There were times when I was on the verge of despair, other times when I felt as if Joyce and I were performing some great cosmic dance. You know, being is its own justification, that sort of thing.'

In fact, I'm as ignorant as a stick when it comes to ideas like being and justification. Philosophy is beside the point, in any event. In Hauptman I recognize a man who needs to talk, a man who wants to put his grief out in front of him so he can take a look at it.

'Yes, I understand,' I tell him. 'Some events are so overwhelming that it takes a while to sort them out.'

He looks at me for a moment before continuing. 'When I finally admitted that I wasn't feeling anything, I asked myself what I was supposed to feel. Relief? Sorrow? Anger? Joy?'

'Joy?'

'My wife is free now, detective, free at last. Personally, I believe she's with her Maker. I believe that whatever sins she may have committed, her suffering has more than balanced the cosmic scales. No one should have to suffer the way she did. It's immoral.'

He goes on to describe his wife's seizures, his body gradually unfolding as he begins to gesture with his hands. He does not cry and his voice, albeit thin, does not tremble. 'I was helpless, that was the worst of it. I could not relieve her suffering. And there were so many ironies.' He hesitates for a moment, then continues. 'You know how, when you see someone in pain, you want to comfort them by touching? A hand on the shoulder, a simple caress? It's instinctive. But Joyce's muscles went into spasm when she was touched, so even that slight gesture was off the table.'

He lights a cigarette and leans forward again, his posture gradually closing. As the silence builds, I find myself caught up in the painting on the wall behind him, the one with the warships. I can't decide if the artist intended the ships to be menacing, serpents in the garden, or if the enormity of the sea and the sky has somehow reduced them to the status of toy boats in a bathtub.

'You used the word *anger* a moment ago,' I finally say. 'Why should you be angry?'

He pulls on the cigarette, draws the smoke deep into his lungs. His eyes close as he releases his breath, then open to stare directly into mine. I'm instantly suspicious. Hauptman's been looking away throughout the interview. Not that I think he's going to lie to me, not necessarily.

'Joyce's physician, Dr Meyer, insisted that Joyce was without consciousness. "I know it looks like she's in pain," he once told me, "and she probably is in pain. But she's not aware of her pain." And though he didn't say it in so many words, that meant the quality of her life was irrelevant. Even convincing him to pre-scribe anti-seizure medication was like pulling teeth. But keeping her alive? That was his mission. He prescribed drugs to maintain her blood pressure, drugs to thin her blood and prevent clots, antibiotics whenever she had an infection.'

32

Hauptman looks away for a moment. When his dark eyes come back to me, they're angry indeed. This is not an academic discussion, not for Charles Hauptman. He's reliving a battle he'll most likely be fighting for the rest of his life.

'One day, Meyer showed up a few hours after one of Joyce's seizures. I was at the end of my rope. I just couldn't take it any more. So I asked him, point blank, "If quality of life is a concept that can't be applied to Joyce, why do you work so hard to keep her alive? Why do you treat her infections so aggressively? Hell, why do you treat them at all?"'

I watch his hands curl into fists as he draws a breath. 'What did he say?' I ask.

'What did he say? One thing you should understand, it's hard to find doctors willing to make home visits in cases like this, even if you have money, so I could only press him so hard. But to answer your question, he became angry. Joyce didn't have a living will or a health-care proxy, so he had no other option. And who was I to question him in the first place? I wasn't his patient. His first obligation was to Joyce.'

'What about hospice? If you wanted to end her suffering, then hospice would seem like a good way to go.'

Although detectives pay at least as much attention to body language as to the words spoken by suspects, they usually pay attention to the wrong body language. Fidgeting, for example, is commonly mistaken for evasiveness, but it indicates only that the suspect is nervous, a state easily

33

explained by the basic situation. Failure to maintain eye contact is another false indicator of guilt. Accomplished liars – hustlers, con men, pure psychopaths and New York City detectives – never look away, not even when their lies are blatant.

But there *are* reliable indicators of deception (though not necessarily of guilt), and one of these, the micro-expression, is particularly helpful. Micro-expressions are facial expressions that contrast dramatically with the overlying emotion being projected by a suspect. Because they typically occur in about one-twenty-fifth of a second, micro-expressions were entirely unknown before some genius of a sociologist ran a videotaped interrogation in slow motion. Then they became obvious, even to an untrained viewer.

The really good news here is that interrogators can learn to spot micro-expressions, despite their brevity, with just a few hours of training. The even better news is that I've had the training. The bad news is that micro-expressions are quite rare and most people, even when they're lying under stress, never display them.

Hauptman appears to be angry. I hear anger in his voice, read anger in his curled fists, compressed mouth and narrowed eyes. All very genuine, as far as I can tell. But then, for a mere fraction of a second, his facial muscles rearrange themselves entirely. His anger vanishes, replaced with a look of such cold calculation it's all I can do not to react.

The expression passes as quickly as it appears

34

and Hauptman finally speaks. 'New York has a hospice law that allows for the withdrawal of life support if there's strong evidence that an unconscious patient would not wish to be kept alive under the circumstances. That's good, right? Because Joyce didn't leave an advance directive, but she told everyone she knew that she wouldn't want to live this way. Only Joyce wasn't on a ventilator, which might have been disconnected, and New York law specifically excludes fluid and nutrition from its definition of life support.'

He spread his hands, palms up, and shrugs. 'Another fucking irony, if you'll excuse my language.'

'OK, I get the point. And you can trust me on this, I know where you're coming from.'

I'm careful to maintain a reassuring tone when I launch into a brief description of my Aunt Margaret's vegetative state. Yes, I feel his pain, feel it and understand it. But what I'm thinking, as my words run along on automatic, is that Hauptman's given me a second motive for murder. He's told me that he wanted to end his wife's suffering and was frustrated because the state wouldn't let him.

'My Uncle Jack,' I tell him, 'he didn't have your strength. He put Aunt Margaret in a nursing home. Now he hardly visits.'

I put out my cigarette after a final pull. I'm tempted to light another, but Hauptman doesn't offer, doesn't seem to notice. Finally, he says, 'Your uncle ... what was his name?'

'Jack.'

'Yes, Jack. Well, I envy your Uncle Jack. Something like this, it takes your life away. I mean literally, detective. Over time, friends drop off, you stop going out, you become more and more isolated. Work and care, work and care, work and care.' He looks down at the cigarette between his fingers for a moment, then stubs it out in the ashtray. 'We could have afforded twenty-four-hour nursing,' he announces, 'only I wanted to care for Joyce myself, at least some of the time. I know it doesn't make sense, given what I just told you, but I've stopped asking myself why. Now I live with my contradictions. I don't expect life to make sense.'

I pick that moment to change the subject. Somebody reached into the ME's office to get the autopsy canceled. I want to know if that somebody was Charles Hauptman.

'I know this must be painful for you, but when someone dies at home without a doctor present to sign the death certificate, the medical examiner usually orders an autopsy. It's pretty much standard operating procedure.'

Hauptman's anger vanishes and he again deflates. Another blow to a man who's already absorbed too many, another cut to a man who's dying the death of a thousand cuts. Charles Hauptman is not a fool. He realizes that his wife's death has aroused the state's suspicions. Why else would a detective be sitting in his bedroom asking questions? But if he already knows there won't be an autopsy, he hasn't revealed it. As far as I can tell, Hauptman's taking me at my word.

36

'By the way,' I ask, 'where's your wife's doctor? Has he been here and gone?'

'I called Dr Meyer right after Joyce died. You know what the bastard told me? He told me he was too tired to come out.'

He gets up, walks to the window, raises the blind, stares out for a moment at the coming dawn. When he turns around, he appears a bit stronger.

'I'm asking myself what I'm supposed to do next. For the past five years, my life has been highly structured. Between work, caring for Joyce and performing all those little tasks that keep a household up and running, I barely had a minute to myself.' He pauses long enough to smile. 'Actually, that's not entirely true. Are you a baseball fan?'

'I watch my share of Mets games.'

'Ah, a Mets fan. Well, I was born the son of a Yankees fanatic. My dad took me to my first game when I was three. By all accounts, I slept through the entire thing.' He pauses again, perhaps remembering better days, then continues. 'The Yankees have been my principal escape for the past several years. I've made it my business to have all my work done, my dinner consumed and the dishwasher loaded by seven o'clock when the games start. Then I retreat to the media room, load myself into a recliner and follow the action pitch-by-pitch. I suppose that doesn't seem terribly profound, but it was the only available escape because I lacked the energy to pursue a social life. It nearly broke my heart when the Yankees didn't make the playoffs this year.'

I offer a short laugh in reply. 'You'll have to excuse me if I'm not sympathetic. The Mets are lucky to make the playoffs once in a decade. But there is a matter I'd like to explore, and if it seems indelicate, I apologize in advance. You said that your wife's doctor thought she was in a vegetative state, but the nurse I spoke to, Nurse Borders, claimed that her patient was able to communicate with eye blinks.'

'Ah, *consciousness*. I wondered when we'd get to that.'

'What made you think we'd get to it at all?'

'Because everyone asks that question when they first hear about Joyce's condition. "Is she conscious?" Personally, I think they were testing my sanity. You know what I'm saying – only a crazy man would take personal responsibility for an unconscious individual, even if that woman was his wife, even if he loved her.' Hauptman looks at me for a moment before turning back to the window. Now, apparently, he's ready to address my question directly.

'First thing, Shirley's wrong about the eye blinks. Believe me, I tried to communicate with Joyce again and again during that first year. Not that I'm faulting Shirley – she was spectacularly devoted to Joyce – but she saw what she wanted to see.'

I stare at his back for a moment. His shoulders are relaxed, his hands limp and by his sides. 'So, you're saying that she *wasn't* conscious?'

'Consciousness is a slippery term, detective. It resists a precise definition. The real issue is communication. If Joyce was able to communicate, she could make her own decisions about her medical treatment.'

He stuck his hands in his pockets and lapsed into silence, but I wasn't finished. I wanted an answer to the question I asked, not the one he chose to answer.

'You're confusing me here. Your doctor claims that Mrs Hauptman was completely unaware, that she couldn't even feel her own pain. Do you agree with him?'

He flinches when I say the word pain, but answers without hesitation. 'I'll tell you what, you give me a definition of consciousness – or awareness – and I'll tell you if Joyce...'

And that's it. The sound of a closing door brings Hauptman to a halt. His eyes narrow and my first thought is that he's going to become angry. But then he flashes a second micro-expression, identical to the first, a look of cold calculation, as footsteps sound on the stairs. A moment later, two men, one elderly, the other young and eager, burst through the door. Both wear overcoats and business suits, despite the early hour.

The older man does not introduce himself. Instead, he locks his eyes on Hauptman, who meets his gaze evenly. The younger man, business card in hand, walks up to me and introduces himself.

'My name is Arthur Allard. I'm Mr Baum's attorney.'

I glance at Hauptman, but he doesn't acknowledge me until I call his name. Then he turns to me and says, 'I'm sorry.'

39

'Don't apologize. You've been very helpful and I'm pretty much finished anyway.' I step in front of the older man and offer my hand to Hauptman. 'We're not going to perform an autopsy at this time,' I tell him. 'And again, I'm sorry for your loss.'

'Thank you, detective,' he says. 'This is my father-in-law, Maxwell Baum.'

Baum doesn't offer his hand. He turns his back instead. I'm not offended, though. In fact, I even manage a narrow smile as I cadge another cigarette on my way out.

Four

I pay a return visit to Joyce Hauptman's room before leaving the house. Joyce is exactly as I left her, one eye open, her mouth slightly ajar, lips turned sharply down at the corners. But I now understand why Charles was evasive when I raised the possibility of his wife being conscious. Joyce's partial awareness, even if proven, wouldn't change a thing. Aware, her death would be even more of a blessing, a mercy killing even more appropriate.

We speak for the slain. I'm talking about homicide detectives. We speak for the murdered, for the victims. As a matter of law, we're the only ones who can speak for them.

A lecturer in a political-science class I took at

40

Queens College many years ago claimed that one characteristic of a modern nation is that the state reserves the use of force to itself. Citizens have no right to revenge, no matter how awful the harm done to them. If they seek revenge, they themselves become subject to prosecution by the state.

I was already a cop, already a detective, when I heard these words, and I was struck by the implied responsibility, especially when the offense is murder. At times over the years, when I worked homicide scenes, I asked myself a simple question: If not me, who?

Up until this moment, when I stand before Joyce Hauptman's ruined body, I've always thought the question to be rhetorical. That's because I'd never been to the scene of a homicide where the victim didn't cry out for justice. This is different.

Suddenly, I entertain one of those nasty little thoughts better left to fester in some unexamined corner of the mind. If I prove that Joyce was deliberately killed, if I arrest Charles Hauptman and the state convicts him, Joyce Hauptman, wherever she is, will not thank me. I will not be speaking for her.

I take another look around, rummaging through Joyce's meds and her supplies, but again I find nothing out of place. This time, however, I'm struck by the cost of maintaining a woman in her condition. Her supplies must run to a couple of grand a month, but they're nothing compared to the price of nursing care. Joyce's LPNs have to be making twenty dollars an hour

41

at the very least. Twenty dollars an hour, times eighteen hours a day, times three hundred and sixty-five days a year? Times five years?

I do a rough calculation in my head and come up with $650,000. And that's without the supplies, or the cost of renting the oxygen concentrator or the air compressor or the feeding pump or the hospital bed.

I leave through the unlocked front door, thinking that if I make a dash for my car I'll get out of the wind before hypothermia takes hold. But I'm brought to a stop on Hauptman's small portico. Every bit of vegetation, trees, grass, flowers and shrubbery is touched with a silvery frost that glistens in the dawn light. The effect is stunning, even beautiful, though I'm initially reminded of a graveyard. I watch a car, a BMW, back down the driveway across the street, its exhaust blowing puffs of steam into the frigid air. The car stops at the end of the driveway and the driver's door opens briefly. A hand with a lit cigarette between the fore and middle fingers reaches out to collect a newspaper lying in the grass, then quickly withdraws.

I head for my own car, a well-used Chevy Impala, start it up and turn on the heater. There's a briefcase on the floor with a yellow pad inside. I retrieve the pad and a pen, then light up the cigarette I filched on the way out. Hauptman was not technically a suspect when I interviewed him and I was under no obligation to read him his rights. Everything he said is on the record. But Hauptman did not sign a formal statement and I didn't record the interview. In a courtroom it'll be my word against his. Though I think the odds against this case going to trial are very long, I want to be able to claim that I wrote up my notes while my memory was still fresh.

That done, I consider heading back to the house, where I could open an official investigation. The house is the 112th Precinct, universally called the One-Twelve, headquarters for the Queens Homicide Unit. But I'm not sure Morelli wants a case file opened under these circumstances. I never had a chance to put the hard questions to Hauptman and it's no surprise, damaging admission or not, that he didn't come within miles of a confession. Plus, I don't know if a crime has been committed. Maybe I should keep my observations to myself, at least for now. I call in to the house, but Morelli's already left. That's to be expected because Morelli's tour – and mine, too – started at four o'clock in the afternoon.

Ordinarily, stamina is one of my assets, but now I'm suddenly tired. I'm thinking about victims in dire need of justice, and of Angel Morales, the killer that my partner and I were trying to run down when Morelli called me. Morales is a genuine bad boy, currently wanted for his involvement in a drive-by shooting that took the life of an eight-year-old girl. Is Morales still walking around? Don't get me wrong. Davy Lowenstein's a great partner, but he's nearing sixty and he's been a cop for more than thirty years. Stamina is not one of his assets. More than likely, he's already in bed.

By the time I finally put the car in gear and start for home, New York is up and running. For the better part of an hour, I battle traffic on Queens Boulevard and the Long Island Expressway, all the way to 5th Street, a block from the East River in Long Island City. The sun is up now and it floods the skyline of Midtown Manhattan, or the little slice I can see as I come down 47th Avenue. It's a funny thing about Manhattan. I love to look at the city, especially in the early morning, but I rarely go there. Queens is my beat and has been for many years, which makes me an official hick by New York standards. It could only be worse if I lived on Staten Island. Even the ravaged Bronx is cooler than Queens.

But I don't mind being an outsider. Being an outsider suits me. I drive down to the edge of the water and park for a few moments. To my left, to the north, the interlaced girders of the 59th Street Bridge suck in the light. Directly across the river, the ice-blue glass of the United Nations headquarters reveals thousands of molten facets. A news anchor on the radio announces the results of the first post-season baseball games. The Mets are not mentioned. In the hunt for the playoffs until the last day of the regular season, they finally crapped out. Now they're busy consoling themselves with every luxury a multimillion-dollar salary can buy.

I finally park the car and head home. Home is a one-bedroom apartment on the third floor of a four-story walkup in a mainly industrial neighborhood. Not much, but I keep it reasonably clean and well furnished. Plus, at nine hundred dollars a month it's a real bargain by New York City standards. I've got some decent prints on the wall, mostly ancient maps, a few posters advertising exhibitions at the Met, and a set of Lionel trains on the windowsill in the living room. My parents gave me the set on my ninth birthday, along with a little engineer's cap. The set's transformer stopped working years ago, but I like the way they look, the black steam locomotive trailed by a coal tender, a mail car, six passenger cars and a cheery red caboose. In the morning, in sunlight, the train appears almost to be in motion.

Not much, like I said, but enough so that I don't feel like a bear that wandered into a strange cave when I come through the door. I'm forty years old and I've lived through many relationships, some short and some even shorter. No wife, though, and no children, so I've at least avoided divorce-alimony syndrome, an affliction common to cops everywhere. Which is not to say that I haven't paid a price, that there aren't days and nights when I feel so far removed from ordinary human life I might as well be on the moon, staring at the blue ball of the Earth, wondering if there's life out there.

But this is not one of those mornings. I've been going for more than sixteen hours and what I am is tired. Still, my curiosity propels me to my computer where I type Charles Hauptman's name into a search engine. I get ninety-six hits, none of them related to the Charles Hauptman who lives in Jamaica Estates. Maxwell Baum's name follows and here I catch a break. I discover a profile published six years before in *Business Weekly*. The story's entitled 'Heir With A Flair' and it's highly flattering. According to the author, Max Baum, grandson of Otto Baum, the legendary entrepreneur, might have been content to live the playboy life, jetting from one pleasure dome to another. Instead, he'd successfully invested in securities, warehousing, real estate, mining and residential construction. Baum's also a founder and board member of the Ship of State Institute, a libertarian think tank devoted to free-market economics. Under Mayor Bloomberg, he served, unpaid, as the mayor's special envoy to the New York Chamber of Commerce.

I shut down the computer and head off to my bedroom where I set the alarm for 1:00 p.m. I don't know exactly what I expected my search to uncover, but I feel oddly satisfied. I've danced this dance often enough to know that I'm committed to the case. If Joyce Hauptman was murdered, mercifully or not, I intend to find out.

An image rises, unsummoned, when I close my eyes, of Charles Hauptman and the cold, calculating look he so briefly displayed. I cling to that image for a few seconds, only to find it suddenly replaced by the ravaged, grieving man I encountered when I first entered the bedroom. I ask myself which is more valid. Charles's face, the deep grooves around his mouth, the sooty pouches beneath his eyes, the deeply felt sorrow apparent in those eyes? Or an expression here and gone in a twenty-fifth of a second? Again, I don't know, but I intend to find out.

* * *

I needn't have bothered with the alarm. My mother calls at noon. 'It's your mother,' she announces when I pick up. 'I only got a minute, but I wanted to touch bases. Are you taking me to church on Sunday?'

I love my mom dearly – we were always close and we've become closer since my father died. But Sarah Shaw is an Irish Catholic's Catholic. While my father was alive, she devoted herself to redeeming his skeptical soul, an effort that did not go unrewarded. Dad made a full confession to Father O'Neill just a few hours before he passed. Now I'm the target of her missionary impulses. Mass on Sunday is fine with me, but confession is a step I'm not willing to take. I don't mind telling God that I'm sorry, but I can't bring myself to believe that the man in the black suit and white collar represents Him.

But Mom hasn't phrased the question precisely in any event. She should be asking me if I'm working, since I always take her to church when I'm off, to church and to breakfast afterward, a routine that's driven more than one lady from my life.

'I picked up a new case yesterday, but I expect to wrap it up pretty quick. I should be OK for Sunday.' I briefly consider discussing Charles Hauptman, but decide to keep the details to myself. My mom is nothing if not opinionated and I'm not up for a lecture on mercy killing when there's no proof that a killing of any kind has even occurred. 'I'm off to the dentist this afternoon.'

47

'You're not...'

'Just routine, Mom, no needle.'

Fear of the needle is why I neglected my teeth as a young man. Personally, I find it amazing that dental researchers haven't developed a pain-killing method more humane than a two-foot-long syringe. These days, dentists can drill a hole in your jaw and screw in a new tooth. They can transform a ragged, ugly smile and whiten the yellowest teeth. But the needle goes on forever.

'So, who are you seeing?'

'Dr Chitterjee, but look, I have to get moving. I just woke up...'

It's not to be. My mother owns a small apartment building, her main source of income since my father died. In years past, she loved to complain about her ungrateful tenants and the rules imposed on her by New York's rent laws. Now she's changed her tune. Families that paid their rent on time for decades are suddenly in arrears, and not through any fault of their own. There are no jobs to be had. If you happen to be employed, like me, that's great. But if you lose your job, you can't survive on unemployment insurance. Not in New York.

'What am I supposed to do, Lenny? I have a mortgage and taxes to pay. I can't have non-performing units. God help me, but I'm gonna have to put the Sanchez family on the street.'

Five

I walk into the One-Twelve a quarter of an hour late. There are six civilians in the anteroom, all waiting to unload their various tales of woe on a pair of uniformed officers assigned to the task of screening complaints. One of the civilians, a woman, has a swollen eye. Another clutches a sheaf of papers which she holds out to me when she spies the gold shield clipped to my coat. I ignore her, passing quickly through an interior door to the heart of the precinct. Or is that the bowels?

I settle for the latter because the question of whether or not the NYPD has a heart is still undecided after a century and a half. But that we're full of shit is not in doubt. Nevertheless, I'm instantly energized when I cross the threshold. The organized chaos of a New York City precinct appeals to me. Besides the obligatory contingent of uniformed officers and a squad of precinct detectives, the One-Twelve houses a homicide squad, a narcotics squad and the anti-terror unit charged with keeping La Guardia Airport safe. I climb two flights of back stairs, my heart growing lighter with each step, past the precinct squad room to the home of the Queens Homicide Unit. The prospect of investigating

Joyce Hauptman's death commands my total attention.

Queens Homicide is housed in four rooms, the squad commander's office, two interview rooms and the squad room. The squad room's walls are covered with wanted posters, union notices and memos from downtown, most of them outdated and none of which any detective I know actually reads. Arranged back to back, the eight desks in the room are old enough to remember Prohibition, when the One-Twelve was originally constructed. But the new computer stations, one to each pair of desks, are a lot more reliable than the battered filing cabinets where case files are routinely misplaced.

There are three detectives and a civilian in the squad room when I arrive. Greg Lato is sitting at his desk. His hands are folded in his lap and he looks half asleep. His partner, Eve Durand, sits across from him, hunched over a computer keyboard. The civilian is seated to the side of Eve's desk.

I've been a cop long enough to remember when paperwork was done on manual typewriters and I pause for a moment to watch Eve's hands drift across the keyboard. Eve types with all ten fingers, even her pinkies, a feat of manual dexterity I can never hope to match. She's keeping up with the civilian, an elderly Asian man wearing a Kangol cap and a thick burgundy parka.

The fourth man in the room is my partner, Davy Lowenstein. Davy's chewing on the end of a pencil, a fairly disgusting habit he acquired when he stopped smoking cigars.

'Our lord and master,' he tells me, 'has requested your presence.'

Morelli's a large man in his late forties with a round face, a permanent five-o'clock shadow and suspicious brown eyes. I know you're guilty, those eyes declare, and it's only a matter of time until my judgment is confirmed. He gestures me to a chair in front of his desk, then leans back in his own chair and puts his hands behind his head.

'What're ya doin' to me, Shaw?'

'Doing?'

'When I spoke to you last night, I gave you a specific assignment.'

'That's true, but...'

'But what do I find when I come to work this afternoon? *Nada*. As in nothing, as in zero, as in over and out. No perp under arrest, no open investigation, not even a fucking memo.'

I shrug my shoulders and assume a contrite expression. 'Sorry, lieutenant, but a deputy director from the ME's office, Jennifer Gold, phoned Singh a short time after I arrived. She killed the autopsy.'

'What?'

I repeat myself. 'She killed the autopsy.'

'Why?'

'Religious objections. The Hauptmans are Jewish. Plus, according to her, there wasn't any clear evidence that a crime had been committed.' I give him a moment to absorb the implications. 'Then we got another bad break when a

51

lawyer showed up. I tried to call you, but you'd already left for home. There's some good news, though. I learned that Joyce Hauptman had two life-insurance policies totaling seven hundred and twenty thousand dollars.'

'Her husband the beneficiary?'

'Yup, and I uncovered another motive, too.' About to toss him a bone, I smile. 'This one's more in line with your thinking, boss. Hauptman admitted that he wanted to end his wife's suffering. He told me that he was frustrated because New York law wouldn't let him do it.'

I take the notes I made from my briefcase and lay them on his desk. 'I wrote these up in my car a few minutes after Hauptman's father-in-law arrived with the lawyer in tow.'

Morelli dons a pair of reading glasses. The glasses must be old because he settles the pages a foot from his eyes before he begins to read. I cross my legs, fold my hands and let my eyes crisscross the room. Morelli has managed to reach into the procurement process somewhere along the line. The desk and the matching bookshelves behind it are new. No gouges, no scratches, no battered corners. He's got a flat-screen monitor for the computer on his desk, and a flat-screen TV with an attached DVD player on a shelf to his left. His various plaques and awards are arrayed on the wall behind him. Photographs of his wife and two children rise from his desk like sails.

'What you got here,' Morelli finally admits, 'what with the nurse claimin' the rash was caused by the victim's meds, it ain't much.'

'I know that, boss. Like I said, I was just getting to the hard questions when the shyster made an appearance. Personally, I don't think Hauptman called him. And I don't think Hauptman had anything to do with the autopsy being canceled. When I brought up the likelihood of an autopsy, he didn't blink.' I hesitate before delivering the last bit of bad news. 'Also, the father-in-law, Maxwell Baum? According to *Business Week*, the prick's not only richer than Donald Trump, he worked as the mayor's special envoy to the Chamber of Commerce.'

'For which mayor?'

'Billionsberg. And Baum founded some kind of Republican think tank, so he's definitely connected.'

Now it's up to Morelli. Will he say, 'Fuck the whole thing, bury the woman and forget about her?' I know that's not what he wants. Morelli has to feel dissed. It was the death inspector, the medical examiner's spokesman at crime scenes, who raised the original questions. Without those questions, Morelli wouldn't have opened an investigation. For a deputy director from the ME's office, a political appointee in a patronage job, to cancel the autopsy without notifying the NYPD first is a slap in the face. But at the same time, Morelli's got to be wondering exactly who this Maxwell Baum is and how much juice he's got. I watch him glance at the phone. Should he call his own bosses at Queens Borough Command? Should he cover his ass?

Morelli picks at a mole on his cheek. 'All right,' he says without looking up, 'you go back to finding Angel Morales. See if you can wrap it up tonight. I'll let you know about Joyce Hauptman before you clock out.'

Davy Lowenstein pushes a box of donuts from his desk to mine as I take a seat. I glance inside to discover a single glazed donut stuck to the bottom of the box. Ten minutes later and even the box would be gone. I watch Davy flick at the crumbs and the powdered sugar clinging to his moustache. Within shouting distance of sixty, Davy's luxuriant gray mustache mirrors a thick head of gray hair that he wears long enough to curl over the tops of his ears. He favors shiny silk shirts, black or navy blue or midnight green, and matching ties and black suits. He calls this pose his Bensonhurst-wise-guy look and he brings it off reasonably well, though not as well as he did seven years ago when he and I first teamed up. Me, I'm wearing a tweed jacket, brown slacks, loosened yellow tie, a white shirt with the top button unbuttoned. I'm your Uncle Lenny, with a badge and a gun.

'You get reamed out?' he asks.

'No, but I didn't get thanked, either.'

If I'd opened a complaint on the night before, as Morelli wanted, his choices would be a lot more limited. Now he can bury the whole thing and never a word on paper to indicate his suspicions.

I outline the case for my partner, as I know he's been waiting for me to do. Davy's a student of policing. He can name every police commissioner, from Clubber Williams to that consum-

54

mate professional, Ray Kelly. He can recite damning testimony from the Knapp and Mollen Commission hearings on police corruption word-for-word. As he listens to me his eyes widen slightly and he leans forward to lay his elbows on his desk.

'So, whatta you make of it?' he asks when I finish.

Oddly enough, though I asked myself this question early on, I never bothered to answer it. I take a minute to consider my response, then say, 'Hauptman slipped up twice with those micro-expressions. At the very least, he was deliberately holding something back. But I don't think he knew the autopsy was canceled. And he didn't seem overly concerned, one way or the other.'

'But somebody did reach in to stop the autopsy. And the religious excuse is a joke. No mezuzah? Lenny, observant Jews have mezuzahs in every doorway in the house. And no yarmulke, no menorah, no talit, no tallis, no Shabbat candleholders?'

'And no Jewish books in the bookcase.'

'Not even *World of Our Fathers*? Hey, pal, the thing speaks for itself.' Davy leans back and spreads his hands apart. Then he wags a finger in my direction. 'Otto Baum, the great philanthropist, is a legend in Jewish circles. He came from a family of German Jews who arrived in the new world before the Jews of Poland and Russia even heard of America. These German Jews had more money and more education when they immigrated. And they were a lot less religious. Trust me, kosher did not appeal to them. What they did was build synagogues on the Upper East Side that you can't tell from a cathedral. Swear to God, you walk by, you think you're passing St Patrick's.'

I'm just about to change the subject. There's a fugitive out there named Angel Morales who needs to be put in a cage and kept there until he's an old man, broken in body and spirit. We have the evidence to do just that, if only we can find him. But the phone on my desk rings before I get going.

My touchtone phone is nearly as old as the precinct, a bulky thing with fingertip-sized buttons and no features. I settle the handset against my shoulder.

'Detective Shaw here.'

'Hello, my name is Theresa Santiago. I got your name from Shirley Borders. I was one of Joyce Hauptman's nurses.'

I recognize the name immediately, but the accent throws me off. Despite the name, Santiago, the accent isn't Spanish, or at least the kind of Spanish I'm used to. There's a sing-song quality that reminds of Pakistan or India, but that's not right, either.

I motion for Davy to pick up the extension. 'What can I do for you?' I ask.

She hesitates, either to gather her thoughts, or to censor her initial impulses. Finally, she says, 'I got your name from Shirley Borders,' she repeats. 'You gave her your card.'

'I did, and thank you for calling. So, what can I do for you?'

'Well, Shirley is saying that she told you that Joyce's rash appears after she began taking ampicillin. This is not so.'

'Really?' Though my little heart is thumping away, I keep my voice calm.

'I had noticed a faint reddening on the upper left quadrant of her back two days before.' She sniffs into the phone, perhaps to indicate her disgust.

'Did you put that in your notes?'

'Yes.'

'And where are your notes now?'

'In the notebook, at work.'

'You all used the same notebook? You didn't keep separate notes?'

'No, we didn't, if that makes a difference.' Her tone is sharp and I find myself suspecting that her sarcasm is a matter of habit, that critical is a way of life for her. 'When Shirley calls me at eleven o'clock last night,' she continues, 'she tole me there was gonna be an autopsy. I tole her, "Good." Now she calls me and she says the autopsy is canceled. This is wrong and I want to know why.'

I almost react. Her voice has risen an octave and resembles the squeal computers make when they talk to each other.

'Don't misunderstand,' I explain. 'We didn't close down the investigation. The investigation is ongoing and I hope to interview you in the very near future. As to the autopsy, that can be done at a later time if necessary.'

The woman cackles, a hideous sound revealing an infantile satisfaction that makes my skin

57

crawl. 'Joyce Hauptman,' she announces, 'was cremated six hours ago.'

'Are you sure?'

'I spoke to Charles this morning, to ask about the funeral. He told me that his wife's body was already at the Bayville Crematorium on Long Island. I've been trying to reach you all day.'

Morelli's pissed and I can't blame him. Cremation is forbidden to religious Jews, an absolute no-no. Whoever reached into the ME's office lied straight out. And why, Morelli wants to know, would he or she do that? Unless he or she wished to destroy evidence, in this case Joyce Hauptman's body?

I have an answer – that to a man like Otto Baum, an autopsy would have been embarrassing, if not scandalous – but I don't offer an opinion. Instead, I offer a bit of advice. Most people, when they imagine cremated remains, think of powdery ashes. In fact, the ash also contains shards of bone. Can that bone be tested for the presence of arsenic? I suggest we call the ME's office for an answer.

'You know someone in the ME's office?' Morelli wants to know.

'Amar Singh, who's already motivated.'

Amar's no happier than Morelli when he hears the news and it takes a while for his initial outrage to dissipate. When it finally does, I ask him about testing the remains for arsenic. He tells me that the human body does, indeed, deposit arsenic in bone and that traces might be uncovered if enough bone survived the cremation fire. But that assumes we can get our hands on the remains, a likelihood that rapidly diminishes when Morelli phones a contact at the district attorney's office. Morelli wants the assistant DA in question to get a court order forbidding Hauptman to dispose of his wife's remains. With a little time, he assures his contact, we can work up a strong enough case to justify seizing the remains for testing.

The ADA passes the buck, the move as swift and nonchalant as it is reflexive. The office of the district attorney will be glad to cooperate if the Medical Examiner goes on the record with his suspicions. But the ME's office is in denial mode, protecting their decision not to perform an autopsy in the first place. They'll act if the NYPD uncovers evidence that a crime has been committed, but not until then. The likely destruction of Joyce Hauptman's remains before that evidence can be produced troubles them not at all.

We sit together in silence for a few minutes after Morelli gives up. From time to time, he glances at the phone on his desk. What do the bosses want? But it's likely that the bosses haven't so much as heard Joyce Hauptman's name. How they might react, if they eventually do, is anybody's guess.

'What do you think?' Morelli finally asks.

What I think is that Joyce Hauptman's better off dead, however she got that way. But that's not what Morelli wants to hear.

'Why don't I interview the nurse, Santiago. It could be she's bogus. If she's not, we can go from there.'

'Good.' Morelli favors me with a thin smile and an encouraging nod. 'But keep it close, Shaw. No paperwork unless I give the OK.'

Six

On the surface, Nurse Theresa Santiago is an attractive woman. She's in her mid- to late thirties and petite, with doe eyes, a lush mouth and a flat, yet delicate, nose. Her ivory complexion is touched with mahogany highlights, especially along her cheekbones. Her black hair flows in soft waves to her shoulders.

But Nurse Santiago does not attract me as I stand in the doorway of her Brooklyn apartment. An underlying tension, like an overly wound spring, dominates her features. Lines fan out from the corners of her eyes and her mouth, wrinkles that I associate with bitterness, and her small nostrils are noticeably compressed. She stares at my ID when I show it to her, her suspicious gaze traveling back and forth, from the photo on the card to my face. Only when she's certain that I'm a bona-fide cop and not some con artist does she invite me in. My first thought is that she's afraid. Immigrants are commonly afraid of authority figures, especially cops. But that's not it. Her high-pitched voice speaks to a self-image hammered together long ago, a self-image that's not about to change. Theresa Santiago is angry, permanently and perpetually angry.

I follow her into her living room, shedding my coat as I come. I'm not surprised by the plastic covers on the sofa and the chairs, or by the oils-on-velvet *Last Supper*, or by a pair of small shrines in the corners. Flickering candles burn in votive candleholders, one to each shrine. The candleholders are glass and ruby red in color, the flames behind them an intense orange.

'Are you Catholic?' she asks.

'I'm Irish. I went to Catholic school.'

The last part isn't true, but I'm guessing it's what she wants to hear. She points to the shrine on our left, to a framed print depicting a nun poised before an altar. The nun stands with one foot forward, her hands extended, palms up. A beaded rosary is draped over the picture frame so that her breasts are covered by the crucifix.

'St Rose of Lima, the patroness of the Philippines. She is famous for her beauty and many men were attracted to her. Some were powerful and some were rich, but she refused them all. Then she retreats into a nunnery and rubs her face with pepper until her skin is red and blistered. St Rose suffered a long and painful illness at the end of her life, but she had only one prayer: *Lord, increase my sufferings, and with them increase Your love in my heart.*'

Though I find St Rose's final wishes to be vaguely un-American, I keep my opinion to myself as Nurse Santiago gestures to the second shrine. This one bears a statue of the Virgin.

'Our Lady of Turumba. Also called Our Lady

61

of Sorrows.'

Our Lady of Turumba doesn't look all that sorrowful to me. Her beatific features are surmounted by a golden halo twice the size of her head and her brocaded robes are nothing short of sumptuous. But, again, I keep my opinion to myself. I'm thinking that Nurse Santiago has an agenda and that she's demonstrating the intensity of her religious beliefs in order to convince me that she's going to be truthful. This, of course, puts me on my guard.

The introductions concluded, I follow Theresa into a kitchen large enough to contain a small table covered with a plastic tablecloth. There's coffee already brewed and there's a plate of cookies on the table. I'm not surprised. For many immigrants (and for poor people in general), offering food and drink to visitors, even cops, is more or less obligatory.

'Sit,' she tells me. 'I'll pour the coffee.'

I take a seat and cross my legs. On the way over, I was hoping that Nurse Santiago smoked. No such luck. The spotless kitchen smells faintly of pine oil and roast chicken.

'I don't want to give you the wrong impression, nurse,' I tell her when she lays a cup of coffee on the table in front of me. 'We haven't stopped investigating. Far from it.'

'You're investigating? How? By letting Joyce be cremated?'

I sip at coffee strong enough to melt the enamel on my teeth, then say, 'I can't discuss the investigation in detail, of course. I can only tell you that the cremation came as a big surprise to us. If it was done in an effort to end the investigation, it's had the opposite effect.'

My comment is rewarded with a genuine smile. I've just provided her with an opportunity to indulge the most basic element of her personality. I encourage her still further with an open-ended question.

'Tell me, what was it like? Working for Charles Hauptman?'

'Actually, I didn't work for Charles. I worked for Max Baum. He was the one who hired us and paid us. He paid for Joyce's medical supplies, too.'

'Really?'

'Yes, but not with his own money. The check I received every two weeks had Joyce's name on it, but was signed by Max.'

I cover my surprise by taking another pull at my coffee. Separate finances? With the father-in-law controlling the purse strings? Well, the Hauptmans' finances wouldn't be separate for long. I'd already seen Joyce's will and Charles stood to inherit every penny. I glance at Nurse Santiago, who's displaying that malevolent smile again.

'Don't ask me why,' she observes, 'but there is someone not trusting Charles Hauptman.'

I stare down at the plastic tablecloth for a moment, at a flock of roosters and hens, at a pig in a pen, at a cow with its face in a tuft of grass. I realize that I've yet to see a single photograph in Nurse Santiago's apartment, no husband, no children, no father, no mother.

'You say you didn't work for Charles. Does

63

that mean he didn't control your day-to-day activities?'

'Charles? Charles was too weak to control anything.'

Theresa launches into a prolonged account of a minor disagreement between herself and Nurse Borders regarding treatment of a small bed sore, which she calls a decubitus. The story's point is simple enough. Charles Hauptman's efforts to resolve the dispute were ineffective, neither woman paid him the slightest heed.

Theresa sits upright in her chair and her eyes never leave my face. She spins her coffee cup on the saucer, spins it in little circles. 'I think,' she finally declares, 'that Shirley was in love with Charles. With Shirley, when we spoke together, nurse to nurse, she always sided with Charles. He could do no wrong. St Charles of Jamaica.'

She sneers again, the right side of her mouth curling down so far I think it might reach her chin. 'In my thinking, Shirley wanted to help him.'

'Help him what?'

'Help him to be rid of his wife.'

My cellphone begins to vibrate in its holder on my belt. Despite the urgency of the moment, I check the Caller ID screen. Davy Lowenstein is on the other end and I decide to take the call. When I set out for Theresa's apartment, my fear was that Davy would stumble on Angel Morales without me being around. Davy has heart, but he's too old for violent confrontations. He's admitted as much to me over drinks after work.

His reflexes are shot and he's lost the snap in his muscles. The way he tells it, nowadays he has to telegraph instructions to his arm before throwing a punch. Detailed instructions. And even then, more often then not, the lines are down.

'Yeah, Davy, what's up?'

'I got him, Lenny. I got Morales.'

'In custody?'

'No, I got a location. In East New York. He's holed up with a hooker and a half-ounce of coke.'

'Where'd you hear this?'

'From his sister, Rose. Seems the family's had enough of little Angel, what with his propensity for mindless violence. They're hoping we'll make him disappear.'

'When are you gonna take him down?'

'Eleven.'

'You book a SWAT team?'

'Negative that. The Brooklyn SWAT team is participating in a city-wide anti-terror drill. Likewise for Queens. They're down by the docks, preventing an amphibious landing. We're gonna have to settle for a few volunteers at the Seven-Five. Should I count you in?'

'What time?'

'Nine thirty.'

'See you then.'

I return the phone to its pouch on my belt and take a cookie. Heavy on the ginger with a very tart orange frosting, it's not half bad. I grab another as I display an apologetic grin for Nurse Santiago's benefit.

'Sorry, but I had to take the call. Now, you were talking about Charles Hauptman getting rid of his wife. That's a pretty serious charge. I'm surprised you didn't call us earlier.'

'I didn't say kill her. I didn't say murder her. But I know he wanted to be rid of her. Think about this, detective. Charles takes care of Joyce for six hours a day. He has also to earn a living and run errands and keep the house in decent condition. It is a very hard life and he's not so young. Plus, Charles was always talking about how Joyce wouldn't want to live this way.'

'Would you?'

Mostly I know how to keep my big mouth shut. Not this time. Nurse Santiago's face reddens and her eyes, already prominent, bulge from her head. For the next five minutes, I'm subjected to a rapid-fire lecture on the sanctity of life, complete with biblical references. Theresa's words fly across the space between us like nails from a nail gun, but I don't protest. I wait until she comes down off her high moral horse, then put her back on point.

'What did Charles actually do, nurse, if anything, to arouse your suspicions?'

'When Joyce had infections, he didn't want to treat them. He said to let her fight off the infection if she could. But Dr Meyer wouldn't go along. I remember what he told Charles because Charles told me right after: "If you don't want her treated, don't call and tell me she's sick."'

'Did Charles take him up on that advice?'

'No, but that's only because Charles knew I

would call the doctor if he didn't. I told him so.'

'And he couldn't fire you because you worked for Max Baum, right?' I let that sit for a minute, then said, 'Did you ever directly observe Charles Hauptman do anything to injure his wife?'

'No, but...'

'Do you think the care he personally gave her was substandard?'

'Charles is not trained, but he does well.'

'All right, tell me about the rash.'

'Wait, one more thing. About two years ago, Charles had called every hospice in New York. He wanted to stop feeding Joyce, but this he can't do in New York. He was very upset.'

'But he didn't do anything about it, nothing you observed?'

'Not that I saw.' Her jaw tightens as she forces the admission between her teeth.

'OK, that's good, now we understand each other. So, tell me about the rash.'

Nurse Santiago brings her hands together and draws a breath. 'Joyce began to show signs of a rash four days ago. In the upper left quadrant of her back. This is two days before she began to take ampicillin. I put this in my notes and I showed the rash to Shirley.'

'And how did she respond?'

'She tells me it's nothing, just as she always says.'

'What about the third nurse, Anna Berevski.'

'Max Baum's little pet? Those two, they are as thick as thieves. Besides, Anna was trained in Russia. What she knew about nursing you could put in a thimble.'

'So, you didn't discuss Joyce's condition with Anna Berevski? That's what you're saying?'

'Anna Berevski is an idiot.'

'That doesn't answer my question.'

Theresa's voice has been rising in pitch throughout the exchange. It now reaches the intensity of an ambulance siren.

'No, I did not waste my breath on that Jew.'

I lean back and smile. I'm not offended, though my partner is Jewish and proud of it. As for Anna Berevski, if the investigation continues, she'll have to be interviewed. As will Max Baum and Charles Hauptman's brother, Terence, and Joyce's doctor. But that's in the future. It's nearing eight o'clock and there's a fugitive to be captured and I'm not leaving my partner to handle it by himself. Still, though I'm not sure it's especially relevant, I have a final question.

'Joyce Hauptman's diagnosis was permanent vegetative state, but Nurse Borders told me that Joyce was at least partly conscious. What was your impression?'

Theresa hesitates a bit too long before answering, as though I asked her a trick question. In fact, I'm only curious.

'Would that make a difference?'

'A difference in what?'

'In whether you ... prosecute the case? Or if she wasn't conscious, will you be saying that she wasn't worth anything anyway?'

I stand up. Again, I'm not offended. But I can no longer rely on Nurse Santiago's answer. I've seen that look so many times in the past, the eyes turning suddenly inward, then flicking off to the left. Theresa needs a moment to recalibrate. What response will serve her agenda? What response will leave her triumphant?

'All right, nurse, I think we're through here. I want you to make yourself available, if I need to speak to you again. And I want you stay away from the Hauptman residence. Understood?'

This time she laughs, a chortle she's been holding in reserve since I walked through the door. 'Am I allowed to attend the memorial?' she asks. 'I am talking about the memorial Charles is having for his wife before he scatters her ashes.'

Nurse Santiago hesitates again, but this time her pause is entirely theatrical. She's got a killer punch line to deliver and she wants to be sure it catches me smack in the face. This is a woman who counts the bruises.

'Before Charles scatters her ashes *tomorrow morning.*'

Seven

We climb three flights of stairs on tiptoes, six large men wishing they were as insubstantial as ghosts, and we tiptoe down the hallway. My adrenaline is definitely up, way up, and my heart beats faster and faster as I approach the door behind which Angel Morales squats with his coke whore. Sergeant Cole Starbuck leads the way, a mountain of a cop bearing a twenty-pound battering ram.

Having volunteered to be first through the door, as Cole has volunteered to take the door down, I'm following directly behind. I'm wearing body armor thick enough to stop any bullet fired from a handgun, and my weapon, a .40 caliber Glock, is aligned beside my right ear. As we come to the door, I slip my finger beneath the trigger guard.

We don't hesitate. There's no point. We know Morales is inside because we had his sister, Rose, call him less than five minutes ago. We know he's armed, too, because he told his sister he was, announcing at the same time that he wasn't going back to prison, that he'd rather die. Then he'd asked her to pick up an ounce of coke at the home of a Brownville dealer and mule the package to his current hideout.

I watch Cole march to the far side of the door, then turn to face me. The uniformed cops following behind come to a stop. Davy's at the rear and I have to wonder if he feels compromised. It's tough shit if he does, of course. The first men through the door have to move quickly and decisively, before the target has time to react. Surprise is the whole point. Surprise and survival.

Cole places the nose of the battering ram directly in front of the door and plants himself, legs apart, knees bent, every movement deliberate. His lips tighten and the muscles in his shoulders and neck swell as the ram describes a clean arc, rising well above his head before descending in a blur. The resultant crash is loud enough to stun, but I've been here before and I'm prepared. When the door flies open I leap into the apartment without hesitation, my Glock extended before me, scanning the room, screaming at the top of my lungs.

'Police! Police! Get down! Get down!'

Angel Morales is sitting, cross-legged, on the floor. He's got a straw in his nose and he's bending over a mirror with a mound of coke in the center. His eyes bulge from his head and his short hair is literally standing on end, but he doesn't move. Behind him, maybe ten feet away, a semi-automatic pistol lies on a small table. To my left, an open door leads into the bathroom. There are no other rooms in the apartment.

I leave Sergeant Cole to handle Morales, who appears to be in shock, and approach the bathroom door. I'm about to demand that whoever's

71

in there come out – my mouth is already open – when a woman explodes through the opening. The woman's holding a .38 caliber revolver in both hands and she empties it as fast as she can pull the trigger. She continues to pull the trigger, the hammer clicking away on the spent shells, while five cops pump eight rounds into her body and another ten into the walls. Me, I don't fire my weapon. I'm standing so close to her when the shooting starts that I'm more afraid of the cops to my rear than the woman in front of me. I jump to my left and hit the deck.

Like most gun battles involving police, this one is over in a few seconds, leaving me and everyone else, including Angel Morales, more or less stunned. I have to take a minute to collect myself before I check on my fellow officers. I find one, a rookie named Everett Bagley, on the floor. There's a bullet hole in the center of his vest which he tentatively probes. Davy and the others have come through unscathed. They're now in the process of cuffing Morales, who's trembling from head to foot.

I approach the woman where she lies a few feet from the bathroom doorway. That she's dead is not in question. Most of her brain is on the shower curtain behind her. Still, I can't take my eyes away. The woman is wearing a T-shirt and panties, both soiled. Her brown legs are broomstick-thin, while her ankles and feet are badly swollen. A line of open sores extends from the corner of her mouth down to her jaw and her slightly crossed eyes, yellowed by jaundice, are shot with jagged red lines.

Davy comes up to stand behind me. He puts an arm on my shoulder. 'Jeez,' he asks, 'whatta ya think got into her?'

Talk about a long night. Any time an NYPD officer discharges his or her weapon, a shooting board automatically, and immediately, convenes. The first members of this board, all ranking officers, appear within an hour. We have a dead civilian here, a female unrelated to the suspect named in our warrant, a female who turns out to be eighteen years old. Before noon tomorrow, her relatives, accompanied by their lawyers, will meet with reporters. They'll swear that Corinne Mariposa was an honor student, that her life was one of infinite possibility until trigger-happy cops stole it away. They'll demand compensation.

It's an old story in New York, but it won't play this time. The recovered forensic evidence, including the bullet in Officer Bagley's vest, supports our claim that Mariposa fired on us. Then there's Angel Morales, who gives an oral statement supporting our version, a statement his interrogators record on videotape. Corinne's prior arrests for prostitution and minor drug possession won't help their case, either.

We're kept apart for most of the night to prevent us from rehearsing our stories. I'm the first to be grilled, probably because I didn't discharge my weapon. Nevertheless, the bosses are harsh and accusing. Surely, there was some precaution that might have been taken, something we might have done to prevent this tragedy. But we made no mistakes. Our procedure might have been taken directly from the Patrol Guide. The resultant chaos was nothing more than bad luck. Bad luck that Corinne was in the bathroom when we took down the door. Bad luck that she had a gun in the bathroom. Bad luck that she'd been up for two-and-a-half days, snorting line after line of coke, becoming more and more paranoid.

'I don't know what she was thinking,' I tell the shooting board. 'I'll never know.'

Still, as I wait for the board to finish with my partner, I find myself returning to the question. What did Corinne Mariposa intend to accomplish? What positive outcome did she hope to achieve? Of course, there's always the possibility that she got over on us, the possibility that she wanted to end her drug-ravaged life and we provided the means. Suicide by cop is a manner of death universally known to police officers, universally known and deeply resented. You wanna kill yourself, the theory goes, show some balls. Put your own gun to your head and pull your own trigger. And leave a fucking note.

It's ten o'clock in the morning and we're parked, my partner and I, a block from Charles Hauptman's house. We've napped on cots in the precinct and we're pouring coffee down our throats in an attempt to refuel, but we're still depleted, emotionally and physically. Nevertheless, duty calls.

Hauptman's garage door rises at eleven. A Lincoln Town Car backs halfway down the drive, then pauses until the door begins to close.

I raise a pair of binoculars to my eyes and quickly focus. Hauptman's driving, with Shirley Borders sitting next to him. Max Baum sits in the rear, alongside a man I don't recognize.

I keep well behind the Lincoln as we make our way through Queens toward the Triborough Bridge. I can afford to keep my distance because I know where Hauptman's going. According to Nurse Santiago, Joyce Hauptman's remains are to be scattered in the Bronx Botanical Gardens.

I'm driving through a light mist, the temperature having risen fifteen degrees overnight. Davy is beside me, half-asleep. I didn't ask for company – he volunteered – so I don't feel especially guilty.

As we head up onto the bridge, Davy comes back to life. He presses his head against the headrest and sighs. Then he takes a pencil from the inside pocket of his trench coat and begins to chew on it.

'I hit her,' he tells me. 'I know I hit her.'

'That right?'

'Yeah, Lenny. I swear. I saw the fuckin' blow-back, every drop, like ripples in water.'

I can't make the image work, but I don't argue. I've never fired my weapon in all the time I've been on the job and right now I'm just glad I'm alive. I'm glad I'm alive and I'm glad the shooting is righteous and that the mayor and police commissioner are both defending us. Three cheers for the good guys.

'Guess what, Davy. When someone's shooting at you, you're allowed to shoot back.'

We're driving along the bridge's center span

with the whole of lower Manhattan to our left. The view is normally spectacular, but today the heavy mist veils the skyline. We might be on the rim of the Grand Canyon for all I can tell.

'You think I don't know that?' Davy breaks the pencil in half and throws the pieces at his feet. 'But I'm pissed. I'm pissed that she made me do it in the first place. Did you hear the way she was howling? It wasn't human.'

In fact, I don't remember Corinne making any sound at all. But I'm not going there. What's the point? Maybe she howled, maybe she didn't, maybe she was singing 'Old McDonald had a Farm'. I'm only sure of one thing. If I hadn't gotten my ass out of the way, some of those rounds meant for Corinne would have had to pass through my body first.

'I killed before,' Davy tells me, 'in Vietnam, in 1972. I was nineteen at the time, a kid just out of high school. After I came back, I remember telling myself that I'd never kill again. Killing was too big for me. I couldn't handle it, justified or not. Then I went and joined the cops.'

He looks at me and smiles. 'Go figure,' he says.

Eight

The funeral procession continues, along the Bruckner Expressway and the Bronx River Parkway to Fordham Road and Southern Boulevard and the parking lot at the Bronx Botanical Gardens. Our pace is slow because Charles Hauptman's not in a hurry. He's staying a few miles below the speed limit although traffic is light. Alongside me, Davy has fallen silent. His hands are folded across his chest and he's staring through the streaked windshield. When I turn into the parking lot, he buttons his trench coat and looks at me.

'So, whatta ya think?' he asks.

'About what?'

'About what you're gonna do here.'

What I'm gonna do is push the envelope for all it's worth. The way the law works, once an item is discarded, it can be seized without a warrant. This is a rule that's mostly been applied to household trash placed at the curb. I don't know about scattered human remains, but I'm hoping they fall into the category of discarded items. Legally, of course.

We watch Hauptman approach the members' kiosk just past the main gate. The rest cross the plaza to purchase general admission tickets.

Davy and I wait until Charles rejoins the larger group and they enter the gardens together. Then we quickly exit the car and follow. As we pass the ticket windows, a security guard raises a hand. He doesn't know quite what to make of us. I can see that much in his eyes. But he backs off when Davy flashes his gold shield and mutters, 'Police business.'

Davy's wearing a tan fedora that matches the color of his trench coat. I'm wearing a black wool overcoat and carrying an umbrella. That we're out of place goes without saying. The few visitors we pass are hardy types wearing rain jackets, thick-soled boots and Australian bush hats. They look ready to hike all the way to China.

Conspicuous or not, the landscape reaches out to me. I'm far from a nature-lover. City-bred and city-raised, I'm more or less satisfied with concrete, brick, asphalt and glass. I've never even had a window box. This is different. The trees to either side are totally unfamiliar. Some have branches that shoot straight up, as if the tree was being attacked by invisible fire. Others form perfect bells, each leaf overlapping the one below. Still others have branches that twist in every direction, like snakes fleeing a predator. Off to my right, a granite outcropping flashes veins of rain-slicked crystal. To my left, white hydrangeas along a stone wall display massive blossoms that bend to the ground. The mist blends every element, trees, grass, rocks and flowers, and the odor of wet earth is all encompassing. I feel myself being drawn into the mix, the effect as seductive as the perfume of the woman standing at the end of the bar. Something in me wants to be absorbed into the landscape, to let go, once and for all.

But I can't, and for good reason. The surrounding beauty may be as undeniable as the beating of my heart, but what I'm doing (and what I intend to do) is just as undeniably ugly. And the ugly part is what they pay me for.

'Imagine if it's all for nothing,' Davy says. 'Imagine if it turns out that Joyce Hauptman wasn't poisoned. If we follow these mourners, collect pieces of the woman they're mourning, and the pieces test negative. Imagine how you'll feel. And the worst part is that we weren't ordered to do this. We're doing it on our own.'

'Thanks,' I say after a minute.

'Thanks for what?'

'For the "we" part. But the truth is that I'd be here anyway. I need to know, one way or the other. There's too much that stinks. Reaching in to prevent an autopsy because it offends your Jewish beliefs, then cremating the body, then disposing of the ashes twenty-four hours later? Talk about evidence of a guilty mind.'

I'm not convinced, and I doubt very much that Davy is, either. We continue to follow the mourners, keeping a hundred yards back, until they turn into a heavily forested section of the gardens. The path they choose rises to the top of a hill and we have to hurry to reach it before they vanish into the deep woods.

'If we go up after them and they retrace their steps comin' out,' Davy observes, 'we're gonna

79

get pinned for sure.'

I'm feeling bad enough without a confrontation, but I'm operating under the theory that the remains are up for grabs once they're scattered. If I have to face down Charles Hauptman to get to them, I'm prepared to deal with the inevitable negativity. I answer Davy by starting up after the mourners, only to fall to one knee after a few hesitant steps. The dirt path is slick with moisture and my Florsheims, with their smooth soles, are uniquely unadapted to the task at hand. I have to find my way on the grassy verge alongside the path, ducking under tree limbs that whip across my coat, leaving pale green streaks on the black wool. It's no better for Davy, who mutters, 'What the fuck, what the fuck,' as he inches his way up the hill.

We finally turn a bend to find Hauptman and his entourage about fifty feet ahead of us. Hauptman's got a plastic bag cradled in both hands. These are the remains of the woman he's cared for all these years and I know he can feel what's left of her through the bag. He lowers his head and groans loud enough for me to hear him through the dense forest on either side of the path. His pain and grief are so evident, his emotions so genuine – and so elemental – my first instinct is to turn away. Then I recall the cold calculating expression he flashed when I interviewed him. Flashed twice.

After a moment, Hauptman lifts himself to his full height and marches into the forest. He takes only a few steps, but I know he's marshaled his nerve and that it's all stiff upper lip now. He's

80

thinking this is the final act. He's thinking that once he accomplishes this last piece of business, the curtain will close. He doesn't know that I'm standing lower down on the hill, doesn't see me duck out of sight, has no idea how bad my bad intentions are.

Davy and I have to wait a good half-hour before Hauptman and the other mourners leave. Fortunately, they don't retrace their steps but continue on along the trail. A few minutes later, my trousers caked with mud from the knees down, I'm at the top of the hill, staring at a band of gray mud that forms a semicircle on the forest floor. I wonder what Charles imagined when he decided to scatter his wife's ashes. Did he envision a fine gray powder rising on a current of air to finally merge with the heavens themselves? If he did, he picked the wrong day because the heavy air is as wet as it is motionless.

I watch Davy pull a notebook from his pocket and draw a crude sketch of the scene. When he finishes, I produce an envelope bag, don a pair of latex gloves and get to work. The ground is thankfully flat. I can squat instead of kneel as I gather small pieces of bone, none longer than a finger. Still, by the time I finish, my shoes and the cuffs of my trousers are an almost uniform gray.

Morelli manages a small smile when I present him with the results of my ingenuity later that afternoon. It's decision-making time for my boss. The bone in the evidence bag I produce

81

can't be logged in as evidence without opening an investigation.

'It was one of those use 'em or lose 'em situations,' I explain, all hard-ass cop now. 'I mean, if I hadn't trailed Hauptman, the remains would be gone forever.' I gesture to the window behind Morelli's desk. The mist has turned to a steady downpour. 'I had to move when I did. There was no choice.'

I go on to recount my conversation with Theresa Santiago, the good and the bad. Santiago, I tell him, is a nasty piece of work, no doubt about it. But if she documented the rash two days before Joyce began using ampicillin, we have to take her seriously. That's especially true because Charles had motive aplenty. He wanted to end his wife's suffering. The work and the stress were grinding him down. Joyce Hauptman's life was insured. A considerable part of her finances – enough to pay for the nurses and her medical supplies – was controlled by his father-in-law.

'I don't know about you, boss, but I want an answer, once and for all. Do we have a crime here or not? If the bones come up clean, we can always close out the investigation.'

'And if they're dirty?'

'Then we got a homicide.' I shrug my shoulders apologetically. 'Meanwhile, I can do a few more interviews, see what turns up.'

Behind me, I hear Davy enter the squad room. He's coming from a bar on Queens Boulevard that makes half-pound burgers from freshly ground sirloin. I have to wait for Morelli to make a decision, but I'm not about to give him anything more to think about. I want to feed my stomach, do the paperwork and go to sleep. It's been a long tour.

But Morelli's surprises me. He tells me to open a file and to stay on the case, and to show no mercy to the mercy killer.

'I don't care if he turned cartwheels takin' care of his wife. Murder is murder. If he was tired of playin' nurse, he shoulda put her in a nursing home.'

Morelli delivers these words without hesitation, his tone so firm I know that he's discussed the case with his bosses at Borough Command. I know that he's covered his ass and I'm not resentful. Now my ass is covered, too.

'Ask yourself this, Lenny, where does it stop? I'm serious here. You might look at Joyce Hauptman's condition and decide that ending her life was the right thing to do because she wasn't conscious anyway. But the next spouse will say it's all right to kill because their loved one's in a lot of pain, or because they've got Alzheimer's and they can't tell their children from their grandchildren. I mean once you start down that road there's no end to who gets killed and who gets to live.'

Nine

I get home a bit after midnight and sleep until one o'clock on Friday afternoon when the phone wakes me. It's Davy. He's pissed off and he wants to vent.

'Did you see the news?' he demands. 'The family and the lawyers and the fucking reverend? Did you hear what they said?'

I haven't, but I know who the reverend is. His name is Clive Carlton and he's a fixture in New York, his presence as predictable as the events he inevitably sets in motion. Carlton will pose a series of questions, then threaten to march on City Hall if he doesn't get answers. His bluster will continue for as long as the media remains interested.

'The pricks are gonna put me on modified assignment,' Davy continues. 'I gotta report to Borough Command on Monday morning. Plus, I have to see a department shrink before I go back to active duty. It's no good, Lenny. What happened in that apartment was righteous and I shouldn't be punished for protecting my own life. I mean, the physical evidence has already been recovered and there's nothing ambiguous about any of it.'

'Did something change overnight? I thought

the bosses were backing you up.'

'They are. The Mayor, too.'

'Then how come you're worried? Once Billionsberg commits himself, he never backs down.'

'There's a principle here, which is eluding you. You're not supposed to punish the victim.'

'Supposed to? Hey, people aren't supposed to rob, rape and kill, either.' I shift the phone to my other ear. 'If you want a principle to live by, try this one: go along to get along. Play your part. Be contrite.'

'I am contrite. Corinne Mariposa was eighteen years old, for Christ's sake. But I been over what happened a thousand times in my head and there was nothing we could do. We had to return fire. She didn't give us a choice.'

I finally see where Davy's going. Guilty or not, he wants to confess. I let him go on, encouraging him now and then with a grunt. After a few minutes, he shifts the conversation to his daughter, Rosalind. Davy can't shake the contrast between Rosalind's robust health and that of the emaciated coke-junkie he killed. By now he's taking full responsibility for Corinne's death, but I don't try to reason with him. I'm listening to his obvious distress and wondering at my own calm. At the moment, what I mostly feel is a powerful need to urinate.

'I'm not reporting to Borough Command on Monday,' he finally tells me. 'I don't need the humiliation. I've got vacation time coming and I'm gonna take it. If that's not good enough, I'll put in my papers.'

He pauses for a long moment, then says, 'It's bad enough I have to risk my life day after day, I don't need to be punished for not lettin' somebody kill me. Cops have a right to live, too.'

I pass the afternoon running errands. I get a haircut and drop off my dry cleaning and pick up a dozen eggs and a pound of coffee. Along the way, I use my cell to make a pair of appointments. The first is with Terry Hauptman, Charles Hauptman's brother. I'm to meet Terry at his place of business, a plumbing-supply house in nearby Greenpoint, at four thirty. The second appointment is with Nurse Anna Berevski, who lives in faraway Coney Island. Though initially reluctant, Anna agrees, when I press her, to an interview in her apartment at seven.

I call in to Morelli at four. I tell him what I plan to do and he tells me to go ahead. 'Anything else?' he asks.

'Yeah, something that occurred to me this morning. According to Amar Singh, the autopsy was called off by a deputy director at the ME's office. Her name is Jennifer Gold.'

'What about her?'

'Well, I was just wondering who reached out to her, Charles Hauptman or his father-in-law, Max Baum. I'd like to know who made the bullshit claim about objecting on religious grounds. Myself, I think it was Baum.'

Morelli is instantly suspicious. About what, I don't have a clue. 'Tell me where this is going?' he demands.

'Hauptman's got the motive, but it's his father-in-law who has the juice. Plus, when I spoke to Hauptman, I got the feeling he didn't know anything about the autopsy being canceled. In fact, I don't think he knew that Singh was planning to order one.'

'Did you put the question directly?'

'No, I danced around it, then the lawyer showed up. But I'm thinking I might approach Jennifer Gold and ask her.'

'We're not sure a crime has even been committed and you wanna go inter-agency? Are you crazy?' Morelli hesitates, perhaps expecting me to apologize for making such an idiotic request. I don't and he continues. 'Keep it in the house, detective. Keep it in the house until I say otherwise. Are we clear?'

Hauptman Contracting and Plumbing Supply is more impressive than I expected. The two-story concrete building, which covers most of a short block of Ash Street near the East River, has been well-maintained. A dozen trucks parked in a fenced yard bear the company logo, a little dude made of iron pipe who brandishes a plunger and winks broadly. A green-and-white sign running the length of the building also bears his likeness.

Somehow, without my noticing, the day has grown steadily warmer. I take off my coat and tuck it in the trunk of the car before approaching the warehouse. I'm looking at a multimillion-dollar operation, but I'm not terribly surprised. There are many similar businesses in New York's obscure industrial neighborhoods, businesses that spurn Manhattan's glitter, their own relentless utility a particular point of pride.

Inside, I find workers loading trucks and fork-lifts patrolling wide aisles stacked with mer-chandise. Off to my right, three men staff a counter loaded with catalogues and price sheets. I approach one of them, a tall Latino bearing indigo tattoos on both forearms, and ask for Terence Hauptman. He doesn't hesitate.

'Yo, Terry, someone to see you,' he shouts before turning to the man standing alongside me.

Out on the warehouse floor, Terence Haupt-man spins around and I instantly recognize him as the fourth mourner. He's younger than his brother and thicker through the chest and shoulders, but the resemblance is unmistakable. Terry's got the same long nose and drooping lower lip and he's even balder than Charles. He's standing next to a forklift and he turns back to the driver for a minute before crossing the fifty feet between us. His gait is quick, his manner alert to every element of the work going on around him. Ball of fire is the phrase that comes to mind, a boss who's everywhere, who routine-ly outworks his workers.

'You the cop?' Though not belligerent, his tone is confident and aggressive. When he extends a hand, I take it.

'Detective Shaw.' I flash my ID and shield. 'Like I said, I just have a few questions. Won't take more than five minutes.'

'Where have I heard *that* one before?'

His sarcasm duly registered, he leads me up a flight of stairs to the company's offices on the second floor. We pass through a large outer room crammed with desks, computers and filing cabinets, then into a room the size of a broom closet. This is Terry's office and it comes as no surprise that he's chosen the little cubicle for himself. He wedges himself into a chair behind his desk and motions me to a facing chair.

'Ya know, I shouldn't be talking to you.'

'And why's that, Mr Hauptman?'

'Terry, please. Mr Hauptman's my father's name.'

'All right, Terry.' I smile and spread my hands. 'So, why shouldn't you be talking to me? Don't you want to help the police?'

The question produces a laugh, genuine as far as I can tell. Then he taps his nose and winks. 'Don't bullshit a bullshitter. You're here because you think something happened to Joyce. I mean, besides her dyin' of natural causes.'

I respond with another smile and a shrug, but I don't speak. Hauptman's a hard-charging man, that much is obvious. I'm hoping he's also a man who loves the sound of his own voice. Sure enough, after only a few seconds, he gets to the point.

'So, all right, I agreed to talk to you for one reason.'

'Which is?'

'Which is to convince you that Charles would never do something to hurt Joyce. Or anybody else, for that matter. He doesn't have it in him. I'm tellin' ya true here, detective. Charles is weak.'

'What makes you say that?'

'He's my brother, for Christ's sake. I grew up

89

with him.'

'And that's it?'

In fact, I'm not expecting Terry Hauptman to somehow implicate his brother. I'm here to nibble at the edges, to establish a few facts before I make a second run at Charles. And I'm not worried about the lawyer, Arthur Allard, Esq. Not only did Charles never indicate that Allard represents him, Charles isn't a suspect because there's no proof that a crime was committed. Though he can always tell me to go fuck myself, he's not entitled to a lawyer.

'Lemme clue you in about Charles.' Terry opens a desk drawer and reaches inside. Right away, I think he's going for a pack of cigarettes. Instead, he pulls out a mint and pops it into his mouth. 'Charles was the first born – he's got me by five years – so he was in line to take over the business. And that was definitely the original plan. Charles worked here every summer, all through high school and college, and he was pretty good at the mechanics, at least according to my father. But it didn't work out for one simple reason: Charles was too soft. A business like this, sometimes you gotta finagle. Skim cash, pad bills where you can, grease property managers, view every customer as a walk-in ATM. Charles he didn't like that much, but he went along.'

'So what was the problem?'

'The workers. Charles wanted to be friends with his employees, he wanted them to like him. Dad made the ugly truth plain. He told Charles, over and over, "These men are not your friends.

They can never be your friends because you have too much power over their lives.'"

'But Charles didn't get the point?'

'He got the point. He just couldn't deal with it.' Hauptman jabs a finger at my chest. 'Take right now, for example, the recession. So far this year, I've laid off seven workers, three drivers, two stock clerks and two of the women who work in the office. You think I don't know they have families to support? You think I don't know they got zero chance of finding another job right now? But if I didn't do it, I'd go outta business and nobody would have an income.'

'But there's still a difference. Between you and them.'

'Which is?'

'Which is that you're never the one who gets laid off.'

'That's exactly right. Call it juice. Charles is not a guy who can deal with havin' juice. Put him in charge and he'll go down with the ship.'

Though I was fairly sure that Terry was speaking in all sincerity, I wasn't convinced by his argument. If Charles was willing to sacrifice his financial interests for his employees, wasn't it likely he'd risk his freedom to end his wife's suffering?

'Tell me, what was Joyce Hauptman like? Before her stroke?'

Terry doesn't hesitate. 'A mouse,' he tells me. 'A fearful little mouse who needed protection. And that's what Charles did, right? He protected the injured maiden like he was born to the task. Martyrdom suited him.'

91

'You say she was injured? How?'

'I don't know the details, but I'll tell you this. Max Baum is a scumbag of the first magnitude. Myself, I think he harassed his wife into the grave. That would be Lola. She committed suicide four years ago.'

'Suicide?'

'Yeah, she cut her wrists in the bathtub.'

I can't say the info doesn't capture my attention, but I'm quick to put it on the back burner. 'Correct me if I'm mistaken,' I say, 'but it appears that you don't think much of Max Baum.'

He rolls his eyes. 'You have a conversation with Max, somewhere along the line he's gonna put you down. He's gotta show you that he's the big dog. It doesn't matter how polite you are. He can't control himself.'

'But your brother works for Max.'

'Max let Charles work at home and that relieves a lot of the pressure. See, Joyce went to a nursing home after she was discharged from the hospital, a real hellhole in Far Rockaway. I know this because I went there with Charles a few times and the place was a horror. But so what? From Joyce's point of view, it didn't matter. That's because Joyce didn't have a point of view.'

'So, you don't think she was aware?'

'Aware? Gimme a break.' He dismisses the idea with an annoyed wave. 'What Charles shoulda done was walk the fuck away. Instead, he visited Joyce three times a week and watched his wife deteriorate. Smart, right? I tell ya, when Charles told me he wanted to bring Joyce home,

I wasn't surprised. But there were problems. How could he take care of Joyce and go out to work every day? Max's offer took care of that, no question.'

I nod to myself, now ready to explore the area I came to explore. 'Ya know, it wasn't bad enough that your brother worked for his father-in-law, Max controlled the purse strings, too. The nurses told me that Max paid them for their services and paid for Joyce's medical supplies.'

'Ah, Lola's revenge.'

'Sorry?'

'Lola was Max's wife. She committed suicide, remember?'

'Right, right. So, what's this about revenge?'

Terry's grin extends from ear to ear. He pulls open the bottom drawer on his desk, this time retrieving a bottle of Wild Turkey and a couple of plastic tumblers. A moment later, we're sipping at our drinks.

'This is a good story, detective, one of the best. It starts about forty years ago when Maxwell Baum, heir to the fortune of Otto Baum, proposes to Lola Pinsky, only daughter of a kosher butcher who immigrated from Poland. Lola's well educated – she has a master's degree from Columbia – but the Pinskys aren't rich. And they're not cultured, either. They live in a Jewish neighborhood in Flushing and attend an Orthodox synagogue where the women sit behind a screen.'

'Sounds like a perfect match.' I shake my head when Terry laughs. 'No, I'm serious. If Max Baum is as bad as you describe him, he'd definitely want a wife he could put down. He'd want to establish his superiority from the outset. What better way than to marry beneath him?'

'OK, I'll go with that. But Max demanded a concession first. He got Lola to sign a pre-nuptial agreement that kept their finances separate. Yeah, he'd pay all their living expenses, but if the marriage broke up, she wouldn't get a dime of his money. Only the joke was on him. Lola peddled real estate for ten years before she opened her first brokerage and she really learned the business. By the time she sold out to American Realty, a year after Joyce's stroke, she was a powerhouse in Queens, Brooklyn and Nassau County. She had twenty outlets and a hundred people working for her. Hey, I'm in business myself. I know how hard it is. My hat's off to her.'

He finishes his drink in one gulp, then crushes the tumbler and tosses it in the waste basket. 'Lola left her fortune to her daughter, every fucking penny. That was the revenge I mentioned. She cut her husband out altogether, which she could not have done without his help. See, unless there's a pre-nuptial agreement, a spouse inherits at least fifty per cent in New York. Max Baum screwed himself.'

I raise my glass and drink. The liquor burns my throat, but settles nicely in my stomach. 'That's a good story. No, make that a great story. But it doesn't explain why Max controls the purse strings.'

'Oh, yeah, that. I almost forgot.' He pushes his chair back until it's touching the wall. 'Lola killed herself about six months after Joyce's stroke. At the time, Joyce was still in a nursing home and obviously incompetent, so the matter was turned over to Probate Court. Now, if Charles had applied for a formal guardianship before Lola's death, Lola's money would have come to him naturally. But he hadn't and Max went into Probate Court first, asking to be made executor of his wife's estate because her husband had a conflict of interest. Charles, he could have gotten a lawyer. He could have fought the motion and probably won. But my brother's not a fighter, detective, which is what I've been telling you from the beginning. He just let it happen and now Max writes the checks.'

'Not any more,' I observe. 'Tell me, how much money are we talking about here?'

Terry shakes his head. 'I'm wastin' my time,' he announces. 'You're convinced that my brother's guilty and you're only lookin' for a way to convict him. Well, fuck you, detective. This conversation is over.'

I stand up, but don't bother extending a hand that he's unlikely to take. 'It's Charles who raised our suspicions, Terry. Charles himself, when he objected to an autopsy on religious grounds, then had his wife cremated a day later.'

For once, I catch Terry by surprise. 'Charles and Joyce religious? That's gotta be a joke. They didn't even celebrate the holidays. Passover, Yom Kippur, Rosh Hashanah? If it wasn't for our mom, they wouldn't be any more important to Charles and Joyce than Arbor Day.'

Ten

Martyrdom suited him. As I make the long drive from Greenpoint to Coney Island, I can't shake Terry Hauptman's judgment. Me, I'm not the self-sacrificing type, the simple fact that I've chosen not to marry being a case in point. Married cops live miserable lives. Family and job are always in conflict and I consider myself fortunate in not having to make that phone call when I'm required to work overtime. I'm talking about the one that brings down an avalanche of guilt. If I choose to work thirty-six straight hours – a fairly common occurrence – I don't have to answer to anyone. My colleagues, on the other hand, would rather face a psychotic on angel dust than disappoint the family again. Crestfallen doesn't begin to describe their expressions when they pick up that phone.

One thing is sure, you can't miss your kid's baseball game or dance recital if you don't have kids in the first place.

As I inch my way south on the Van Wyck Expressway, I envision Charles Hauptman rising to the same set of demanding tasks, day after day after day. I imagine him permanently depressed, his eyes perpetually downcast, his heart always heavy. But martyrdom suited Charles Hauptman, at least according to his brother, as did sacrifice and a regimented life, a life with every minute accounted for. So, maybe I'm completely off base. Maybe it was freedom that he dreaded. Maybe he feared escape.

I push Charles Hauptman's suffering to one side as I pull off the Belt Parkway at Coney Island Avenue. A killer's suffering isn't really a cop's business anyway, not unless he hopes to exploit that suffering. I had a job to do and I intended to do it. As always.

Coney Island and the bordering neighborhood of Brighton Beach have long been magnets for post-Soviet immigrants from Russia and Ukraine. Seven- and eight-story brick apartment houses dominate the architecture, with a few low-income projects tossed into the mix. Most of the buildings are as featureless as Terry Hauptman's warehouse in Greenpoint. This is not to discount the ocean-front boardwalk and what's left of the amusement parks that made Coney Island famous. But Anna Berevski lives many blocks from the ocean, in a gray building on a treeless road lined with parked cars. As in-structed, I call her from the street – her intercom isn't working – and she buzzes me inside.

When the elevator door opens on the seventh floor, Anna's waiting for me. She's standing in the doorway to her apartment and she's scowl-ing.

'You are late.'

'Traffic.' I scoot past her before she can bar my way. 'Sorry.'

'Please to not disrespect me,' she says, her accent as thick as pudding. 'I am not to be disrespected.'

I watch her shut the door and turn to face me. She's a short woman, maybe thirty years old, with a rounded belly and no ass whatsoever. Her short black hair, as stiff as wire, clings to her scalp as though attached with a staple gun.

For a moment, we stare at each other without speaking. I know she's trying to read me, but I don't mind. I'm thinking more about why – if she's prepared to tell the truth, the whole truth and nothing but the truth – she feels the need to make an assessment.

'So, please, say to me what is so important that it cannot wait until tomorrow,' she demands.

'I'm off tomorrow, likewise on Sunday, so it'd have to wait until Monday.' I shrug. 'What could I say? I got a boss, he wants what he wants. Like you, right, you and Max Baum?'

I haven't forgotten Nurse Santiago telling me that Berevski is Baum's pet and the question is designed to catch her off-guard. It doesn't.

'You are listening to this bitch, Santiago,' she accuses. 'But you are wasting your time. Santiago is crazy to find fault with everyone.'

'When you say "crazy", do you mean enthusiastic? Or insane?'

Berevski's black eyes don't waver. 'Her notes, you should read them. Patient has some new disease every week. How many times pneumonia, I couldn't even count so high. Bedsores she has by the hundreds. And always the other nurses are ignoring these terrible complaints.'

Anna Berevski's living room is so cluttered that I have to clear the debris off a chair before sitting down. There are clothes everywhere, some obviously dirty, some with price tags still attached. Piles of opened mail, magazines and newspapers cover every horizontal surface, including the counters in the kitchen. On the floor beneath a window, three tarnished samovars rest side by side, while a pair of gilded icons lie flat on coffee table. In a corner, unopened boxes of electronic goods – televisions, sound systems and laptop computers – form three columns that rise nearly to the ceiling.

I pull a notebook from my jacket and flip the pages for a moment before speaking. 'Now, tell me if I've got this right. Nurse Borders called you shortly after Joyce Hauptman's death. She told you the medical examiner intended to perform an autopsy. Then you called Max Baum.'

Nurse Berevski's eyes turn inward for a moment and I know she's deciding whether to lie or tell the truth. Her problem, should she choose the former, is what lie to tell. What lie to tell and if I'll find out anyway.

'One thing here is wrong,' she says. 'It is Mr Baum who is calling me, not me calling to him.'

'But you told him the medical examiner was planning to do an autopsy.'

'For why do I keep this secret?'

'No reason. I'm just establishing the sequence of events.' In fact, Anna is not only confirming a hunch – that Max knew about the autopsy – she's confirming Nurse Santiago's claim that Anna was close to Max Baum. As Nurse Borders was close to Charles. 'Nurse Borders told me that Joyce had a rash and diarrhea. Is that correct?'

'Yes.'

'When did these symptoms first appear?'

'Two or three days ago. After she is taking ampicillin. This rash, I have seen it before. Also the gastroenteritis. Every time patient takes antibiotics, she is having this.'

'What about the original infection? Did Dr...' It takes me a second to come up with the name. 'Did Dr Meyer provide the diagnosis?'

Anna Berevski's laugh is dismissive. 'No, Shirley calls doctor after Joyce runs temperature for two days. Prescription for ampicillin is made over telephone. Doctor is never coming.'

'Correct me if I'm wrong, but ampicillin is mostly used for tooth infections. How did Nurse Borders know the infection was in Joyce Hauptman's mouth?'

'Joyce's urine was clear. Also for her lungs.' Anna's responses are coming quickly now, and she's volunteering information. 'Understand, please. Patient had chronic infections in mouth. This is how it happens when there is no dental care for many years. Joyce's teeth could not even be properly brushed because of her contractions. Charles is wanting to have all her teeth removed, but he cannot find oral surgeon to do this operation. They say her breathing is compromised and anesthesia is too risky for patient who is not conscious anyway.'

'Is that what you think? That she was unconscious?'

'Ach, this question again, as if it matters.'

'Please, nurse, just tell me what you think.'

'This is not so easy. Sometimes I ask Joyce to turn her head or lift her arm and she does. Her eyes, too. When she looks at me, sometimes I am thinking she sees me. But when I ask her to squeeze my hand, there is never a response.'

'What about eye blinks?'

'This is craziness you heard from Shirley.' She taps a fingernail against her teeth, a gesture I'm unable to interpret. 'Understand, please, how it is between Charles and Shirley. Shirley is in love with Charles, so if Charles is thinking Joyce is aware, she thinks the same.'

'Did Nurse Borders tell you that she was in love with Charles Hauptman?'

'No, she never says this right to my face. But I think Shirley and Charles are lovers. I see this by how he looks at her.'

Nurse Berevski stands by the door throughout our little conversation. Though the apartment is warm enough to make me sweat, her arms are folded across a fluffy wool sweater and her unwavering stare is cool and calculating.

'Did Charles Hauptman ever express a wish to end his wife's suffering?' I ask.

'I have heard him one time arguing with Dr Meyer. This is perhaps a year before. Charles does not wish to treat his wife's infection, but doctor will not go along. He writes prescription and hands it to Charles. He says if prescription is not filled, he cannot be doctor to Joyce.'

'And Charles? What did he do?'

'Charles must have doctor. If there is not

101

doctor for writing orders, nurses will quit.'

'So, he filled the prescription?'

'He has no choice. He cannot care for wife by himself.' Anna's expression softens momentarily and she looks down at her feet for a moment. Then she nods once before speaking. 'For wanting Joyce's life to end I cannot be condemning Charles. When she is having a seizure, it is terrible to see. Doctor says she is not aware of suffering, she is not conscious. But is dog conscious? Is bird conscious? Is reptile conscious? These animals would be put out of misery if their suffering could not be cured. Why is only human allowed to be in endless pain?'

Fortunately, I don't have to answer the question. A man emerges from an inner room. Older than Anna by at least fifteen years, he wears boxer shorts and a wife-beater T-shirt and his arms are thick with muscle. His mouth is twisted into a scowl but he doesn't look at me as he crosses to the refrigerator and opens the door.

'This is brother, Leonid,' Anna says.

Brother Leonid doesn't acknowledge his sister. Or me, for that matter. He opens the freezer compartment and removes a bottle of Stolichnaya and grunts with apparent satisfaction. Watching him, I feel an urge to knock the smirk off his face, but there's no guarantee I'll come out on top should I make the attempt. I'm a pretty big guy – over six feet and nearly two hundred pounds – but everything about him, including scars on his forehead and jaw, indicates a relish for combat. His nose has been broken so many times it lies nearly flat on his face.

Still without speaking, Leonid disappears into the bedroom, closing the door behind him. Anna stares after him for a moment, her eyes slightly narrowed, her lips pursed. Then she looks at me.

'We are finished, yes?'

'Can't wait to get back to Leonid?'

As with Charles Hauptman, I get lucky. For a fraction of a second, Anna Berevski's face turns to stone, displaying a calculated ruthlessness that goes well beyond the routine contempt she's exhibited up till now. I think back to a Russian I arrested last year, Sergei Yalnikov. American prisons, he told me, are paradise compared to Russian gulags. As American cops are, relatively speaking, angels of mercy.

'I am asking you nicely when you walk in to not disrespect me,' Anna declares, her tone matter-of-fact, her calm fully restored.

'Sorry, I lost my head. But I only have one more question. Charles was responsible for Joyce's care for ... I believe it was six hours a day.'

'Six, yes.'

'How would you rate the quality of the care he gave her? Did you ever observe any sign of neglect?'

'Never.' She unfolds her arms and moves toward the door. 'This do not doubt, please. Everything nurses do for Joyce, he is also doing. Charles is always loving his wife.'

'Loving her enough to kill her?'

She hesitates before answering, bringing a finger to her lips. 'I think, in the end, Charles would do anything to stop the suffering.'

Eleven

I hang out in Coney Island long enough to visit the original Nathan's hotdog stand on Surf Avenue. I buy a couple of chilidogs, an order of fries and a soda, and carry them, along with a pile of napkins, to a bench on the boardwalk. A crescent moon hangs low in the east. What little light it casts skips over the incoming surf to fall into my lap. For the next few minutes, while I stuff my face, I listen to the waves pound the white sand, the odor of the sea as pungent as the heavily spiced chili on my hotdog.

A life-is-good moment, no doubt about it. Made even better because my work on the Hauptman case is pretty much done until the lab completes an analysis of the bone samples. I'm thinking that Nurse Santiago was telling the truth about Joyce's rash, that it probably showed up before Joyce began taking ampicillin. But I also believe Anna Berevski. Theresa Santiago was given to uncovering problems that didn't exist and her own notes will discredit her. As a potential witness, she's pretty much useless.

This is bad news, which I'll have to convey to Morelli, whether he wants to hear it or not. But I'm unconcerned. More and more, I'm hoping the whole case will go away, that the cremated bone fragments will prove to be untestable, that even if they test positive for arsenic they'll be inadmissible in court. My basic claim – that I was merely collecting trash when I recovered them – sounded pretty good when I made the decision to go ahead. But from a legal point of view, I may very well have been robbing a grave.

I finish my fries before starting on the last hotdog. By now, both hands – and my lips, too, no doubt – are dripping chili. I'm leaning forward, hoping to save my shirt and tie, and my mouth is on fire from the hot sauce I added. But I persevere, wiping my hands and face, tossing the soiled napkins into the Nathan's bag, tossing the bag into a trash basket. Then I walk out onto the beach and spend a moment listening to the ocean. I'm remembering Anna Berevski's question. Why are suffering animals routinely euthanized while human beings are left to linger in pain? I suspect it's because most people believe that's the way God wants it. The only other answer is money. Unconscious patients generate lots and lots of dollars for the medical profession. My Aunt Margaret's nursing home runs to more than a hundred grand a year. Joyce Hauptman's bills, given her one-on-one nursing care, had to be twice that.

Eventually, I admit that I don't have any answers, not to Anna's question, or to why the New York Police Department is conducting an investigation in the first place. I tell myself that I'm just doing my job, just following orders. The answer fails to convince me.

I watch the foam rush toward me as wave after wave breaks on the sand. I'm thinking that no one ordered me to follow Charles and his entourage to the Botanical Gardens. No one told me to collect those bone fragments. I might have buried the investigation forever. I might have, but I didn't. I might have, but I couldn't.

I write up my notes in the car, both interviews, with Terence Hauptman and Nurse Santiago. I leave nothing out. Charles Hauptman had motive upon motive for killing his wife. So what? There's no smoking gun here, and no proof that a crime has been committed. Hopefully, it will remain that way and I can return to my chosen profession, catching murderers.

On a whim, I pass by Charles Hauptman's mini-mansion on the way back to headquarters. A mistake, as it turns out, because I discover eight trash bags, an IV pole and a pair of tray tables at the curb. The bags are large and black and obviously contain more than the usual household trash. By all appearances, Charles is moving on.

Though I have some doubt about the legitimacy of collecting Joyce Hauptman's remains, there's no legal obstacle here. There's no legal obstacle and I know that arsenic is deposited in human hair. As I know that hairbrush I saw when I wandered through Joyce's bedroom, should it be nesting inside one of the bags, will provide a smoking gun that no court will reject. Assuming that Joyce Hauptman was murdered.

It's take it or leave it time. Collect the trash or allow the Department of Sanitation to haul it away in the morning.

Without making a conscious decision, I put the car in gear and attempt a getaway. But it's no use. I'm a cop and I can't let go. I turn left at the end of the block, turn left again at the end of the next block, then make another left and another until I'm back in front of the Hauptman home. I'm telling myself that I'm a complete asshole even as I get out of the car, pop the trunk and fill it with trash bags. I do notice the front door when it opens and I do see Charles emerge, but I don't stop until he comes within a few feet and extends a pack of cigarettes.

'Thanks.'

'You're welcome.'

Charles appears even more haggard. He's standing beneath the outer leaves on an enormous maple tree and the pale orange light cast by a streetlamp falls on him in soft, nearly indistinct patches. I light the cigarette and pull the smoke into my lungs. The first hit makes me dizzy, as usual, and I lean back on the front fender.

'So, you think I'm a murderer.' The way Charles speaks the words, it's not a question.

'Mr Hauptman, if you were a suspect, I'd have to inform you of your constitutional rights, which you notice I haven't done. That's because there's no definitive proof that a crime's been committed, only enough suspicion to warrant a half-assed investigation.'

My good deed for the day. I'm telling him that anything he says can be used against him. I'm warning him to keep his mouth shut. Not that he listens. No, Charles needs to talk. I can see the truth in his eyes. The emotions cascading through his heart and mind are too powerful. He can't contain them.

'I came out here to tell you that I didn't kill my wife,' he says.

'Thanks for sharing.'

Charles manages a rueful smile. 'I suppose that doesn't count for much.'

'Actually, there's nothing you can say that'll help you here. If you hated her? That's motive. If you loved her? That's motive, too. Plus, I know that you would have let her infections go untreated if Dr Meyer hadn't opposed the idea, and that you would have discontinued nutrition and fluids if the law allowed it. Myself, I don't blame you.'

'What if I tell you that I was prepared to care for Joyce indefinitely?' He jams his hands in his pocket. 'What if I tell you that I enjoyed caring for her?'

I watch a car enter the block and accelerate past where I'm standing, the stink of its exhaust lingering for a moment. I'm wondering what I'm supposed to do here, forbid him to speak?

'How much?' I ask.

'How much?'

'How much was the estate your wife inherited worth? In round numbers.'

'Before the recession, nearly twenty million. Now I don't know. I can't get a clean accounting from Max.'

'Can't get an accounting from Max? You'll forgive me for saying so, but from what little

I've heard, the man sounds like a total prick. Why did you let him get control of your wife's money in the first place?'

'Actually, Max did me a favor.'

'How's that?'

'As Joyce's guardian, he not only had to account to the court for every penny spent on her care, he had to pay all of Joyce's bills and meet a payroll every Friday. This was a headache I didn't need.'

I blow on the coal at the end of my cigarette, watch it turn bright orange. 'Plus, of course, even if you had the money, you wouldn't have it.'

'Exactly. If I'd opposed Max, I might have been appointed Joyce's guardian. But so what? I'd have no more right to that money than Max. It would always be Joyce's. It would never be mine.'

'Until she died. Until now.'

As I speak the words, I'm thinking I got off a pretty good shot. Not so. Charles nods and smiles.

'I'm not surprised to hear you say that, detective. But the simple truth is that I didn't need Joyce's money. I don't gamble or drink or use drugs, and I never have. If you dig a little deeper, you'll find that I'm perfectly solvent. I pay my bills every month and I have no debts outside of a small mortgage on my home.'

The cigarette I hold between my thumb and forefinger has burned halfway down and I'm wondering if I can drag out the conversation long enough to cadge another. 'Were you and your wife religious?' I ask.

'No, not at all. Joyce was an editor at a travel magazine, the *Intrepid Wanderer*, and we traveled all over the world. We were planning a trip to southern Africa when she fell. Literally, detective. We were sitting on the floor sorting through a pile of brochures when she disappeared forever. One minute there, the next gone.'

'If she was gone, why did you care for her? Why didn't you let someone else do it? And why did you tell me that you thought she was conscious?' I don't wait for an answer. 'Look, you objected to an autopsy on religious grounds, an autopsy that would have established a cause of death. Now you're telling me that you and your wife weren't religious. What am I supposed to think?'

'I didn't have anything to do with that.'

'But you know about it, Charles, and you know who made the claim. So, why don't you tell me? Then we'll both know.'

'I did...' Hauptman takes another step back. 'She suffered so much, detective. You have no idea, no idea at all. Did she really deserve this last indignity? To be put on a slab and cut into pieces? What if it was someone you loved? How would you feel?'

'That's not an answer.'

'Max had the clout,' he finally admits. 'He made the call.'

'But you had no objection to the bogus claim?'

Charles shakes his head. 'I knew nothing about the religious objections he raised. By the time I found out, Joyce had already been cremated.'

110

'Less than twenty-four hours after her death.'

'Her last wish.'

'Pardon me?'

'In her will, Joyce specified that she be cremated upon her death and her ashes scattered in the forest at the Bronx Botanical Gardens. We loved the gardens, detective. We loved them.'

I'm trying to work up some righteous indignation, but I can't. I'm thinking that he's been imagining the sequence for years, the cremation followed by the formal scattering of her ashes. And he's right, too, about the autopsy. I've witnessed many autopsies and the word 'indignity' is way too mild for what happens on that table. If it was someone I loved, I'd do everything in my power to prevent one.

'Did you ever stop to think,' I ask, 'that Max's interference only raised our suspicions?'

The question seems to revive him. He squares his shoulders and turns to face me dead-on. 'I didn't kill my wife,' he informs me, 'so I'm not worried about what you might or might not find. You want my garbage, you can have it.'

'I've already got your garbage.' I take the last bag and toss it onto the back seat. 'But if you can spare another smoke, I'd be happy to take advantage of your generosity.'

I carry the loot back to the One-Twelve and clear a space in the basement. Then I photograph the garbage bags and number them, one through eight. It's ten o'clock and quiet, the only sound the snoring of Patrolman Elman Schneider, the precinct's property clerk. Elman's asleep inside his chain-link cage fifty feet away.

Along with all of Joyce Hauptman's meds, I bag and label a used feeding tube, a used, though empty, urine-collection bag, a used feeding bag, three pair of latex gloves and a hairbrush. These items will go to the lab for testing. The rest, the dozens of items still in their original packages, I return to the numbered garbage bags. Then I awaken Patrolman Schneider, who's not altogether happy about my interrupting his nap.

'Jeez,' he tells me as he takes possession of the garbage bags, 'I hope there's nothing in here that's gonna rot. That would be a health code violation.'

His remark gives me an idea and I quickly climb the stairs to the third floor where I discover one of my colleagues, Eve Durand, at her desk.

'Morelli in his office?' I ask.

'Yeah, the prick.'

I suppose I should ask her what's wrong, but the truth is that I don't want to know. I locate the case file in a filing cabinet and bring it to my desk. Sure enough, the entries are out of order. Morelli's been busy. But I don't care. Let him look wherever he likes. I've done my job.

In the old days, before the job linked our computers to the outside world, almost every inquiry involving public information necessitated a trip to some city, state or federal agency. Now I let my fingers do the walking. I reach into the Department of Health's computer for its licensing records, entering the names of the three nurses employed by Max Baum. Shirley Borders and Theresa Santiago are properly licensed, but Anna Berevski's name does not appear in DOH files.

Encouraged, I reach into NYSIIS, the New York State Identification and Intelligence System, a database that includes the state's criminal records. Again, Borders and Santiago come up clean. Not so the Berevskis. Leonid passed two years in an upstate prison, having pled guilty to assault in the second degree. More than likely, given the plea bargain, the original charge was assault in the first degree.

Leonid's sister, by contrast, has only a misdemeanor conviction on her record. For practicing as a nurse without a license. In fact, she's still on probation. If she'd attempted to work in any hospital or nursing home, or for Medicaid as an independent provider, she'd have been spotted immediately. But Max was paying the nurses with his daughter's money. No city or state agency was involved.

I carry the information into Morelli's office, where I describe my night's work in detail. He's not happy with my assessment of Nurse Santiago, but I point out that the nurses' opinions really don't matter now.

'In fact, when you think about it, if Joyce Hauptman was poisoned, all three of them are suspects. They had opportunity.'

'How would they get arsenic into her?'

'Through her feeding tube, which is how she received all her medications.'

'You can put a pill through a feeding tube?'

'No problem, as long as you crush it first.'

He considers this for a moment, then says, 'What about the Russian nurse?'

'Berevski?'

'Yeah, should we contact her probation officer?'

'I don't think so, boss.'

'Why not?'

'Because if we do, we'll have nothing to threaten her with later on.'

Again, Morelli pauses to consider the ramifications. Then he says, 'I've got a friend in the lab who can expedite the testing. Until then, we wait. But you did good work, detective. Without your initiative, there wouldn't be anything to test. Congratulations.'

Twelve

I'm supposed to spend my Saturday night hunting up, if not a girlfriend, at least a sexual companion. But I don't have the heart for it. I eat a stir-fry assembled from leftover meatloaf and rapidly softening vegetables culled from my refrigerator's vegetable bin. Then I wash the dishes and scour the sink. By eight o'clock, I've settled in to watch the Boston Red Sox play Tampa Bay in the championship round of the baseball playoffs. The formal introduction of the players reminds me that neither the Mets or the

Yankees made the playoffs this year, which does not improve my sour mood. To make matters worse, the game is lopsided, with Tampa Bay's hitters pounding Tim Wakefield's knuckleballs early and often.

I make it through the bottom of the fourth inning before I admit that I'm too restless to sit still. Then I grab a windbreaker and head for a cop bar on Queens Boulevard, not far from the 59th Street Bridge. My partner, Davy, is standing at the end of the bar. Good news. I don't have to be anything with Davy. We've been together long enough for him to recognize, and tolerate, my every mood.

'What're you drinkin' tonight, Lenny?' the bartender, Roy Maloney, calls out from the end of the bar.

'Draw me a Bass ale.'

Davy waits until I take my first sip, then says, 'I been on leave for one day and I'm already goin' nuts. And I'm makin' Rita nuts, too. Swear to God, Lenny, I'm not designed for leisure. My mind won't stop turning. First I see the entry, then Morales bent over the cocaine, then Corinne Mariposa comin' through the bathroom door. And the worst part is that it never changes. It's the same movie, over and over, so what's the point?'

'I think it's called the healing process. You wait long enough and it eventually stops.'

'That's fine, but I gotta find somethin' to do. Either that or fucking explode.'

One thing about Lenny Shaw, he's always ready to help a friend in need. I nod sagaciously

115

and say, 'Well, there is something, a little matter that's been ticking away at the back of my mind. According to Charles Hauptman's brother, Max Baum's wife – her name is Lola – committed suicide. She cut her wrists in the bathtub.'

'When did this happen?'

'A few years ago.'

'And you're suspicious?'

'Lola Baum was worth millions, Davy, and her husband didn't know she'd willed everything to her daughter.'

'You want me to poke around?'

'Yeah, see if she left a note.'

On a small flat-screen TV above our heads, the playoff game between Boston and Tampa Bay continues. The game's in the seventh inning with Tampa Bay up 12–2. The game may be a dud, but the picture on the little set is incredibly sharp, the colors so bright they appear unnatural.

'You wanna make a trade?' I ask.

'What for what?'

'Your post-traumatic stress for the Charles Hauptman case.'

Davy shakes his head. 'I don't see why you're worried about Hauptman. Even if he's arrested and the state finds a jury willing to convict, Charles won't get more than five years.'

'Only five years? That's all?'

'Partner, you're lookin' at this through the wrong microscope. The assembly and the state senate wrote the law on mercy killing. Their members were elected by the people, just like the governor who signed the law into effect, whoever he was. You're a cop, Lenny. You can't ignore the law because it happens to be inconvenient. Cops aren't allowed to decide which laws are just and which unjust, and for damn good reason. The last thing this city needs is thirty-seven thousand penal codes.'

I like Davy's little speech well enough. On the surface, his reasoning is sharp enough to convince. But I don't live on the surface and neither does he. The two of us, we commonly allow criminals to remain on the street. We even have a name for this class of lawbreaker. We call them snitches.

I'm about to point this out when the door opens and a woman strolls inside. Somewhere in her thirties, she has blue eyes and auburn hair that rolls across her shoulders.

'Doesn't take much to divert your attention,' Davy observes. 'But if you dropped a Viagra before you left home, you wasted your money. Her name's Merle Brink and she's a lesbian. Do you know Valerie Impellateri, from Borough Command? She walked out on her husband six months ago.'

'Sure.'

'Well, Valerie and Merle, they're an item.'

Lieutenant Valerie Impellateri, as if summoned, walks into the bar. She's in full uniform and she winks at me before joining her girlfriend. I don't know what to make of the wink, but I entertain a very brief fantasy in which Valerie invites me to a threesome. This fantasy is the highlight of my evening.

* * *

'They put Margaret on a ventilator last week,' my mother tells me. We're having breakfast in a diner on 21st Street in Long Island City, coming from Mass at St Anthony's. The diner is huge and packed and the buzz of a hundred conversations surrounds us.

'She can't breathe on her own?'

'Not any more.' My mom is in her sixties, but still vigorous, still going out to work every day. Except for a few shallow lines at the corners of her eyes and mouth, her skin is smooth and she maintains her figure by working out three times a week.

'Is that good news or bad?'

'Good. The way the laws are written, a patient in a vegetative state can be removed from a ventilator and allowed to ... expire.'

I recall my conversations with Charles Hauptman and the nurses. New York State law permits the removal of life support in hopeless cases, but specifically excludes food and nutrition from the definition of life support. As long as Aunt Margaret was able to breathe without the aid of vent, she had to be kept alive.

'So, what happens next?'

'That's up to Jack.' My mother's lips curl into a dismissive sneer. 'The bastard.'

Though Uncle Jack hasn't divorced his brain-injured wife, he's moved to western New Jersey and lives with his lover, a woman many years his junior. I spoke to him about his choices at a wedding two years ago and I had a hard time faulting him when he insisted there was nothing he could do for Margaret.

118

'I can't make her better,' he told me. 'There's no medicine on the planet that can make her better. And I can't comfort her, either. So what's the point of my sitting by her bed for an hour every two weeks? What does she gain? What do I gain? She's not a shrine, for Christ's sake.'

A waiter shows up, interrupting our conversation. He lays a western omelet and a side of bacon in front of me, and eggs benedict in front of my mother. I've spoken to Mom about ordering eggs benedict in a diner, where the sauce is cooked up in factories and shipped in five-gallon drums. I even offered to take her to a decent French restaurant where she could sample the real thing. But she's not interested.

'The thing about it, Lenny,' Mom notes after a few minutes, 'is that I can't even start the process. Jack's still her husband. The decision to go ahead is up to him. And he's gonna have to meet with the hospice staff and do a lot of paperwork.'

'So, you want me to call him?'

Mom smiles a perfectly innocent smile, a smile of great satisfaction. The last time she and Jack spoke, they nearly came to blows. 'Would you?' she asks. 'There's a hospice in Manhattan, on the west side, that'll take her.'

I spend the next few minutes, while my breakfast rapidly cools, jotting down the name and phone number of the hospice, the extension of a social worker already familiar with the case and Jack's phone number in New Jersey. That done, I get back to work, responding to Mom's occasional remarks with little more than grunts, until

I finally spread the last of the butter on what's left of my English muffin. Only then do I get down to business.

'Here I am, on the one hand trying to arrange for the death of my aunt, while on the other trying to put a man in jail for doing exactly the same thing to his wife. And for exactly the same reason.'

'You should have walked away from that case,' Mom observes. 'This business, it's not for cops.'

'Oh, all of a sudden you're a liberal?'

Mom's always been a law-and-order fanatic, but she doesn't rise to my challenge and I know she's given the matter due consideration. 'There's no way you can write a law that covers every single possibility,' she insists. 'There's always gonna be exceptions.'

'Maybe so, but this isn't one of them. The law covers this situation exactly. And I don't recall seeing you trying to end Margaret's life on your own. Why does the law bind you and not Charles Hauptman?'

'But that's just it, Lenny. I should have done something and I would have, too, except that I was scared I'd get caught. I mean, we're talkin' about my sister.' She pushes her plate to one side and sips at her coffee. 'Margaret was always the most daring, more even than my brother. You climb into a tree, she'd climb higher. You make a loop-the-loop on the swings in the playground, she'd make two. And dance? She could dance all night.'

I watch my mother's eyes drop to the coffee in

120

her cup. Mom's a stalwart type and I know this isn't a side of herself she likes to display. She broke down right after my father's sudden death in an auto accident. For the first few days, her eyes were wild with grief and she couldn't sit for more than few minutes at time, not even at the wake. She looked as if she'd been seized by a spirit, that she'd been invaded. But she threw it off within a couple of weeks, telling me she was tired of feeling sorry for herself.

'All right, enough with Charles Hauptman,' I say. 'The evidence is in the pipeline. Whatever decisions I made, I can't take 'em back now.'

'Good, let's discuss your Uncle Jack.'

Our waiter comes over to drop the check on our table. Most likely, he wants to be rid of us. The waiting area by the front door is crowded. But Mom isn't taking the hint. 'Bring me a cheese Danish,' she tells him, 'and if you can get someone to refill my coffee, I'd be grateful.'

Then she turns back to me. 'Can we talk strategy here? About Jack? Because the way I'm thinking, we're gonna have to use dynamite to get him off his ass.'

I listen politely, but her strategy, which involves a half-dozen relatives, goes in one ear and out the other. Within minutes of returning home, I call Uncle Jack and lay out the situation. I'm not surprised when he takes down the phone number of the social worker at the hospice, or when he promises to call on the following morning.

'You tell yourself that life goes on,' Jack explains. 'You tell yourself that life is short and you'll be gone soon enough and you better learn to enjoy the life you have before it's too late. But last week, on Maggie's birthday, I cried like a baby.'

Thirteen

The toxicology results come back in mid-week. They're waiting on my desk when I arrive on Wednesday afternoon and they're unequivocal. Joyce Hauptman's bones, hair and feeding tube have all tested positive for arsenic sulfide. I stare at the numbers for a moment, but they're absolutely meaningless to me and I quickly move on to a second fax, this from the Office of the Medical Examiner. The manner of Joyce Hauptman's death is now officially a homicide.

At this point, I'm supposed to take the news to Morelli, but I don't. I want more information about arsenic poisoning before Morelli's decides what to do next. I make a five-thirty appointment with a toxicologist at the ME's office in Manhattan and leave the precinct immediately. Still, I'm ten minutes late when I enter Dr Rania Herzog's office.

Dr Herzog's a stunner, at least on first impression. Her features are perfectly balanced, her pale skin flawless, her teeth small and square and very, very white. Ordinarily, my antennae would already be twitching. But there's something off about her as well. Maybe it's the cat's-eye glasses on a chain, or the frumpy black dress with the padded shoulders, or the ragged part in her not-too-clean hair. But whatever, my first instinct, to pour on the charm, is quickly replaced by a resolutely businesslike demeanor.

'Sorry to be late, doctor. These days, what with lane reversals on the bridges and tunnels, it's as hard getting into the city during rush hour as it is getting out.'

She folds her hands and makes a little tsking noise with her tongue. 'Yes, fine, shall we get on with it? How can I help you?'

'I've never dealt with a case of arsenic sulfide...'

'Realgar.'

'Pardon?'

'The common name for arsenic sulfide is realgar.'

'When you say common, do you mean it's easy to get?'

'Fairly easy. Arsenic is a naturally occurring mineral. It's mined for industrial use in several countries and it's a common byproduct of other mining operations.' She drums her fingers on the table, a practiced gesture that runs from the pinky on her left hand to the pinky on her right. 'For example, the slag produced by coal mining is inevitably contaminated with arsenic, likewise for the ash produced when coal is burned.'

'That's interesting, doctor, and I suppose my suspect could have acquired arsenic from an industrial source. But it's very unlikely. Charles

Hauptman's an accountant who works from home.' I flash a quick rueful grin. 'Tell ya the truth, I was hoping he got the poison from a can of bug spray.'

'Sorry to disappoint. A less toxic form of arsenic is sometimes found in agricultural pesticides, but arsenic, in any form, is banned for use by the general public.'

'Then how would Hauptman acquire enough arsenic to poison his wife?'

Dr Herzog turns to her computer. Keys flash, the mouse clicks, until she finally swivels the monitor to face me. 'As I said, realgar is a mineral, a crystal. In its purest form, its red color is finer than the red of a ruby. Realgar is used, by the way, to add the color red to fireworks.'

I register the words, but most of my attention is on the screen. Herzog has opened an eBay web page displaying fifty-nine realgar specimens up for bids, some for a little as $1.99.

'Can I assume that a search would uncover other outlets for the sale of realgar?'

'Certainly. Or you might purchase the mineral at any gallery specializing in crystal. Realgar is collectible.'

Means, motive and opportunity, the three legs of the homicide stool, the legs that hold up the case. It's been clear, from the outset, that Hauptman had motive and opportunity. Now I know the means was readily available and that's bad news for Charles.

Dr Herzog stands up and offers her hand. Time for me to go. 'Have you handled a case of arsenic poisoning before, detective?' she asks.

'Can't say I have.'

'Then you need to know something. The presence of arsenic in bone and hair means only that an individual was exposed to elevated levels of arsenic prior to death. What can't be demonstrated from an examination of bone and hair is that arsenic caused your victim's death, or even that her overall health was negatively impacted.'

'But the ME pronounced the manner of death as homicide. How—'

We end as we began, with Dr Herzog interrupting me. 'Manner of death is a term of art, detective. We have the end-stage symptoms – the rash, the gastroenteritis and the erythematous papules observed by the death investigator on the decedent's arm. We have traces of arsenic in the feeding tube, her bones and her hair. We have the hasty cremation and disposal of the victim's remains. On balance, we think it's very likely that she was deliberately poisoned.'

'But you can't be certain?'

'No, we can't.'

I'm about to leave when a thought occurs to me, one I might have already considered. 'The rash and the papules? Can I assume the death investigator documented them?'

'They were photographed.'

'Great.'

Dr Herzog shakes her head. 'The rash and the papules might have been caused by other conditions, as the defense will surely argue. An examination of the liver and the kidneys at autopsy, on the other hand, would have been definitive.'

* * *

125

I take everything to Morelli, the ME's fax, the lab's fax and my conversation with Dr Rania Herzog. I'm more disgusted than surprised at Morelli's joyous response, even after I point out Herzog's caveat. The presence of arsenic in bone and hair doesn't prove that arsenic is the cause of death.

'We got the son-of-a-bitch now, Lenny. Despite everything.'

I assume 'everything' refers to the cremation and the scattering of Joyce Hauptman's ashes, which Morelli – like Herzog – assumes to be evidence of a guilty mind. But if Charles was out to destroy evidence, why did he leave the hair-brush and the feeding tube standing at the curb where I could pick them up? Why didn't he flush Joyce's hair down the toilet? Why didn't he cut the feeding tube into tiny pieces and flush that, too?

These questions tickle the edge of my consciousness as I sit across from Morelli, as I bask in his enthusiasm.

'You done good, Lenny,' he tells me, not for the first time. 'If you hadn't followed your instincts, this prick would've walked away. I'm gonna recommend that you be kicked up to detective, first grade.' Still grinning, he shakes his head. 'You'd figure a guy like that, educated and all, would have more sense. What he should have done is put his wife in a nursing home. But some of these jerks, they think they're smarter than the cops. They think they can't get caught.'

Morelli doesn't wait for my response, or request my advice about what to do next. He calls

126

in an assistant district attorney to draw up a search warrant for Hauptman's residence. Most ADAs have a cynical attitude when it comes to search warrants, which require probable cause and a judge's signature. That's because cops generally request the right to conduct a search on the merest suspicion. But not this time. ADA Miriam Khan is so pleased when I present her with the lab work and the ME's conclusion that she adds Hauptman's computer to a list of items to be seized, along with the nurses' notes. The night-court judge is impressed as well. He signs the warrant after merely glancing at its contents.

I'm back at headquarters at ten o'clock, listening to a plan of action Morelli cooked up in my absence. The scene of the crime, Joyce's bedroom, will be processed by the Crime Scene Unit. Searching the rest of the house will fall to a trio of detectives culled from the unit's day shift. My job is to finally pry a confession out of Charles Hauptman.

'Give it everything you've got, Lenny. Tear this jerk a new asshole.'

I want to point out that the only real jerks in this equation are looking into each other's eyes, but I hold my tongue, as I hold off on expressing my resentment at Morelli's devising a strategy without my input. I'm the primary investigator, after all.

'When is all this going down?' I ask.

'Tomorrow morning, six o'clock. Two cars for the detectives, a CSU van, and two squad cars. When Hauptman looks out of his window, I want him to see the majesty of the law rolling down the block. I want him to shit his pants.'

I could go home and return, but I don't see the point. There's no one to go home to. It's near midnight when I finish the paperwork and I head for one of the cots laid out in a room on the fourth floor of the building. There's a shower on the fourth floor, as well, and hangers for my suit. Now, when I display my lawful majesty for Charles Hauptman's inspection, I'll look presentable.

Mostly, I'm a great sleeper. Nothing prevents me from drifting off within minutes, not even sagging cots, not even knowing my back will hurt when I get up. But not tonight. Tonight I wake up at four o'clock, restless from a dream that fades before I catch hold of it, and I don't go back to sleep. I roll around for an hour, annoyed with myself, then shower, dress and head for the squad room. There I scrounge a cup of coffee and discover a pair of detectives from the day tour asleep at their desks. Morelli's in his office, holding his cellphone to his ear. When he spies me looking in, he hangs up and motions me to a chair.

'Have you given any thought to how you'll approach Hauptman?' he asks.

In fact, the right approach is too obvious to state. And it has nothing to do with the tearing of assholes.

I know why you did it, Charles, in your place I might have done the same thing. And maybe I'm even wishing the lab results had come back negative, or at least inconclusive. But they

128

didn't, Charles. They came back positive and now's the time for you to come clean. Believe me, you're gonna feel a lot better when you do.

I smile at Morelli and sip at my coffee. 'Ask me that question when I get to the bottom of this mug. Right now, my brain's still on hold. But what were you thinking, lieutenant?'

Morelli scratches at his five-o'clock shadow, which is now almost a beard. His little brown eyes are bloodshot and feverish. 'Forget what I said before about tearing the bastard a new one. You gotta come on sympathetic.'

Fourteen

Majesty or not, Charles Hauptman isn't impressed when our little convoy rolls to a stop in front of his house. That's because he's asleep, a factor Morelli omitted from his calculations. I have to pound on the door and ring his bell for a good five minutes before he makes a bleary-eyed appearance. By this time, the silhouettes of his curious neighbors fill a half-dozen windows.

I hand Charles a copy of the warrant and push past him. Three detectives, four uniformed officers and a trio of paper-suited crime scene cops trail behind. Charles is wearing a plaid bathrobe and a pair of lined deerskin slippers. His comb-over has fallen to one side and now hangs below his ear, a gray fringe to echo the little fringes on his slippers. He doesn't bother to read the warrant. He doesn't protest or threaten to call his lawyer.

'I'm gonna make a pot of coffee,' he announces. 'You want?'

'Sure.'

Charles leads me into the kitchen where he removes a can of Maxwell House coffee from the refrigerator. I have to admit that I'm disappointed. Given the size of the room, not to mention the granite counter tops and the Subzero appliances, I was expecting something more exotic.

'Hope you like your coffee strong,' he says.

'Strong is fine.' I hesitate before taking a card from the inner pocket of my suit jacket. 'I'm afraid, at this point, I've got to read you your rights.'

I do exactly that, in a bored, sing-song voice. All very routine is the message I hope to convey. Let's get this done so we can move on to more interesting matters. Finished, I hand him the card and a pen.

'If you'd sign on the bottom, where it says that I informed you of your rights and you understand them, I'd be ever so grateful.'

Charles signs with a flourish, then hands the card back to me. I shove it into my pocket where it will hopefully be forgotten. Behind me, I hear my crime-scene cops head up the stairs to Joyce's bedroom. A moment later, my three detectives enter the kitchen.

'Which way to the basement?' Mayford Allman asks.

I point to a door on the other side of the room, then glance at Charles. As far as I can tell, he has no idea how much trouble he's in. We listen to the detectives clump their way down the wooden staircase, listen in silence. Then we're interrupted again, this time by a uniformed officer named Sharon Rodriguez.

'Where do you want us?' she asks.

'Outside in your cars. And it's OK if one of you makes a coffee run. Just don't talk to the neighbors. And don't carry any food into the house.'

Sharon ignores my scolding tone. Life doesn't get any better than this, not for cops. She all but salutes. 'Ten-four, detective.'

Charles waits until we're alone, then says, 'I need to use the bathroom. Is that all right?'

I can't refuse permission, the poor slob just got out of bed. But I'm supposed to accompany him, in case he's intent on destroying evidence. Instead, I raise my hands defensively.

'Hey, no problem, and if you'll leave a cigarette behind, I'll be in your debt forever.'

'Sorry, detective, I gave them up two days ago.'

When Charles returns fifteen minutes later, his comb-over in place, I've helped myself to a mug of coffee. Charles fills a mug, adds milk and sugar, finally carries his mug to the breakfast bar.

'What are you hoping to find?' he asks.

'Arsenic sulfide.'

131

'Realgar.'

'Say that again.'

'Arsenic sulfide is also called realgar.'

'How do you know that?'

'I used to collect crystals. Small exemplars for the most part, but very pure.'

'Used to?'

Charles blows on his steaming coffee. 'After Joyce's stroke, I lost interest and sold out.'

'Did you have realgar in your collection?'

'I didn't, but only because realgar breaks down when exposed to light. See, in its purest form, realgar is ruby red and stunningly beautiful. It would be part of every collection if it didn't turn yellow over time. That's why it can't be displayed. You have to keep realgar in a box.'

'Really? Is realgar easy to get, then?'

'Sure, you can buy it from any large gallery. In fact, I wouldn't be surprised if it was sold online, maybe on eBay.'

Though I nod enthusiastically, I'm thinking that Charles Hauptman is a complete jerk. If he'd possessed and handled realgar when he had his collection, he could explain away traces of the mineral uncovered by the search. As it now stands, any trace of arsenic sulfide will condemn him. And the worst part is that his response – like his readily signing the card, and his failure to challenge the search warrant, and his apparent ease – is one I'd expect from an innocent man.

'So, what are you telling me here?' he asks.

'That arsenic sulfide was found in your wife's hair and in fragments of bone recovered from the Bronx Botanical Gardens.'

Hauptman's features sag for the first time. To me, observing, he seems genuinely perplexed. Then he relaxes. 'I don't believe you,' he announces. 'I know that cops are permitted to lie.'

I open the search warrant and point to the second paragraph on page two. 'The warrant is based on those test results. Without them, we wouldn't have probable cause for a search.' I give it a beat, then continue. 'Look, Charles, you can trust me here, nobody from my side wanted this, not me, not my boss, not his boss. If there was a way out, most likely we'd take it. But those lab reports? Once they're generated, we can't just sit on our hands.'

'Spare me, detective. If you wanted to drop the matter, you wouldn't have carted my garbage away in the middle of the night. Or collected pieces of my wife's remains.'

'Listen to what I'm telling you. The NYPD didn't start this process. You did, when you got your father-in-law to prevent an autopsy.'

Charles opens his mouth, perhaps to repeat his claim that Max Baum acted alone, but I rush on before he can speak. 'You remember Amar Singh? The death investigator? He's not a cop, Charles. He works for the Office of the Medical Examiner, a completely independent agency. Establishing cause of death is the ME's primary function and it's the ME who ruled Joyce's death a homicide. Once that happened, the NYPD had to act.'

Still unconvinced, Charles reaches inside his bathrobe to scratch at the long gray hairs on his chest. 'Am I under arrest?' he asks.

133

'No, as I already mentioned, you're not under arrest.' Again, I resort to a lie. The case against him is entirely circumstantial and we don't have enough evidence to make an arrest. But Charles can't know that. 'Look, if this was some kind of brutal murder, I'd be taking you out in handcuffs. This you can believe. But it's not and nobody thinks you're a threat to society.'

'How do you know that? Maybe killing Joyce has stirred something in my reptile brain. Maybe I'm drunk on death.'

'Actually, what I think is that you're a good man who got dealt a bad hand, a hand you were forced to play.'

'God, how I hate that. A good man? Give me a break.'

'But you are, Charles, whether you like it or not.' I gulp down a mouthful of coffee. 'Your wife was in a nursing home. You could have left her there. You could have walked away. Instead, you brought her home.'

'Are you married, detective?'

'Nope, never took that step, though I've been close a time or two.'

'Why's that?'

'Commitment phobia, pure and simple.'

'So you didn't want to take those vows. You know the ones I'm talking about, right? In sickness and in health, from this day forward, till death do us part? You didn't want to take them and I don't blame you. If I'd been aware of their true scope, I wouldn't have taken them myself.'

'I hear you, Charles, and just like I said, you're a good man. But that vow, in sickness and in

134

health, doesn't mean you have to provide personal care.'

'And I wouldn't have, either, if what the nursing home provided wasn't closer to personal neglect.' He leans toward me. 'Like most patients in her condition, Joyce was unable to cough up the secretions in her lungs. They had to be suctioned out every so often, a procedure that takes about a minute. No big deal, right? Yet I'd come to visit in the morning and find her half-drowned in her own phlegm. And it's not like I didn't complain. Hell, I even threatened to personally sue the head nurse. But I might have been talking to the wall.'

'Why didn't you move her to another facility?'

'Because neglect in nursing homes isn't about laziness. Believe me, I watched the staff closely and everybody worked hard. The problem was understaffing. There just weren't enough aides and nurses to do the job.' He hesitates briefly, then his eyes retreat. 'If Joyce was neglected in the morning, even though the staff knew I was coming, what treatment did she receive at midnight when there was no one around to see? I became obsessed with this question. I'd lie awake at night, knowing there was no one to protect her, that she was alone and defenseless. I'd imagine her struggling in the dark, unable to complain, unable to ring the call button, hour after hour after hour.'

I nod, drop my eyes to the top of the breakfast bar, shift in my seat. My suspect's eyes have filled, though he's not actually crying. This is exactly what I want and I simply wait him out.

135

'After a few months of this,' he finally says, 'I knew I'd have to make a choice. Watching Joyce suffer, day after day, was beyond me. I had either to bring my wife home, or abandon her.'

'And that you couldn't do.'

'No, I couldn't. I couldn't abandon her any more than I could murder her.'

'Do you think it's murder, Charles?' I don't wait for a reply. 'Pretend we're not discussing Charles Hauptman. Pretend we met somewhere and I told you about a woman in your wife's condition, about how she was suffering. Pretend I told you that her husband ended her suffering in the only possible way. Would you call that murder?'

Charles Hauptman doesn't get to answer this question. Footsteps sound on the basement stairs and Mayford Allman's round face appears in the doorway. He's a black man with a huge and ready smile, but he's not smiling now.

'Lenny, you wanna come down here a minute?'

The timing is off, but I can't complain. I asked Mayford to interrupt if he found anything significant. I shrug, then ask Charles to join us. 'You have every right to watch the process,' I tell him.

We file down the stairs, through the paneled room with the dusty pingpong table and into the tool room at the far end of the house. Another detective, whose name I don't recall, is holding a metal file. Caught between the file's criss-crossed serrations, a dozen ruby-red particles glisten like sugar on a cookie. There are other

136

particles, as well, on the floor and on a workbench.

Charles looks like somebody hit him with a baseball bat. He's that stunned. 'I haven't been down here for months,' he finally announces. 'I don't know anything about this.'

I acknowledge the comment with the tiniest of shrugs, then lead Charles up the stairs and into the living room. We take seats across from each other, him on the couch and me in an easy chair large enough to hold a giant. Behind Charles, Otto Baum's portrait dominates the wall above the fireplace. I stare at Otto for a moment before deciding the artist missed the mark. Between the walking stick and the straw hat, Baum looks more like a playboy than a robber baron.

'What was it like, living with Otto all these years?' I ask. 'I'm thinking about the paintings in your bedroom and that screen with the cranes.' I gesture to the portrait. 'This can't be to your taste.'

'You've got it wrong,' he tells me. 'I've grown very fond of Otto. Otto's not going anywhere.'

'Be that as it may, I'm having a problem imagining him a dapper don, a playboy, which is what he looks like in the painting.'

'That's acute. Otto Baum was as single-minded as a hungry snake.'

I'm waiting for more, but Charles abruptly changes the subject. 'If I passed a polygraph test,' he asks, 'would that convince you that I didn't kill Joyce?'

'A polygraph can definitely be arranged.'

'That's not what I asked you.'

'Polygraphs are a trap, Charles. They're good at detecting lies, but terrible at detecting truth. Most likely, either the results will be deemed inconclusive or you'll flunk altogether. And that's especially true if the examiner works for the state. What's more, negative results will be leaked to the press in order to poison the jury pool. It's a no-win situation.'

'You still don't get it, detective. I'm asking you personally. If I pass, will you accept the fact that I didn't kill my wife?'

'OK, let's say you do pass and I'm a hundred per cent convinced that you're innocent. So what? At this point, the medical examiner, the district attorney and my own bosses are all involved. That means the case will go forward no matter what I believe. And something else you might want to consider. Joyce was murdered, Charles. Somebody killed her. And you're the only one who had a motive.'

Charles hesitates briefly, then says, 'My father-in-law will inherit Joyce's money if I'm convicted. That gives him millions of reasons for wishing her gone.'

'No, no.' I shake my head. 'You need to find another way. What you did is forgivable. Hell, it's even honorable. I admit that, Charles. And what I think is that you'll have more supporters than you can count once the story comes out. But not if you continue to deny what happened. You know that cliché? Throw yourself on the mercy of the court? In your case, you need to throw yourself on the mercy of the public. It's not only the best bet, it's the only bet. The evidence against you is overwhelming.'

But Charles isn't buying. 'You asked me a simple question. If I didn't kill Joyce, then who did? But I'm not the detective here. This is a question you should be asking yourself. I'm only hoping you will.'

I rise, walk over to the window and part the drapes to look out on a crisp fall morning. With the first heavy frost weeks away, the sloping lawn before the house is still green, still growing. A border of impatiens between the lawn and the sidewalk is in full bloom, its flaming petals as red as the little crystals in Charles Hauptman's basement. Out beyond the flowers, my four uniformed officers are gathered around the hood of a cruiser, drinking coffee and munching on goodies from McDonald's. As I watch, Officer Rodriguez shakes out a Virginia Slim and lights up.

'The answer isn't out there,' Charles tells me.

'No?' I let the drapes fall, but don't turn around. 'You think I'm jumping to conclusions?'

'Aren't you?'

'Well, let's see about that. Let's do an objective analysis. First, we have the motives. The burden of caring for Joyce was overwhelming and her suffering unbearable. Plus, you stood to profit from the substantial insurance policies on her life, not to mention the millions she inherited from her mother. Second, we have the means. You were familiar with realgar from your collecting days and you knew how to get your hands on it. Third, we have your actions following Joyce's death. You had your father-in-law use political influence to avoid a routine autopsy. You had Joyce cremated within a day of her passing. You scattered her ashes twenty-four hours after that. Fourth, we have the known physical evidence. Traces of arsenic sulfide were found in your wife's hair, in her bones and in her feeding tube. Fifth, we have the untested physical evidence found on the tools in your basement.'

I finally turn to face Charles. I'm expecting him to appear defensive, but he's sitting with his legs apart, his hands on the couch at his side. His eyes are calm and unafraid. My best move here is to let the silence build, to force a response. I want Charles to face the situation. I want him to decide that admitting guilt is the only way out. But I'm interrupted when Mayford Allman calls to me from the top of the stairs.

'Hey, Lenny, you wanna come up here a minute? There are some things you need to see.'

What I need to see, and what Charles also gets to see, are traces of the same red substance found in the basement. This time the red crystals appear in the cuffs of a pair of trousers hanging in the bedroom closet, then again in the crack between the wall and floor in Joyce's empty sick room. There's not much, but the color is un-mistakable.

I lead Charles back downstairs and into the living room. Far from upset by the discoveries, he's smiling as he pulls at his droopy lower lip.

'Those trousers, they're my fat pants,' he

declares. 'I haven't worn them since I lost thirty pounds two years ago. Check the waist if you think I'm lying. I believe they're a size forty.' He pauses, but only for an instant. 'And now, if you don't object, I'd like to phone my attorney.'

Fifteen

I get home at three o'clock on Thursday afternoon, strip down to my shorts and fall into bed. I awaken at ten, stuff a ham sandwich down my throat, then go back to sleep at midnight. This is a mistake because it's eight o'clock in the morning when I open my eyes and now I'm wide awake and wondering what to do next.

Like my partner, I'm no good at leisure, even when there's something to do besides watch doom-and-gloom news shows. Millions out of work, the stock market at an all-time low, the Taliban running riot in Pakistan, food pantries overwhelmed, a record number of families applying for shelter. After a few minutes, I shut down the TV and cross the room to stare out through the window at a steady downpour. I watch the rain sweep across the asphalt, moving from north to south, watch angry clouds that descend almost to the roofs track the same journey. I know that cold air will rush in behind the rain. Here comes winter, ready or not.

Lieutenant Morelli and I have an understanding. With the city's economy in the tank, overtime pay has become a thing of the past. As far as the NYPD's concerned, I'm supposed to show up at four o'clock in the afternoon and go home at midnight. That's fine if you're a patrol officer, fine for Vice and Narcotics and Traffic. But murder has its own schedule and no homicide detective clocks out when there are leads to be followed, witnesses to hunt down, suspects to be interrogated. Our most immediate bosses, squad commanders like Morelli, have adjusted. They now compensate us with flexible schedules. You work twenty-four hours straight, you get the next day off, with the payroll division none the wiser.

Bottom line, I don't have to be on the job until Monday afternoon. I suppose I should be thankful, but I've been running for days, running at top speed, and I can't just grind to a halt. If I had a family, there'd be plenty to do. Families are always backed up on the chores, husbands and wives always in need of relief. Briefly, I imagine myself preparing a healthy dinner for the kiddies while my supremely grateful spouse enjoys a hot bath. But the fantasy does nothing to improve my prospects and I gather up my coffee mug and head for the computer and my address book.

I start with Sally Abraham and run all the way through to April Willenski. What I want is a three-day hookup. A hundred miles to the north, the fall foliage is at its peak. A bed & breakfast, long walks through the forest, hearty New England dinners, bouts of intense sexual activity.

What's not to like?

What's not to like is that there isn't a woman among the many female listings who hasn't broken off with me, for good and forever. I try one number, Carol Roga's, only to discover that it's been disconnected.

I finally give up. I stuff my soiled laundry into a black garbage bag, don a hooded raincoat that reaches almost to my ankles and head off to a laundromat on Vernon Boulevard. I bring a book with me, Philip Dick's *Clans of the Alphane Moon*, hoping to finish the last fifty pages. Unfortunately, my little brain is spinning faster than the washing machines across the room. I'm remembering Charles asking me not to give up on him and the little speech I made in return, the one listing the evidence pointing to his guilt. Without exception, everything I told him was true. True, but unfair. There's an equally persuasive side to this story, which I conveniently left unspoken. I don't feel particularly guilty – all's fair in love, war and police interrogations – but I can't ignore the facts, either.

I'm the only customer in the laundromat actually washing clothes. This early in the morning, the real action is at the front of the store where laundry is being dropped off by a parade of men and women on their way to work. Four workers scurry about with these drop-offs, filling machines, adding soap and bleach, shifting clothes from washer to dryer, folding and stacking. The workers are Latinas, the tallest among them no more than five feet, and they don't stop for a minute. From above, on a shelf, a cheap stereo plays pop mariachi tunes.

The woman standing behind the cash register in the front manages the laundromat. Running up on thirty years old, her name is Felicia and she's Dominican. I know this because she's gorgeous and I flirt with her whenever I cadge cigarettes outside the store. Now she glances my way and smiles. Felicia has a husband, a transit worker, and two young kids. Maybe she's flattered by the attention, but she's definitely not interested in a fling with a middle-aged gringo.

I turn back to the spinning machines, listen to the various rumbles and clanks, the scratch of zippers against the metal sides of the drums. I know that I'm now as obsessed with Charles Hauptman as Davy is with Corinne Mariposa. My obsession is more rational, though. When Corinne charged out of the bathroom, Davy had no choice. That's not the case with Charles. His guilt is not beyond doubt, the place it should be, at least in a cop's mind, before an arrest is made. Especially for a crime as serious as murder.

In the first place, Charles Hauptman's actions following the death of his wife are as much evidence of an innocent, as a guilty, mind. True, he had his wife cremated within twenty-four hours, but he also invited the nurses to be present when Joyce's ashes were scattered. If not, I would never have known what happened to Joyce's remains. Any sane murderer would have dumped the ashes at sea.

The hair evidence and the feeding tube fit this same dual pattern. Charles tried to get rid of his wife's medical supplies at the earliest opportunity. That's not in question. But not only didn't he destroy the relevant evidence, he placed the trash bags at the curb on the night before a scheduled pickup. If it was me, I'd have waited until the garbage truck was rumbling down the block. If it was me, any potentially incriminating material would have been disposed of inside the house, including the crystals found in the basement and cuffs of those trousers. Maybe the crystals were small, but their color made them extremely conspicuous.

Once I get going, I can't stop. For instance, I checked the trousers we seized and they were size forty, as Charles claimed. I also looked through his computer, which wasn't password protected, searching a stored history of visited websites that stretched back for two months. I found nothing to incriminate him, no visits to sites that peddled crystals, no visits to sites that described the effects of arsenic or any other poison. And Charles, I have to admit, isn't the only motivated actor in this play. Max Baum has much to gain from his son-in-law's conviction.

My washer shuts down with a final clunk, distracting me from thoughts I'd rather not be having. I gather my wet laundry and carry it across the laundromat to an empty dryer. I know I'm supposed to separate my laundry, but I never do. I just stuff the load into a single large machine, add quarters then grab my coat and head for the door. Felicia sees me coming. She gathers her own coat and quickly follows.

'Ya know,' she tells me as she produces a pack

of cigarettes, 'you owe me about a thousand dollars.'

We're standing beneath a narrow canopy, listening to the rain pound the canvas above our heads. The traffic along Vernon Boulevard is heavy, most likely because the entrance to the Queens Midtown Tunnel, a few blocks away, is congested. Off to the east, a bolt of lightning streaks down to earth, so far out to sea the rumble of thunder fails to reach our ears. I accept the smoke Felicia offers, pausing long enough to run it beneath my nose before I light up.

'You've got my eternal gratitude,' I announce. 'I can't believe you'd exchange that for money.'

'I'd exchange just about anything for money. People who say money is the root of all evil should try livin' without it.' She pulls on her cigarette and shakes her head. 'Tito got laid off. We're gonna have to live on his unemployment insurance until one of us finds a job.'

'What about your salary here?'

'The only reason I work here is because the hours are flexible. I need time off in the afternoon to see about the kids. But I'm gonna have to start lookin' around for a real job. Anyway, what about you? You catch any interestin' murderers lately?'

Maybe my mother's right, maybe I need to start going to confession. As it is, I hastily unburden myself, describing the Hauptman investigation and my personal misgivings. Apparently, I strike a nerve. For Felicia – and I expect for millions of other Americans – Joyce Hauptman's story is personal.

'My grandpa,' she tells me, her tone wistful, 'lived at home for a couple of years after he had his stroke. He wasn't in a vegetative state, but he was mostly confined to a bed or a wheelchair. Plus, he could barely talk and he couldn't swallow food. *Mi abuelo*, he was big man. Carin' for him was no picnic, you could believe that. And he suffered, too, with cramps on his paralyzed side. I seen him cryin' more then once. When he finally passed, his daughters were mostly relieved.'

'But they didn't do anything to make it happen?'

'Not that I know of.'

It's three o'clock in the afternoon and I'm across the street from Max Baum's corporate headquarters in a brick townhouse on East 63rd Street in Manhattan. There's no real sign, only the words Baum Capitol Management on a tarnished bronze plaque to the right of an oak door. The door glistens, even in the fading afternoon light, and I have to wonder if it's been polished. I'm standing across the street, one eye on a double-parked Mercedes and one on the door. The black Mercedes is long and sleek and the window glass in the back is opaque. Not so the front window, through which I can see Leonid Berevski's profile. Though I'll admit the chauffeur's cap is a bit incongruous, the flattened nose and jutting brow are entirely familiar.

I'm assuming that Berevski's more than a chauffeur, that he also guards Max's body. I don't know why Baum needs a bodyguard, but I intend to find out. As I intend to find out why Baum made a three-thirty appointment with me, but is now coming through the door of Baum Capitol Management a half-hour early.

Berevski is out of the Mercedes in a flash. He circles the car, his stride quick and graceful, reaching the back door on the passenger side as his boss crosses the sidewalk. I arrive at the same moment, drawing the startled attention of both men when I place myself between them.

'Hey, Mr Baum, you remember me, right? Detective Shaw?' I flash an ingratiating smile. 'We have a three-thirty appointment?'

Unlike his son-in-law, Max Baum has a full head of hair, no comb-over necessary. Green enough to startle, his eyes rake my face. The look is hard, as he intends it to be, the sort of look an overseer might bestow on a slave. But I detect a hint of amusement, too. Or maybe I'm just focused on the half-smile. Max has a thin mouth, the lips almost bloodless, but the tug at the left corner is unmistakable to a trained observer. There's only one smile that doesn't include both sides of the mouth, a smile of contempt.

I endure the scrutiny without complaint. I'm not intimidated. Besides, I'm playing a game of my own. I'm standing with my back to Leonid. This is not the sort of dismissal a man like Berevski appreciates.

'Yes, I remember.' Max's voice is soft, almost somber. 'Unfortunately, a small matter came up that needs my attention. Didn't my secretary call you?'

'Not yet, but I'm sure she will as soon as she thinks you're gone.'

'No need for that, detective.'

But Max's timing is off. My phone rings and sure enough it's Max's secretary canceling our appointment. I drop the phone into my pocket and shrug. If anything, Max's smile has expanded. I've caught him in a lie, but he couldn't care less.

I know Max can tell me to fuck off. There's no law requiring him to cooperate. But he's not going to do that. The temptation to play with me, now that I've confronted him, is too great.

'Before I go any further,' I tell him, 'I just wanna say that I'm sorry for your loss.'

Max takes a moment to consider the statement. I've reminded him that the woman whose death I'm investigating is his daughter. He's supposed to be in mourning. He's supposed to care about whether she was murdered. Finally, he says, 'Can you return in an hour?'

'I can if you'll be here.'

'You have my word.'

Sixteen

I spend the next hour in an internet café on Third Avenue nursing a cup of coffee while I run a general search for realgar. I'm looking for some as yet unknown tidbit but come up empty. Arsenic sulfide is a mineral, it's naturally occurring, it's collectible, it's deadly. Thanks for sharing. I get luckier, though, at the very end when I enter Max Baum's name in Google. On a business site, I find an article published in 2003 entitled 'Skyrocketing Entrepreneur'. The story notes Baum Capitol Management's acquisition of the Americana Fireworks Corporation, but it's mainly focused on Max, himself. There's a photo of Max at the head of the article, his smirk firmly in place, his green eyes as dismissive as I remember them.

The rain has started up again by the time I leave the café and walk the short block to Max's office. Not content with his little victory, he keeps me waiting for another twenty minutes before I'm shown into his sumptuous office. As I shake his hand, I can't help comparing the carved desk and upholstered chairs, the coffered ceiling and the brass chandelier, with Terry Hauptman's little cubicle at Hauptman Contracting and Plumbing Supply. They might as well be living on different planets.

Baum motions me to a chair, then drops into the ergonomic leather chair behind his desk. Well into his seventies, his starched white shirt is only a shade lighter than his perfectly barbered hair, which is only a shade lighter than his soft papery skin.

'Now, detective, what can I do for you?' He folds his hands and lays them on his inlaid desk, revealing immaculately clean fingernails.

'Believe me, I get no pleasure from telling you this, but it's becoming more and more likely that your daughter was murdered.' I let my words hang out there for a moment, then add, 'Almost certainly by her husband.'

'I've spoken to Charles, and to his attorney. No need to fill me in on the details. As for Charles, I suppose you have your duty to perform, but I have a hard time condemning him, guilty or not.'

'The moral issue, Mr Baum, is between Charles and his God. The state, on the other hand, has other interests. But don't let me waste your time. I just have a few questions and I'll be gone.'

'Ask away, detective. I'm here to help.'

'OK, first thing, according to the nurses, you hired and paid them. Is that right?'

'It is.'

'Did the money come from the estate left to Joyce by your wife?'

'Yes, that's correct.'

'Now, Charles and his brother both told me that you filed a petition in Probate Court to gain control of your wife's estate after her death.

Did you?'

Though Max's smirk widens slightly, his jaw tilts up. I'm being impertinent and he's annoyed. 'I did,' he tells me.

'And that's because Charles couldn't be trusted with his wife's money.'

'I don't see where this is going.'

'I was just wondering why you felt that your son-in-law was untrustworthy. I mean, everybody I've spoken to agrees that Charles was devoted to Joyce. What led you to conclude that he might steal her money? You did give him a job, right? At Baum Capitol Management? So you must have trusted him on some level.'

But Max has had enough. He dismisses the question with a wave of his hand. 'This is none of your concern.'

'Family disputes involving millions of dollars aren't my business? OK, if that's the way you want to leave it. Now, you were responsible for hiring the nurses. Have I got that right?'

'Hiring and occasionally firing.'

'Can you tell me where you found them?'

'I used several employment agencies.'

'Is that how you found Theresa Santiago?'

Max shivers, his smile now touching both sides of his mouth. 'A sour woman, Theresa. But punctual. Unlike many of the nurses who came and went over the years, she never missed her shift. And, yes, I found her through a small employment agency.'

'And Shirley Borders?'

'Shirley began working for Charles before I became involved.'

'What about Anna Berevski? Did the employment agency know she was unlicensed? Did they know she'd already been convicted of practicing without a license?'

I finally catch him by surprise and he pauses long enough for the delay to be unmistakable. He needs time to consider his response.

'Anna was recommended to me by her brother.'

'Your chauffeur?'

'Yes, Leonid.'

'And you didn't check her credentials?'

'No, detective, I didn't.'

I nod and scratch an ear. 'Mr Baum, did Charles ever express a desire to end his wife's suffering?'

'Many times.'

'How about you?'

'Excuse me?'

'You visited often. You saw how your daughter suffered. If the law allowed it, would you have chosen to end her life?'

'Without hesitation. As I said, I don't condemn Charles, even if he did what you suspect him of doing.'

'Tell you the truth, as a citizen, I don't either.'

'But you're a police officer, too.'

'I am. Now, tell me, do you know what realgar is?'

For just a second, his smirk vanishes, replaced with a tightening of the lips and a narrowing of the eyes I associate with true anger. I've thrown him another curve ball and he doesn't like it.

'Real...'

'Realgar.'

'No, I'm afraid I don't.'

'Realgar is another name for arsenic sulfide. We found traces of it in your daughter's bones and her hair.'

'In her bones?' The smirk is back. 'And how did you acquire Joyce's bones?'

'I collected them in the Bronx Botanical Gardens. And I know what you're thinking. You're thinking what I did was distasteful. But you can trust me on this, Mr Baum. Picking bone fragments out of the grass is nothing compared to searching through a dumpster that's been sitting behind a butcher shop for a couple of weeks. Say in mid-August.' I wave away his response. 'But that's beside the point. Realgar has a number of industrial uses, among them to add the color red to fireworks. You own a company that manufactures fireworks, which gives you easy access to arsenic sulfide.'

The smirk no longer sufficiently contemptuous, Baum actually laughs. 'Am I a suspect, detective?'

'Not as far as the police are concerned. It's your son-in-law's attorney you should be worried about.' I lean over the desk and drop my voice. 'Although certain items are still being tested, we're virtually certain that your daughter was deliberately poisoned. And even if the case against Charles is circumstantial, it's very compelling. In fact, I don't see how Charles can be acquitted without offering up another suspect. That would be you, Mr Baum. In addition to a stated wish to end your daughter's suffering and the substantial estate you inherit if Charles is convicted, you had access to the poison used to kill her. Keep in mind, any good defense lawyer will attempt to show that the circumstances in a circumstantial case implicate someone else. I don't think it's gonna work, personally. The state will prove that Joyce was exposed to arsenic sulfide over a period of weeks, when you didn't have access. But after the details of your wife's estate become public, you'll be the subject of nasty conjecture for many months, if not for-ever.'

'And how will that happen? The details be-coming public?'

'You'll excuse me saying so, Mr Baum, but that's a very naive question. Celebrity trials are as much about showcased leaks as courtroom procedure. Your son-in-law's attorney will brand you a villain long before the trial actually starts.'

Max brings his right hand to his chin, then strokes his neck three times before dropping his hand to his lap. The gesture seems to me tender, almost loving, and I wonder what it was like for Joyce, growing up with a father who reserved his affection to himself. Unlike the ravaged Charles Hauptman, Max is fresh as a daisy, his daughter's murder having no detectable effect on his well-being.

'I see what you mean, detective. The situation may very well become ugly. But Charles is entitled to defend himself at trial, so I suspect there's no avoiding the sleaze factor.'

'There's one way, Mr Baum. You can take a polygraph test. I realize it's an inconvenience, but it would establish your innocence before the media circus begins.'

I lean all the way back in my chair, lace my fingers behind my head and cross my legs. Those green-on-green eyes have turned inward, the suggestion having taken Max completely off guard. He needs a little time and he buys it with a question.

'I thought lie-detector tests were inadmissible in court?'

'That's no problem. We'll just leak the results when your name comes up. You know how it goes. Max Baum was fully cooperative. He volunteered for a polygraph, which he passed. We've eliminated him as a suspect. By the time the trial begins, every potential juror will know the facts.'

I don't expect Max to agree and he doesn't. He tells me that he'll consult his attorneys (I note the plural without changing expression) then get back to me. It's pretty much what I expected and it doesn't prove a thing. Max Baum has to be in charge. He can't allow himself to be manipulated. If there's to be a polygraph examination, it will be on his terms.

'Well, I'm out of questions for now,' I tell him. 'But if there's something you want to add, I'm here to listen.'

Although I'm expecting a quick dismissal, he jumps in with both feet. 'About Anna Berevski. If you say she's unlicensed, I have to assume she is, but she was a very good nurse.'

'How do you know that?'

'Charles was quick to complain about in-

156

competent and unreliable nurses. He never complained about Anna.'

'I hear what you're saying, but Anna Berevski broke the law once and got probation. Now she's broken it again.'

'Are you telling me that she'll be arrested?'

I shrug. 'It'd be different if her testimony was important, but she only repeated what the other nurses already told me.'

'Will she go to jail?'

In fact, I have no idea, having never arrested an unlicensed nurse. 'I'm not a judge and I won't be sentencing her, but she's still on probation, so the first thing she'll get is a probation hearing. At that time, she might be ordered to complete her original sentence, whatever that was. And you can take this one to the bank, the judge who presides over that hearing will not be happy to learn that she repeated the same offense.'

My own little triumph in hand, I rise and offer my business card. 'If there's anything else you think of, anything I should know, give me call.' I wait for Baum to accept the card, then head for the door, only turning back after I pull it open.

'There is one more thing, actually, which I almost forgot. Who arranged to cancel the autopsy, you or Charles?'

'I did, at his request.' Max is sitting back in his chair, perfectly relaxed. He's smirking, but he's been smirking all along. His eyes continue to dismiss me, but they've been dismissing me all along. Now he takes a last shot.

'You've asked me a goodly number of questions,' he calls to my retreating back. 'Now let me ask you one. If I killed my only child, intending to place the blame on Charles, would I have prevented the autopsy necessary to establish his guilt?'

I leave Baum Capitol Management at the height of the evening rush and fight my way over the 59th Street Bridge and back into Queens, all the way to the offices of Dr Fred Meyer in South Jamaica. Though barely a mile from Charles Hauptman's mini-mansion in Jamaica Estates, South Jamaica is a notorious black ghetto, a neighborhood of shuttered stores and run-down homes that was making a comeback just a few years ago. Now, like the rest of the city's poor neighborhoods, South Jamaica's reversal of fortunes is obvious at a glance.

Meyer's offices are housed in a storefront clinic. A sign across the front of the building reads GARVEY MEDICAL SERVICES. Clinics like Garvey are the last line of defense for the urban poor in New York. All but the most dedicated physicians refuse to accept Medicaid patients because the reimbursement rates are so low. Dr Meyer echoes these sentiments as he explains why he didn't respond when Charles called him after Joyce died. He gestures to his crowded waiting room and says, 'Joyce Hauptman didn't need me. These people do.'

Meyer is a tall, gangly man, somewhere in his forties. His face is round, his neck crêpey. He looks like he hasn't slept in weeks. We're standing in a bare-bones examining room. Through the open door, I can see ten or fifteen patients, mothers with children for the most part, sitting on wooden chairs. In a far corner, an elderly woman with a curved back leans so far forward that her head is only inches from her knees.

Meyer's failure to attend Joyce's death is extremely significant. People die at home every day, from heart attacks and strokes and cancer and a dozen other diseases. When they do, uniformed patrol officers are routinely charged with assessing the circumstances, as Officers Carter and Bonilla did when Joyce Hauptman expired. If they discover a physician in attendance and no obvious signs of violence, the medical examiner isn't notified. The body is simply released for burial or cremation.

'I've only got a few minutes.' Meyer gestures at his waiting patients. 'As you can see.'

'I'll be brief,' I assure him. 'I was told that you prescribed an antibiotic for Joyce Hauptman a short time before her death. That right?'

'Yes, ampicillin.'

'Did you examine her beforehand.'

'No, I relied on the nurse in attendance.'

'And that was...?'

'Nurse Borders.'

'Was Nurse Borders the one who reported the subsequent rash?'

'Yes, and I prescribed Lotrisone, as I have many times.'

A boy in the waiting room, a toddler, begins to wail. We've been speaking for less than a minute, but my time is already running out.

'No disrespect, doctor, but is this standard procedure, not attending a patient's death, prescribing over the phone?'

'I have fifty-five homecare patients who are too sick to come to the clinic. Without me, they'd be in nursing homes. Can I give them the quality of care that Americans with insurance take for granted? No, I can't. But if you don't mind, I want to know exactly what you're doing here.'

'I'm investigating Joyce Hauptman's murder. I thought you knew.'

Meyer brings one hand to his mouth and leans against the examining table for support. He's surprised, certainly, but I can't dismiss the possibility that his eyes, when they jerk away from mine, are also afraid.

'Are you sure?' he finally asks.

'The medical examiner's made his ruling. Joyce Hauptman's cause of death was arsenic poisoning. Her manner of death was homicide.'

'But you can't suspect Charles. He was devoted to his wife.'

'Devotion may have been his prime motive, doctor. But let's not convict the man before he's even been arrested. Right now, I'm conducting an investigation. Your name came up in several conversations I had with Charles and the nurses. I'm here to verify the facts they presented.'

I wait until Meyer nods, then continue. 'According to the nurses, Charles suggested that his wife's many infections not be treated, but you refused to go along. Can you verify that?'

'Conversations between Charles and myself are privileged, detective.'

'Why? Charles wasn't your patient.'

'As far as I'm concerned, he spoke for my patient.'

'That's not the same thing.'

Meyer shoulders square as he draws himself up to his full height. Though he doesn't speak, not right away, I know he's made a decision. I'm about to be put in my place.

'Charles Hauptman honored the vows he made to his wife on their wedding day as no other man I've ever met. I'm not going to do anything – and I mean *anything* – to help you put him in jail.'

Righteous anger is the easiest emotion to fake, closely followed by sympathy. Is Meyer faking? There's something about his stance that doesn't sit right and I decide to take him down a peg.

'But you already have,' I tell him. 'You've helped us.'

'How?'

'By not getting off your lazy ass when Charles informed you of his wife's death at eleven thirty in the evening. If you'd been there to sign a death certificate, no death investigator would have been called, no investigation begun. If you'd been there, it would've been bye-bye Joyce and nobody the wiser.'

I'm expecting Meyer to become angrier, but his expression softens and his response comes a little too fast. 'My work week runs between sixty and seventy hours. I couldn't get out of bed that night. I just couldn't. I never thought, not even for a second, that Mrs Hauptman's death was other than natural.'

My smile is anything but sympathetic. 'Just one more question and I'll be out of your hair. You were paid for your services by Joyce Hauptman's trust fund, with Max Baum signing the checks. That means your patient wasn't on Medicaid and you could charge whatever you wanted. I was wondering just how much that was?'

'My fee, detective, was – and is – none of your business.'

Seventeen

I'm in Dooley's Tavern, a cop bar in Forest Hills, when Sergeant Marie Burke walks in at half past eight. The twice-divorced Marie Burke is the epitome of the grizzled NYPD sergeant. She's heard all the bullshit stories ever concocted by patrol officers who aren't where they're supposed to be, or doing what they're supposed to do. She's been the object of every known variety of abuse that irate citizens can bestow on a cop. She's witnessed violent death in all its many horrendous forms. The resulting tension is apparent in the deep lines that separate a pair of supremely mistrustful eyes.

Marie works out of the 110th Precinct and she's been at the scene of a number of homicides when I roll up. Though we've never so much as flirted, she smiles and joins me at the bar.

'I sent the kids to my mom and dad for the night,' she tells me halfway through her first beer. 'God knows I love 'em, but there are times when a girl's just gotta get away.'

Besides me and Mike Dooley, who's working the bar, there are only three patrons in Dooley's Tavern. They're watching the World Series at the other end of the bar and they're wearing wedding rings on their left hands. That makes me, I suppose, the default setting.

I'm not insulted. Marie Burke is what my mom calls stocky. Her shoulders are broad and she's thick through the waist without actually being fat. By reputation, she's dead game in a brawl, a cop's cop. My hope is that she'll be dead game in bed, too, a disciplined woman who's got her priorities straight.

'I heard,' she tells me, 'that you were mixed up in that shooting, where the girl was killed.'

'I was there all right.'

'You pick up a beef?'

'No, the shooting was righteous. But I didn't really have anything to do with it. Where I was standing when the shooting started? If I didn't get out of the way, I would've been caught in the crossfire, no doubt about it. I would've been a victim of friendly fire.'

'You got off easy. I shot an armed robber once, in 1995, in the Bronx. The round knocked him on his ass but didn't kill him. Me, I was a long time gettin' over it. I don't why, because the perp was a hardcore knucklehead and deserved worse.'

163

'You sound like my partner. Davy fired off six rounds and now he can't stop kickin' himself in the ass. The bosses put him on leave, which was probably the worst thing they could've done. I've got him helpin' me out on this really strange case, just to give him something to do.'

'Strange? How?'

'I've got a suspect, I can't make him a bad guy, even if he actually killed his wife, which I'm not sure he did.'

Marie's a street cop, her career devoted to handling emergencies of one kind of another, but she enjoys a good mystery. Her eyes don't leave mine, nor does she stop nodding, until I finish a quick summary. That's when Davy walks in. He comes straight toward us, stands for an introduction, then finally orders a Dewars and water. I've come to Dooley's at his request.

Davy waits for his drink and takes a sip. Ordinarily, we'd find a quiet spot to have a private conversation. But not only am I not moving, I'm standing distinctly closer to Marie than to my partner. Davy gets the point, though his expression doesn't change.

'I took a peek at Lola Baum's case file down in Records Division,' he tells me.

'The file was already swept out of the precinct?'

'Her death was ruled a suicide one day after the autopsy and the case was closed.'

'Did she leave a note?'

Davy shakes his head. 'Not only that, her blood-alcohol level was point three-nine. She might have been unconscious.'

'But there was no investigation?'

'Not so's you'd notice. Max was interviewed, but he had a rock-solid alibi. He was in London, on business. As for Lola, she had hesitation cuts on her wrists, which you'd have to be pretty clever to put there if you were gonna kill her.'

Hesitation cuts are tentative incisions commonly made by citizens bent on suicide as they marshal the courage to finish the job. And Davy's right. You'd have to be very clever even to know about hesitation cuts.

As my thoughts begin to turn, my attention falls on a Budweiser sign, an antique, on the wall behind Davy. A woman in classical dress stands at the center of the sign, both arms raised above her head. She wears gilded armor over her breasts and she's surrounded by a dozen cherubs. I can't determine the sex of these cherubs, their groins being covered by lengths of strategically placed ribbon, but each cradles a very phallic bottle of beer in its arms.

Something's tickling the edge of my brain, an intuition that I can't draw far enough inside to identify. I sense a rising anger. What do I need this for? Charles and Max and all the rest of it? As soon as the lab results on the material recovered in his home are completed, Charles will be taken into custody and the media alerted. Charles the saint? Charles the murderer? Oprah will have a field day, especially if there's a trial, in which case I'll get my fifteen minutes of fame when I testify.

'You wanna hear something funny?' Marie asks.

'Anything.'

'My mom, she's in her seventies. When she had a mini-stroke last year, I downloaded a living-will form and printed it out. This is not something it's easy to talk about with your mother, trust me on that, but Mom didn't hesitate when I finally got the courage to show it to her. No, she gave it back to me the next day, all filled out.'

'What did she write?' Davy asked.

'She wrote that she wanted to be kept alive, no matter what.'

Davy lifts his glass. 'I'll drink to that.'

I'm a veteran of the weekend hookup and I know enough to remain sober. Not so Marie. By the time we get to my apartment at one o'clock, she's barely able to walk. I lay her down on my bed, and take off her shoes and a turquoise necklace before covering her with a blanket. Then I retreat to a pull-out couch in the living room. I'm disappointed, no question, but I'm not a scumbag. No matter how horny, I reject the very idea of sex with blow-up dolls or unconscious women. Call me St Lenny. One of a pair with St Charles.

For the next fifteen minutes, I try to interest myself in a replay of the World Series game, but I can't concentrate. That's because Lola Baum's ostensible suicide is too intriguing to ignore. Yes, Max Baum has an ironclad alibi, but there's still Leonid Berevski. Would Leonid kill for Max? Instinctively, and without hesitation, I answer the question: yes, if the money's right.

166

The real question is whether or not Leonid could have gotten to Lola without being detected. I flash back to Davy's remark about the hesitation cuts. You'd have to be very clever to put those cuts on Lola's wrists before you killed her. As you'd have to be very clever to frame your brother-in-law for the murder of his wife. Too clever for Leonid.

At two o'clock, I shut off the TV and the light. I'm still fairly agitated, but I fall asleep within a few minutes, only to awaken from a dream at sunrise. The dream remains vivid long enough for me to capture it whole. There's Corinne Mariposa emerging from the bathroom. There's me pouring bullet after bullet into her torso. There's no one else in the room.

Just what I need.

The smell of coffee brings me to full consciousness. I'd forgotten all about Marie, but now I'm suddenly hopeful. I stagger into the bathroom for a quick shower and a slug of mouthwash, emerging fifteen minutes later in trousers and a T-shirt just as Marie comes out of the kitchen. Marie's carrying a tray loaded with coffee and buttered toast and she's wearing one of my terrycloth robes. The robe is carelessly tied, but I somehow lack the moral strength to call this oversight to her attention.

For the next twenty minutes, while I sip at my coffee, Marie engages in a ritual foreplay that I'm loath to interrupt. Leaning forward, crossing her legs, pulling the edges of the robe together only to let them fall apart. She ends the game by quoting Mae West.

167

'Is that a gun in your pants,' she asks, 'or are you just glad to see me?'

'Both.'

'Both?'

'Yes, I'm glad to see you. And, yes, what I've got in my pants is definitely loaded.'

We eat and we fuck and we bullshit over a bottle of dark rum until noon on Sunday when Marie takes off to gather her kids. We make no specific plans for the future, but I'm thinking we'll get together again. Not that I see our relationship deepening. Marie has a whole other life, a domestic life that holds no interest for me. As far as I'm concerned, kids are someone else's problem.

I take my mother out to dinner that night, compensation for skipping Mass. I'm understandably tired and I don't contribute much to the conversation, which doesn't slow Mom down. Uncle Jack, she tells me, has had a change of heart. He's contacted the hospice and is going full steam ahead with the necessary paperwork and interviews.

'It's the prayers, Lenny, all those rosaries I told finally payin' off. But you wanna hear something funny?' She spears a black olive with her fork and jabs it in my direction. 'Now that it's really happening, I got this sick feeling in the pit of my stomach. I'm thinkin' maybe this isn't right after all.'

I slide a marinated shrimp into my mouth and chew methodically. I'm trying not to laugh. 'So?'

'So I spoke to Marty on the phone. He told me I have no legal standing and I should mind my own business. Can you imagine? I'm the one who visited Maggie all these years and now I'm supposed to mind my own business.'

Marty Shaw, my cousin, is an attorney. Mom calls him whenever she's in need of free advice.

'He's right, Mom. There's nothing you can do now.'

'I know that. But it's hard to say goodbye, even if you've been sayin' it for years. It's just hard.'

Eighteen

I wake up on Monday more exhausted than when I fell asleep. Corinne Mariposa still haunts my dreams, but now she's lying in a hospital bed, her body as contracted as Joyce Hauptman's, and I'm squeezing the trigger, again and again and again. As if my Glock holds as many rounds as an assault rifle.

I'm pissed off, thinking I don't deserve this self-abuse. But there's also a little voice asking me why I thought I'd get off scot-free just because I failed to discharge my weapon? I don't have an answer, except to get my ass in gear. Twenty minutes later, I'm out of the house.

I pick up coffee on the way to my car. I'm

heading for Hauptman Contracting and Plumbing Supply. As witnesses go, Terry wasn't all that cooperative, but I'm pretty sure the questions I intend to ask, about Lola Baum, will pique his curiosity. My goal here is to gather as much information as possible before I report to my boss at four o'clock. Or maybe I've simply become as obsessed with the case as I apparently have with Corinne Mariposa. I've been a cop for a long time and I've never put a man or a woman in jail when I had real doubts about their guilt. I'm not claiming sainthood, far from it. Guilt or innocence was just never in doubt. Until now.

Terry Hauptman's little business is humming along when I arrive, every worker busy. Needless to say, he doesn't celebrate my arrival.

'Jesus,' he declares at my approach, 'the bad penny.'

'I just have a few questions, Terry. Won't take longer than fifteen minutes.'

'Hey, business is finally pickin' up and I don't have fifteen fuckin' seconds. Besides which, there's no law requires me to answer your questions in the first place.'

'Well, these particular questions, I think they're gonna interest you. They're about Lola Baum.'

When Terry's eyes narrow, his caterpillar eyebrows crawl down almost to his cheekbones. 'Lola, huh? Does that mean you're finally gettin' the message?'

'It means I have some questions about Lola Baum.'

'OK.' He glances at his watch. 'Give me

fifteen minutes.'

He takes ten, then leads me through a rollup door large enough to accommodate an eighteen-wheeler, all the way to a vendor peddling coffee and donuts from a van parked at the curb. I accept a container of coffee that I don't want and follow Terry to the edge of the building where he turns and leans against the wall. We're well into October, with Halloween only seven days away, but the morning is summery. The temperature's risen into the seventies and the weathered brick wall, flooded with sunlight, is warm to the touch.

Terry closes his eyes and raises his face to the sun for a moment before turning to face me. 'Your fifteen minutes have already begun,' he announces. 'Tell me what you want.'

'For starters, you can describe Lola. What was she like?'

'Lola was a ball of fire when she was on her game. She could do the work of ten people.'

'What about when she was off her game?'

'You listen to Max, he'll tell you she was bipolar.'

'Did she drink?'

'Like a fish. Had a wooden leg, too. I guarantee, you try to match her drink for drink, you're gonna be the one under the table. Or you woulda been, when she was still alive.' Terry waits for a sanitation truck to pass and turn the corner. 'Look, I only saw Lola from time to time, mostly before she and my brother got married. After that, I avoided the Baum family whenever possible.'

171

'And that's because...?'

'Because Max is so obnoxious. And I'll tell ya somethin' else. I know Charles didn't kill Joyce. I know because he doesn't have it in him. But Max? If he thought he could profit, he wouldn't hesitate.'

'That's a big jump, Terry, from obnoxious to murderer. But let's get back to Lola. You say you never saw her depressed?'

'Sometimes she was quiet. You'd ask her a question, you'd get a one-word answer. But I'm like that, too, at least according to my wife. Sally complains that she can't get a word out of me when I'm in a bad mood.'

We're interrupted by one of Terry's workers, a short man wearing a toupee so ratty it'd look more natural at the end of a mop handle. Ever the respectful civil servant, I step back to let the man confer with his boss. I'm thinking that maybe Lola's .39 blood-alcohol level has been accounted for, but that doesn't mean she was conscious when her wrists were slashed. In fact, if she habitually drank herself to sleep at night, her drinking problem would have presented Max with an opportunity. Clever Max, who already knows about hesitation cuts.

I can smell the East River, a short block away from where I stand. I'm old enough to remember when the river smelled of chemicals and sewage. No more. I can taste the salt on my tongue and the river's odor is the odor of the sea, of fertility and decay so intermingled they've become one and the same. For some reason, I recall the airliner that landed in the Hudson River a few years

172

ago. The pilot was very wise to choose the placid Hudson instead of the East River. That's because the East River isn't a river. It's a tidal basin separating Manhattan and Long Island. When the tides are running, the velocity of the water approaches six knots and standing waves appear around every bridge abutment. Sully Sullenberger's jet would have been torn to pieces if he'd chosen the wrong river.

Hauptman's worker retreats a moment later and I rejoin Terry. His smile is so broad and proud I half expect him to hand me a cigar. 'See that guy, detective? He's one of two workers I rehired this morning.'

'That's good. Maybe, what with the extra money comin' in, he'll be able to buy himself a new hairpiece.'

'Actually, I think he inherited the one he's got from his father.' Terry pauses, still smiling, then says, 'It's good you're checkin' out Max. That chauffeur of his? The guy scares the piss out of me, and I'm no punk.'

'You know Leonid?'

'I know his type well enough. Half the contractors in New York are tied to the Mob.'

'Are you saying that Max is tied to the Mob?'

'The Russian Mob, maybe. So, whatta ya say we wrap this up. I gotta get back to work.'

'Fine by me. Did Charles ever discuss his mother-in-law's suicide with you?'

'If you wanna know what Charles was thinkin', why don't you talk to him directly?'

'I can't, he's got a lawyer. That's why I'm asking you.'

'Yeah, OK, lemme say this. Any questions about Lola's suicide were forgotten when the terms of her last will and testament were announced. Charles told me that Max went crazy.'

'So, what you're saying is that Max didn't know his wife left her money to Joyce until after her death.'

'According to Charles, absolutely.' Terry pushes himself away from the wall. 'Anything else?'

'Yeah, one thing. What happened to Lola's body?'

'She was cremated and her ashes scattered. At sea.'

I walk the half block to the East River and stare across the water at the Empire State Building which towers over this low-rise section of mid-Manhattan. Assuming he was being honest, Terry's given me a lot to consider. I'm forced to question his truthfulness because he never asked me if his sister-in-law was poisoned. I have to assume that he's in touch with his brother and he already knows.

I fish out my cellphone and my notebook. Usually, I prefer to confront witnesses face-to-face – lies are much harder to detect over the phone – but the question I have for Nurse Shirley Borders is simple enough. I want to know if Max Baum checked her credentials.

'Yes,' she tells me, 'he did, and I was none too happy. I came to Charles at the beginning, while Joyce was still in the hospital. But Max said the court wanted the names of all the nurses and their provider numbers.'

I thank Nurse Borders, hang up, then call Theresa Santiago. She confirms Shirley's account without hesitation. Max Baum demanded that she submit a copy of her credentials, including her Department of Health photo-ID card, before she got the job.

'Were you hired before Lola Baum's suicide?' I ask. 'Did you know her?'

'A drunk,' she answers. 'This woman, if you light a match, her breath will catch fire.'

I pick Davy up at noon and we drive to Park Avenue in the heart of Manhattan's affluent Upper East Side. Sometimes called the Gold Coast, this section of Park Avenue is as upscale as New York gets. It's also home to Max Baum, who owns a duplex penthouse in the Ashley, one of the Avenue's many limestone apartment houses. Lola Baum once lived here, too.

That Max continued to occupy the apartment after his wife's suicide is beyond cold, but I have to accept the fact that his alibi can't be challenged. That leaves a single question to be answered. Could someone else have gotten to her on the night she died?

The uniformed doorman charged with protecting the Ashley's residents, including Max Baum, confronts us before we reach the building's outer door. He's a tall man with a full head of stiff gray hair which he's jammed beneath his doorman's cap. Although his attitude isn't exactly confrontational, he's not letting us into the building, either.

175

Davy and I flash our badges at the same time and the man's attitude softens. We still don't belong here, of course, but we can't be dismissed.

'Who do you want to see?'

'You.' Davy's wearing his favorite wise-guy outfit, a black double-breasted suit over a navy-blue shirt and a silver tie bright enough to be a mirror. 'What's your name?'

'Ben.'

'OK, Ben, we just have a few questions about the building's security.'

'How so?'

'Well, I'm assuming there's a twenty-four-hour doorman to watch the front entrance.'

'Of course.'

'What about the elevator? Do you have an operator?'

'Until ten o'clock at night. After that, the tenants are on their own. But, look, maybe you should speak to the building manager.'

Davy ignores the suggestion. 'What about when you have to use the bathroom, or eat a meal? Do they let you off?'

'I get the super to cover for me, him or one of the men who work for him.'

'What about late at night, when the super's asleep? Did you ever work the late shift?'

'Yeah, when I first came on board. But, look...'

'So, what did you do when you had to go to the bathroom?'

He shrugs his shoulders, a violent gesture that sends his epaulets flying. 'I locked the front doors and took care of business. But nobody could have gotten in without a key.'

'What about through the garage? Can you monitor the garage from the lobby?' Davy spreads his hands defensively. 'I'm only askin' because when my partner drove around the block, I noticed that the entrance to the garage is on the side street, not on Park Avenue.'

A cab pulls to the curb and Ben hustles over to open the door. He offers his arm to the elderly woman who emerges, then guides her across the sidewalk and through the lobby, his manner somehow both familiar and servile. I'm wondering if this is a doorman skill learned through experience when Davy taps me on the shoulder.

'Check out the flowers, Lenny.'

Park Avenue is a two-way street with the uptown and downtown traffic separated by wide medians that run the length of each block. These medians have been turned into mini-gardens by the Fund for Park Avenue, a civic organization with deep, deep pockets. There are cherry trees at each end of the median that fronts the Ashley, trees connected by a lake of densely packed red flowers.

'Begonias,' Davy announces. 'I could only wish the begonias in front of my house grew like that.' He pauses, then says, 'I had a look at Lola's autopsy report earlier this morning.'

'And?'

'Lola died between three and four o'clock in the morning. Her body was discovered by her maid, who called the super when nobody answered her knock. At the morgue, the pathologist who did the preliminary examination found zero evidence of a struggle, no bruising, no scratches. If Lola was murdered, she woulda had to be helpless when it happened. But get this, the ME never ran a full tox screen. They checked her blood for heroin, cocaine, barbiturates and alcohol, but that was it.'

There's a class of drugs called diazepines that are easily dissolved in alcohol and would not have been detected by the ME's limited toxicology tests. Usually called date-rape drugs, compounds like Rohypnol, Restoril and Valium incapacitate the victim, making her unable to fight back even though partially conscious. They affect memory as well, rendering later claims unreliable, especially when taken with alcohol.

Davy and I are thoroughly familiar with benzodiazepine, having worked a date-rape case less than a year ago. That Lola's bottle might have been spiked, that she might have drunk herself into a profound stupor is a possibility not lost on either of us.

The elevator door opens and Ben rushes up to us. 'I only have a few minutes,' he announces. 'I have to go help Mrs Havanian with her bags.'

'Good, because I just have a few more questions. Now, I asked you about the garage. Do you have surveillance cameras in the garage? Can you monitor the garage from the lobby?'

'No, and no.' Ben leans a little closer and his voice drops to a whisper. 'The assholes on the board of directors, they've got enough money to buy their way into paradise, but they won't spring for a decent security system. There's a camera over the door outside the building and a camera where you insert your keycard to open the garage door. And that, my friends, is it.'

'What about the stairwells?'

'Look, it's not easy getting into the building. The garage is for residents only and the front entrance is monitored pretty close. Plus, if you did get inside, you'd have to deal with the elevator operator and the maintenance people.'

Davy shakes his head. We've answered the question we came to ask and it's time to go. At three o'clock in the morning, if you had a key to the garage, you could enter and leave with no one the wiser. That Lola Baum was murdered is at least possible.

'You said there's a security camera by the garage?'

'The garage door won't open until you insert a key card into the card reader. When you do that, you're looking directly into a camera.'

'Who has the tapes?'

'DVDs. The set-up's digital. And that would be the building manager, George Finkel. He works at Freeman Associates on Lexington Avenue. Freeman specializes in managing high-end apartment buildings. They're the ones who hired me.'

Davy sticks out his hand. 'Appreciate the time, Ben. You've been great.'

Ben's relief is obvious as he smiles and takes my partner's hand. 'Hey,' he tells us, 'anything to help the police.'

As we start back to my car, Davy glances over at the flourishing begonias. The sun is high now, the crimson blossoms flooded with light. 'One more thing,' he announces, 'about Lola.'

'And what's that?'

'She was dressed when they found her in the bathtub.'

Nineteen

I don't know why somebody would get into a bathtub full of water if they intended to slash their wrists, but I do know that it happens. As I know that people who kill themselves in the bathtub, whether by cutting their wrists or drowning, are almost always dressed. And that's especially true of women. Apparently, they don't want to be found naked. It's too humiliating.

The hesitation cuts? No sign of a struggle? Dressed in the bathtub? A husband with an air-tight alibi? It's no wonder the ME signed off on the suicide.

But we don't talk about the case as I drive my partner home. We talk about Corinne Mariposa, or at least I do. I tell Davy about the dreams, adding, at the end, 'Ya know, I was right on top of her and I can't stop thinkin' I could have done something, maybe reached out, grabbed the gun.'

'You weren't on top of her, Lenny.' Davy's voice is gentle, but firm. 'You were at least five feet away. I oughta know, I was standin' right

180

behind ya.'

When I think it over, I realize that he has to be right. Corinne flew out of the bathroom, gun blazing. If I was as close to her as I remember, she couldn't have missed me. Yet I can't shake off an image that has the muzzle of her gun within inches of my chest. And I can't stop believing that I could have taken the gun away, given the fact that I was wearing a vest that would easily stop a round from her .38 revolver.

I get to work early, at three o'clock, and quickly write up a series of DD5s to cover my interviews with Terry Hauptman, the doorman at the Ashley, Max Baum, Shirley Borders and Theresa Santiago. These I also add to the case file, both the paper files, which I return to a filing cabinet, and the digital file on my computer.

I'm expecting Morelli to go ballistic, if not actually postal, when I admit that I've opened a new line of investigation without telling him. In the old days, he could pull the DD5s with no one the wiser. Digital entries are a lot harder to delete. For one thing, you can't access the case file without using your password. That makes you accountable, which is not a state of affairs to which NYPD bosses ordinarily aspire.

But Morelli falls back on his tight-ass morality when I finally confess. He bites at his lower lip, his eyes narrowing with outrage.

'You tellin' me the husband was framed? The guy who cared for his wife every day for years? He was set up by his father-in-law?'

'I'm sayin' maybe.'

181

'Maybe Baum killed his wife? Maybe he killed his daughter? Lenny, you're talkin' psychopath here.'

'Max Baum has a motive in both cases. Look, boss, I had Davy check out Lola Baum's autopsy report, strictly off the record...'

'Davy Lowenstein? He's on administrative leave.'

'Yeah, and he's goin' crazy with nothing to do. But let me just go through what I've got so far.' I began to tick the items off on my fingers. 'First, the pathologist who did the autopsy ran a very limited tox screen before signing off on the suicide. Second, security in the building where Lola died is a joke. Third, Max Baum owns a fireworks company, so he had access to realgar, which is used to make the color red. And get this – Baum's still livin' in the same apartment where his dearly beloved killed herself. Whatta ya think he did, hire one of those disaster clean-up companies? Restoration guaranteed? Lola Baum lost several quarts of blood before she died. That bathroom must've been right out of a slasher movie.'

Morelli brings his hand to his chin. He raises his eyes to the ceiling and closes them for a moment. This is my boss's decision-making posture and I respect his moment of contemplation by keeping my big mouth shut. Finally, he folds his hand and drops them to his lap.

'Ya know,' he says, 'I've taken a pretty hard line with regard to mercy killing. And I don't have any problem sending Charles Hauptman to jail if he killed his wife. But if he didn't kill her?

If he was set up? Lenny, I wouldn't care if Max Baum was the fucking mayor, this is not something I can walk away from. Poke around a little bit more, see what you can find. I gotta be sure.'

Assistant District Attorney Roy Carmody is of a different opinion. He's a supervisor in charge of the District Attorney's Homicide Bureau. In New York, the district attorney is an elected official, independent of the both the mayor and the police department. Though mindful of the obvious – prosecutorial success requires the NYPD's cooperation – the lawyers who work for the DA have minds of their own. Carmody has an arrest warrant, too, preliminary tests on the various materials recovered in the Hauptman residence having come back positive for arsenic sulfide. The state is now prepared to take Charles into custody.

'The media's going to be notified as soon as an arrest is made,' he tells me. 'The perp walk should be a real zoo.'

Carmody's referring to the march from the back door of the precinct to the bus that transports detainees to Central Booking. If a particular suspect is deemed newsworthy, reporters set up a gauntlet, using cameras and microphones instead of clubs and tomahawks to inflict their injuries. To my mind, the ordeal is a form of shaming, though I've run across many a perp who didn't have an ounce of shame in him.

Well, it's my fault and I have no right to protest. Charles is going to be subjected to every

183

humiliation associated with the arrest process, from the perp walk to the strip search to the holding pens beneath the courthouse. The forces now moving him along are a lot bigger than Lenny Shaw, even if he set them in motion. But I'm positive by nature and I sense a final opportunity.

'If you don't mind,' I tell Carmody and my boss, 'I'd like to make the arrest without back-up. I think Hauptman will talk to me.'

'Why would he do that?' Well into his fifties, Carmody's button nose and pointy ears are imprinted with the map of Ireland. As are the twinkle in his blue eyes and the broken capillaries on his cheeks and his nose.

'Because he wants me to believe that he's innocent.'

Carmody rubs at his jaw for a moment, then says, 'Hauptman's represented by counsel. Nothing he tells you would be admissible.'

'What if I read him his rights again? What if he signs the little card waiving his rights?'

'Then maybe, depending on the judge.' Suddenly the twinkle returns to Carmody's eye. 'But what you can't do is interrogate him, detective. Whatever information you want, he's got to volunteer it.'

Charles stares at me for a moment, his expression grim, then steps back to allow me into the house. He gestures to the living room. 'Cigarette?' he asks.

'You started smoking again?'

'Be kind, don't rub it in.'

In fact, I'm overjoyed. I light up and take a seat in a club chair facing Otto Baum's portrait above the fireplace. A bottle of single-malt Scotch rests on a coffee table in front of the couch, a twenty-year-old Laphroaig that naturally draws my attention.

'Up for a drink, detective?'

'That depends on how you feel about the fact that I have a warrant for your arrest.'

'So soon?'

'What could I say? You're about to become a celebrity.'

'My fifteen minutes. I can't wait. But I'm not holding a personal grudge. And I'm not angry, either. In fact, mostly I feel like I'm looking at my life through the wrong end of a telescope. I feel small.'

He pours two fingers of Scotch into a stubby glass and hands it to me. There's something different about him, but I can't put my finger on the change for a minute. Then I get it. The comb-over is gone, replaced by shorter hair combed from front to back.

I sip at my Scotch and puff on my smoke. I'm feeling sorry for Charles. There's no smoking at any of the city's jails. He's about to go cold turkey for the second time in a week.

'You confronted my father-in-law,' Charles says, his tone far from accusing.

'I didn't confront him. I interviewed him. How could I not? We're talkin' about his daughter. Most likely, the prosecutor will ask Max to testify. But I'm not supposed to talk to you, Charles, because you're now represented by counsel. In fact, if you do want to talk, I'm supposed to have you sign a waiver of your rights. But I'm not going to do that. No, I'm gonna tell my boss that you clammed up right away.'

'Why?'

'Because I don't think you're likely to confess.'

'I won't confess because I didn't kill my wife.'

'There ya go.' Suddenly I realize that the artist who painted Otto Baum's portrait got him exactly right. The supercilious expression, the faint smile, the cocked straw hat, the jaunty cane. The message is simple enough: I'm playing you for a fool and I want you to know it. The portrait might just as easily have been of Otto's grandson, Max.

'So, what's up with the hairdo?' I ask.

'This?' Charles runs his fingers over his hair. 'My attorney thought it was time for a new look.'

'Well, you made a wise choice, which is not to say you've transformed yourself into Brad Pitt. Tell me about Lola.'

The question takes him by surprise and he draws back for a moment before a smile lights his face. 'Lola stood up to Max. I don't know anyone else who can make that claim.'

'Including Lola's daughter?'

'Especially her daughter.'

'So, what happened? To make Lola contemplate suicide? According to your brother, she was a ball of fire.'

'Joyce's stroke happened. Joyce's vegetative state happened. I was lucky, detective. I didn't have time to fall apart. I had too much work to do. But Lola? Joyce was the love of her life. Without Joyce, Lola could barely function. She stopped going to work, then sold her business, which left her with nothing to do but drink.'

I find myself becoming angry. Charles has a bad habit of saying the wrong thing. Lola now seems a perfect candidate for suicide.

'Tell me about Anna Berevski. Did you know she was unlicensed?'

'Anna was a good nurse.'

'I'm asking if you knew she didn't have a license.'

'I knew.'

'And that was OK with you?'

'Max asked me to take her on, as a personal favor. Do you know about Leonid and Max?'

'What about them?' I stub out my cigarette, finish my drink.

'Going back five or six years, Leonid was on the maintenance staff at the Ashley. His claim to fame is that he saved Max from a serious beating when Max was accosted by a homeless man, a paranoid schizophrenic as it turned out. The man hit Max with a fence post and was about to hit him a second time when Leonid intervened.'

Charles lifts the bottle of Laphroaig and raises his eyebrows. 'You want?'

I wave him off and he refreshes his own drink before setting the bottle on an end table next to a photo album. In silver, across the front, there's a single word, spelled out in satin: WEDDING.

'Leonid would have been a hero except for two things,' Charles continues. 'He lost control,

187

beating the man nearly to death, and the incident was witnessed by twenty schoolchildren on a field trip. Under the circumstances, Max couldn't keep Leonid out of jail. But the lawyer Max retained got the charges reduced. Leonid was sentenced to two years instead of the eight or nine he might have gotten. And when he came up for parole, Max offered him a job and found him a place to live.'

'The grateful thug with the unlicensed sister. Very convenient.' I remove the handcuffs dangling from my belt and drape them across my thighs. 'Of course, you realize that aside from you and Max, no one had a motive to harm Joyce. If it wasn't you, it has to be him.'

Charles attempts a shrug, but doesn't quite bring it off. He looks worried, as well he should. I know I'm being manipulated and I'm halfway to letting the system take its course. Then I glance at Otto. That supercilious look with the little sneer? Pure street. You think I'm bluffin', motherfucker, all you got to do is take that step. Ain't nothin' between us but air.

'Finish your drink,' I tell him, 'because I only have one more question, the one I came to ask in the first place. If Max is trying to frame you, why would he reach out to prevent the autopsy?'

'I don't know, detective, but those pants – and I'm sure you checked them out – are a size forty. No way could I have worn them in the basement while I ground up realgar to put through my wife's feeding tube. And there's no way I'd have left traces of realgar on that file or on the floor. There are lots of people out there who think I'm insane, or at least a schmuck, because of what I did for my wife. But I seriously doubt if you'll find many who think I'm stupid.'

'Probably not, Charles, but I don't have time for a canvass. For now, I've got other things to do. I want you to stand up and put your hands against the wall so I can search you. Husband of the year or not, you're going to jail.'

Twenty

I'm sitting in Dooley's Tavern on Sunday evening at seven o'clock, six days after Charles Hauptman's arrest. I've spent the entire week searching for a cop killer named Mario Ballestera, one of a hundred cops assigned to a special task force. The hunt was relentless, the tactics heavy-handed, but Mario wasn't apprehended until Saturday, and not by us. Ballestera was seized at a cousin's house in Boston by the FBI's Fugitive Apprehension Unit. Score one for the FEEBs.

My companions of the moment, Marie Burke to my right and my partner to my left, raise their glasses and I join them in a toast. We're celebrating Davy's imminent return to active duty, three days after he finally worked up the courage to visit a department psychiatrist. To his surprise, after a brief interview, he was ruled sane enough to defend the public good.

'All along,' Davy tells us, 'I thought Dr Grabow was gonna run me through every horrible thing that happened in my entire childhood. You hear what I'm sayin', right? Some of that stuff, it's embarrassin' to talk about. But I had it all wrong.'

'How so?' Marie says.

'All she asked me was if I was havin' nightmares and if I was losin' my temper.'

'And what'd you say?'

'I said no, of course.' Davy drains his beer and holds up his stein for another. 'I told her I met with my rabbi after the shooting and everything's fine.'

'You don't have a rabbi,' I point out.

'But that's just it, Lenny. Dr Grabow didn't care. That's what I mean when I say that I had it all wrong.' He shakes his head. 'Look, I'm sittin' on my ass and gettin' paid. For the job, that's a total loss, especially with the hiring freeze. The shrink, she works for the department, so puttin' cops back to work is her number-one priority. I woulda had to exhibit delusions not to be declared fit.'

A television at the end of the bar is tuned to NY1, the city's cable news station. Joyce and Charles Hauptman are the stars of a special report that's been running for a good twenty minutes. The case has stirred up a hornets' nest that's been hovering just beneath the radar screen since 2001, a kind of unsettled debt. That's when a woman in a permanent vegetative state named Terri Schiavo caught the attention of the general public. Her husband, Michael, want-

190

ed to pull her feeding tube, legal under Florida law. Her parents, the Schindlers, were vehemently opposed. They claimed that Terri was at least minimally conscious, that she'd been a pro-life Catholic, that her husband was only interested in her estate, that he physically abused her while she was healthy.

By the time it was over, the President, George Bush, along with his brother, Jeb, the Governor of Florida, had intervened to postpone the removal of Terri's feeding tube. The Florida legislature wrote a law giving Jeb the right to intervene, a law deemed unconstitutional by the Florida Supreme Court. Not to be outdone, Congress wrote a law of its own, also declared unconstitutional, giving jurisdiction to the federal courts. Politicians of all stripes eventually became involved, as well as clergy from every major religion this side of Haitian Voodoo.

The case dragged on for months, propelled by the Republican base, a base Republican politicians feared offending. Throughout, and by a large majority, the American public believed the decision to be a family, not a government, matter.

The first irony, not lost on the NY1 anchor, Cal Woodman, is that Joyce Hauptman would have been allowed to die under Florida law. New York, supposedly the most liberal state in the nation, allows the removal of a ventilator, but not a feeding tube. The second irony, missed by Cal Woodman, is a lot more relevant. Though Charles has been the recipient of an outpouring of sympathy, especially by other caregivers, nobody's questioning his guilt.

As for Charles, he hasn't been standing still. On Tuesday morning, the day after his arrest, his attorney was in court demanding a speedy trial. Three days later, he was granted bail on the condition that he not leave his home without the permission of the court. By Friday afternoon, that home was surrounded by reporters and Charles was essentially re-imprisoned.

I know all this – we all do – because the story's been repeated, over and over and over again, on television newscasts, on *The View* and *Oprah*, in the news and editorial pages of every newspaper, on radio call-in programs throughout the nation. My name's out there, too. Though I managed to remain in the background at the press conference following Hauptman's arrest, the information packet distributed to reporters named me as the arresting officer. My home phone's been ringing off the hook. Not my cellphone, though. My cellphone's not registered anywhere. It originally belonged to my mom and I buy minutes over the counter when I need them.

Earlier in the day, I had a very depressing after-Mass lunch with my mother. The Sanchez family, she informed me, were evicted on Friday afternoon. The kids were bawling, the parents, too. Mom had evicted tenants before, of course, deadbeats for the most part, or jerks who were terminally disruptive. But the Sanchez family had been with Mom for a decade, paying their rent on time, month after month, year after year.

'I carried them for eight months,' Mom told

me. 'I even tried to get them into Section Eight, the federal program. But they're immigrants, Lenny, and they're not eligible. I mean, for God's sake, it'll cost the city four times as much to keep them in a shelter. Does that make sense?'

Marie Burke's not in Dooley's Tavern because of Lenny Shaw. She's merely stopping off for a drink after finishing her tour. She's not interested in Charles Hauptman, either. Marie's been around for a long time and she knows how the system works. Now that an arrest has been made, the criminal-justice industry will grind away at Charles until he admits guilt or a jury renders a verdict. Dismissing the charges, absent a confession from someone else, is out of the question.

'All you can think about is going back to work,' Marie tells Davy. 'Me, all I can think about is my vacation. If I was lucky enough to be on administrative leave, I'd research every symptom of post-traumatic stress disorder and work 'em until my pension kicked in.'

'What could I say?' Davy presses his hand to his chest. 'You don't get to work Homicide unless you're a little obsessed. When I'm on a job, I feel like I'm where I'm supposed to be.'

Marie finishes her drink and rises. 'Speakin' of where I'm supposed to be, time to fetch the kids.'

I follow her out of the bar and into a wind too cold for a long conversation. 'What happened,' I tell her, 'over last weekend...'

'You wanna do it again?'

'Yeah, now that you mention it.'

She looks into my eyes for a moment, then pats me on the chest. 'I need a little time, you know, to build up a charge. Then we'll see. You're not partial to kids, are ya?'

What am I gonna say? Yeah, I love the little rug rats? But Marie doesn't wait for an answer. She winks, turns on her heel and marches off to her car.

Davy's got a surprise for me when I come back inside, photos of the bathroom where Lola Baum died. He lays them out in a cross with the center photo of Lola as the responding officers found her. Lola's head is against the back of the tub, one eye closed, the other slightly open. Her arms are folded across her abdomen and the long vertical cuts that caused her death are fully displayed. Surrounding her body, the stained bathwater is the color of pink champagne.

The other eight photographs are of the bathroom's walls, ceiling, floor and fixtures. I stare at them for a moment, just to be sure.

'First mistake,' I say.

'That it is, lad.'

'Not that it matters.'

'No?'

'Without a body to exhume, we'll never prove that Lola didn't kill herself. Even if Leonid's face turns up on the surveillance camera in front of the garage. It won't matter unless we get a confession.'

Davy and I continue to stare down at the photos. I don't know what he's thinking, but I have to wonder how the asshole detectives who reviewed the scene could have missed the obvious. The deep wounds on Lola's arms run from near her elbow to within a few inches of her wrist. That blood spurted from these wounds is undeniable. That inflicting them must have been extremely painful is equally undeniable. True, people determined to kill themselves will endure almost any amount of pain in their quest for oblivion. That doesn't mean they remain unmoving throughout the process.

But there's no blood on the walls or the floors or the fixtures or the ceiling. This is clearly impossible if Lola's injuries were self-inflicted, since one arm must have been spurting blood when she cut the other. That alone would have left spatter on the wall and the floor.

'I'm imagining that he gave her something like Rohypnol,' Davy finally says. 'I'm imagining that she was partially conscious.'

Stephen Park shows up at ten o'clock. The son of a Korean father and an Irish mother, Park works for one of the city's tabloids, the *Daily News*. He's a veteran police reporter and we've conspired on a number of occasions. Like many detectives, I'm not above using a reporter to get my version of events before the public. But I didn't invite Steve to meet me at Dooley's Tavern. In fact, I've been trying to avoid the press.

Park walks directly to our table. He nods to Davy and says, 'Hey, Lenny, I've been to every cop bar in Queens lookin' for you.'

'That mean you're gonna pay me the money you owe?'

'What money?'

Like many Eurasians, Park seems to have inherited the best of both worlds. His skin is the color of new ivory and his dark eyes, rounded at the center, taper exotically. His hair is dark and curled at the ends, an asset he maximizes by wearing it long enough to conceal the collar of his denim shirt.

'Just kiddin', Steve. What's up?'

'You tell me. You're the lead detective.'

'What could I say? We released what we have at the press conference. The hair, the traces of arsenic sulfide in the house and the feeding tube, the victim's condition.'

I'm not telling the truth here. At the last minute, the bone evidence was held back. The bosses weren't anxious to explain how the fragments were collected and I don't blame them. The truth is too ugly for a public already sympathetic to Charles Hauptman. Nevertheless, the bone evidence is mentioned in the affidavit supporting the search warrant and the facts will eventually become public.

'If the case is open and shut, why does the medical examiner's report list the cause of death as undetermined?'

Davy shoves his chair away from the table and stands. 'Lenny, you want my advice, you'll tell this gentleman of the press to take a hike. Me, I'm off to the little boy's room, though I'm neither little, nor a boy.'

Good advice, but I'm not listening. I've been

196

drinking for the past three hours and I'm imagining Lola Baum in the bath, Leonid Berevski leaning over the edge of the tub, knife in hand. Does he inflict the hesitation wounds first? Or does he wait until she's dead? I glance at one of Mike Dooley's antique trays mounted on the wall. A nurse occupies the center of the oval tray. She wears a white apron that drops to her feet, and carries a tray bearing a filled mug and a bottle of beer. The brand name appears above her head, Prima-Tonic. The beer's motto, The Food Drink, rims the edge of the tray beneath her feet.

Steve's using a technique familiar to cops. Throw out an interesting tidbit of information and hope the subject becomes talkative. From my point of view, the only interesting part is that Steve's gotten access to the medical examiner's report. Still, I'm first to speak.

'What's the number-one rule for trial lawyers? Never ask a question unless you already know the answer? I'm sure you've already put that question to whoever leaked the information.'

Steve flashes an embarrassed smile, displaying teeth so white, given his ongoing cigarette and caffeine addiction, they can only be veneers. 'Bottom line,' he declares, 'you can't even prove that poisoning was the cause of Joyce Hauptman's death.'

'Proving's not in my job description. What I do is I collect information, then pass it on. Prosecutors do the proving. And by the way, if you saw the autopsy report, then you know the manner of death.'

'Homicide.'

'Be kind of unlikely that she happened to die of natural causes while she was in the process of being poisoned.'

'Not impossible, though, a point Hauptman's lawyer is bound to make at trial.' Park hesitates, but I don't respond. 'What I'm hearing, there was a financial motive, too, maybe an inheritance.'

Another piece of the puzzle not revealed at the press conference. The motive here was different, though. Circus trials in New York follow an unchanging pattern, part of which involves calibrated leaks designed to influence the jury pool. Charles is getting a lot of positive press. Time to bring him down.

What I should do is confirm the information. Why not, since it's accurate? Park and I communicate on a two-way street. In effect, we hold each other's markers. All I have to do is nod my head and the little arrow swings to my side of the ledger. But maybe I've had one too many. Or maybe I'm still thinking about Lola. In the photo Davy showed me, she's wearing a T-shirt and a pair of gym shorts, as though she didn't want to ruin her good clothes. Another nice touch.

'If you're gonna pursue the money angle, you should take a look at Max Baum,' I say after a minute.

'The father-in-law?'

'Yeah, if Charles Hauptman's convicted, Max gets every penny.'

Steve's first instinct is to smile. The corners of his mouth actually twitch. This is a big story and he can smell a Pulitzer Prize at the end of it. But he doesn't want to come too eager. I watch him stand, watch him shove his hand into his coat pocket as he plays his hole card.

'You up for a smoke?' he asks.

Twenty-One

We start out on separate missions early the next morning. Davy's off to interview Jennifer Gold, the deputy director at the ME's office who canceled Joyce Hauptman's autopsy. We want to get to her before her role becomes public. Me, I'm driving out to Coney Island, my aim to re-interview Nurse Anna Berevski. I haven't told her I'm coming, but when she finds me at her door, she doesn't blink.

'You are here to make arrest?' she asks.

'You've been speaking to Max.' I push past her into the apartment. 'And now you can speak to me. I want to hear your side before I make that phone call to your probation officer.'

'What side is this?'

'You tell me, Anna. Tell me why I shouldn't call your probation officer, why I shouldn't take you into custody.'

'What have I done? I am good nurse. I have to make living. In Ukraine, I was nurse in hospital for eight years.'

'Then why can't you get a license?'

'Board of Health refuses to accept my credits from nursing school. They are saying my school is not meeting American standards. I ask what about work I do in hospital? But Ukraine hospital is also not good enough. I must start over. How I am to make money while starting over is not explained. How I am to get money for classes also. They are not giving away education to immigrants.'

She pauses for a moment, tears of frustration welling up to cloud her green eyes. I'm sympathetic, although my expression doesn't change. Charles told me that Anna was a good nurse and I have no reason to doubt his word, and no confidence in a bureaucracy like the Department of Health to make a reasoned judgment.

'Let's say that I let you walk. Let's say I don't call your probation officer and I don't pursue the second offense. What would you do then? Except go right back to practicing without a license?'

I walk into the living room and take a seat. Anna follows along. The first part – if I let you walk – has stirred her imagination. She sits across from me and shakes her head, her stiff hair following along, steady as a helmet.

'I have money I am saving since first I work for Max. Plus, my brother will help me.'

'Now that he's out of prison?' I shake my head. 'No, forget that. You're telling me you'll go to nursing school, right?'

'Yes, I will get degree and license.'

I respond with a sarcastic shrug. The apartment is as messy as I remember, though the stack of electronic goods piled in a corner has disappeared, as have the three samovars beneath the window. I know that Anna's hustling me. I know that she and her brother are criminals in their hearts, minds and souls. So what? My little wedge – the threat to call her probation officer – is way too small to elicit a confession to murder, even assuming Anna played a part in Joyce's death.

'Why people in America are so hard?' Anna laments. 'In Ukraine, most peoples have nothing, but they are not hard like this.'

'Does that mean you'd rather be arrested in Ukraine than in New York?'

Her eyes flicker, becoming, just for an instant, afraid. Nothing could please me more. If something ugly awaits her in the homeland, if she's afraid of deportation, so much the better.

'Why don't we start with your hours? What days did you work, from when to when?'

Under my questioning, a picture of the nurses' regimen gradually emerges. Anna worked four nine-hour shifts during the week and a double on Sunday. Charles, according to her, was a great boss. He disappeared into his office a few minutes after she arrived at one o'clock in the afternoon, leaving her to her duties, which were virtually unchanging. Anna bathed Joyce, changed the sheets on the bed, delivered medications and nutrition on a schedule established by Dr Meyer, finally emptied the urine-collection bag and logged the volume shortly before her relief arrived. Taken together, these tasks consumed about two hours of her shift. The rest of the time, she sat in a plush recliner and watched television. Both chair and TV set were supplied by Charles, who also provided soft drinks, coffee and access to a microwave.

Anna's smiling by the time she's finished. I haven't asked any compromising questions and I've accepted every word she's said. That's about to change, though.

'How often did Max visit his daughter?' I ask.

Anna raises a finger to her chin, her think-it-over posture. 'When Max comes it is mostly on Saturday when I am not working.'

'If you weren't working, how do you know he came on Saturday?'

'From Shirley, who works this shift. Shirley is hating Max. She complains that she is like servant to Max.'

'Why didn't Max visit on Sunday?'

'On Sunday, Charles goes for dinner at brother's house.'

'After caring for his wife until one o'clock in the afternoon?'

'Yes, after.'

'And Max never came by when Charles wasn't there? Never? He didn't come, maybe, to see you?'

'What is this you are saying?'

'Just answer the question, Anna, and don't lie to me. You lie to me, I'll be standing at the departure gate when they put you on a plane to Odessa.'

Anna's out of options. I've asked a big question and she has to come up with an answer. She squirms in her seat, literally, and her lips tremble with indecision as her hand rises to her mouth. There's no reason for any of these behaviors if the simple truth would serve her interests. Clearly it won't and I'm not surprised when she settles for buying a little time.

'Once when Joyce is running fever, Max comes in right before me.'

'Was Charles there?'

'I don't ... Wait, I remember. He was there.'

'What about when Charles wasn't there? Did Max ever visit when Charles wasn't home?'

But Anna's got her ducks in a row, her priorities straight. 'No,' she says, the lie hanging in the air like a half-deflated party balloon, 'not to best of my knowledge.'

I come down the stairs, cross the lobby and open the door to find Leonid Berevski on the other side. Leonid's wearing a black suit and a black tie over a white shirt, his chauffeur's uniform minus the hat. Though his expression is grim, not to mention challenging, I can't resist a little jab.

'Hey, Leonid, I almost didn't recognize you without the cap.'

He grunts once, then says, 'What you are doing here?'

'What am I doing here?' The first thing I learned on the street, absorbed within days of graduating from the Academy, was to never back down. Better to take a beating than show fear. I step forward, putting my face a few inches from his. 'I'm doing whatever the fuck I want to do. How is it your business? Unless you want to tell me where you were on the night Lola Baum died.'

As it turns out, Leonid doesn't want to play. When I put my hand on his shoulder and push him to the side, he slides over, only the anguished look in his flat blue eyes revealing his inner turmoil. Somewhere along the line, most likely in jail, he learned that fighting cops or prison guards is a losing proposition.

'One time,' he tells me as I stroll on by, 'we meet again.'

I don't reply. I have to meet Davy on Lexington Avenue and 93rd Street and I'm already late. We're going to visit George Finkel at the offices of Freeman Associates. If the surveillance DVD made on the night Lola Baum died still exists, we mean to have it.

Unfortunately, Mr Finkel is unimpressed by our determination. He's a short man in a very expensive suit that almost conceals the ring of flab around his waist. Bald on top and maybe five-five, he wears gold-rimmed glasses thick enough to stop a bullet. He pushes these glasses onto the bridge of his nose and shakes his head.

'You're wasting your time,' he tells us.

'Why's that?'

'Our clients expect us to protect their privacy, detective, and we do. Now, of course, if you were to subpoena the DVD, that would be another matter.'

'How do you know we're investigating one of your clients? Maybe we're investigating a street crime.'

'I'm sorry, but there's nothing I can do.' Finkel

makes a little washing motion with his hands. 'And I suppose I should warn you, a subpoena will have to be reviewed by our attorney. It's unlikely we'd fight the subpoena, but the review will take about a week.'

Davy's wearing a light-blue suit, a pink shirt and a salmon tie with angled black stripes. The tie is too wide to be fashionable, but fashion's not what Davy's about. 'You understand, Mr Finkel, if the DVD were to disappear, you'd be charged with destroying evidence.'

Finkel responds with a raised index finger and a sly smile. 'Since you haven't revealed the date of the particular DVD you're after, I feel that you're worrying needlessly.'

'It's that week, while you're attorney reviews the subpoena, that's got me nervous. But why don't you give me the name of your attorney? Maybe the DA will contact him directly.'

'The firm is O'Brien, Crowe and Wilensky.'

Finkel delivers this information with a straight face and I'm thinking that maybe he doesn't know that Charles Hauptman has hired a new lawyer to represent him, a man named Howie Mankel, or that Mankel is a partner at O'Brien, Crowe and Wilensky.

We leave the offices of Freeman Associates at two o'clock, which gives us just enough time for a quick meal before we report to work. We're both hungry, as it turns out, and we don't talk business until we finish our burgers. Then, over coffee, I run him through my conversations with the Berevskis.

'I think the nurse was lying about Max not coming to visit when Charles was out of the house. As soon as I find the time, I'm gonna talk to his neighbors. Maybe we'll get lucky.'

'And then what?'

A good question. Lying to the FBI is a crime under the federal statutes. Martha Stewart went to jail for lying to the FBI. But there's no law against lying to a New York City cop and I decide to change the subject.

'So how did you make out with Deputy Gold?' I ask.

'She wasn't there and she's not comin' back. Jennifer Gold resigned her position as of nine o'clock this morning. She's now represented by an attorney.'

'Did you call this attorney?'

'Yeah, her name's Noel Sanchez. She told me that her client has decided to exercise her right to remain silent. I pointed out that Gold is a witness, not a suspect, but the shyster didn't budge. "I'll tell you same thing I told the district attorney's office," she said. "If subpoenaed to appear before a grand jury, Ms Gold will appear. Beyond that, she wishes to be left alone."'

Left alone? Not after I make a call to Steve Park. I'd left Gold's name out of my conversation with Steve because I felt sorry for her. Max had used the woman, then left her dangling, a casualty of war. But not now. I'm going to present Deputy Director Jennifer Gold to Steve as a kind of long-term investment. I give him the scoop of the year and he gets to buy my drinks for the rest of his life.

Twenty-Two

It's Halloween. I know this only because I see costumed children on the sidewalks as I drive to work. Otherwise, I'd be oblivious.

This early, with school barely out, most of the children are very young. They're major-league cute, as well, even to a jerk as child-unfriendly as Detective Shaw. Lots of princess and ballerina costumes, lots of ghosts and goblins, lots of little girls in mom's make-up. Back in the day, I was always a pirate. Mom would adorn me with a mascara mustache that curled back over my cheeks and plop a tricorne hat on my head. An ostrich feather jammed beneath the hatband, a black eye-patch and a wooden sword completed the look.

'Shiver me timbers, trick or treat.'

Curiously, as I make my way from traffic light to traffic light, I have a clean memory of my first Halloween. I couldn't have been more than five or six, maybe even younger. Knocking on a stranger's door was nearly as intimidating as the prospect of a fistfight with Sean Malone, who lived next door. But I quickly adjusted my attitude when those strangers dropped handfuls of candy into the pillowcase I used for a booty bag. Candy? My mom wasn't a health nut, but she drew the line well short of Hershey and Snickers bars. Ice cream was a once-a-week treat, if I was good.

The wind has died down and the late-October sun is still bright enough to warm the sidewalks. The children hurry along, dancing around their adult caretakers. Thus far, I've had a bad day. First, Anna Berevski claimed that Max only visited the Hauptman residence when Charles was there. Then we struck out on the surveillance DVD. Now, if we hope to pursue the manner of Lola Baum's death, Davy and I will have to get a subpoena, which can only be drawn up by one of DA's prosecutors.

Morelli isn't in his office when we arrive. He's at a meeting of squad commanders in Manhattan. I pass the time by writing a DD5 covering our interview with Anna. I'm just finishing when Davy motions for me to pick up the phone extension on my desk.

'Hey, Jimmy,' he says to the man on the other end, 'would you repeat that for my partner?'

'Sure. A couple of years ago, when the economy tanked, Baum Capitol Management had three projects, residential towers, in the ground. One was on the Lower East Side in Manhattan. The other two were on the Brooklyn waterfront. Through some miracle, Baum salvaged enough financing to complete the projects, but most of the units are still unsold. He came within an eyelash of bankruptcy, at least according to my boss.'

'How can I verify that?' Davy asks.

'You can't, not without a warrant to search his

records. Baum Capitol's not a publicly traded company. It's just Mad Max and his leveraged personal fortune...'

'Mad Max?'

'Friend to none, enemy to all. Business as warfare by other means.' Jimmy chuckles down low in his chest. 'When it looked like Baum Capitol was going over the edge, nobody shed a tear, not on this end.'

The squad room's humming away. Greg Lato and Eve Durand have a suspect in the box. Greg's standing outside the room, observing through a one-way mirror. He'll be the bad cop, if it comes to that. Eve is inside with the prisoner, yakking away. Stamina is Eve's strong point.

Bud Alston and Caesar Corso are sitting on opposite sides of a desk only a few feet away. They're having an animated discussion over a stack of crime-scene photos. But I'm not listening to their conversation, any more than Caesar and Bud are listening to me and Davy. Our desks are little islands of privacy. Unless asked for our opinions, we tend to mind our own business.

'So, who's Jimmy?' I ask when Davy hangs up.

'Jimmy Teague, my partner from fifteen years ago.' He takes a pencil from his desk and begins to chew on the eraser. 'Jimmy was always a hard worker. Ambitious, too. He got an accounting degree and an MBA from Fordham, goin' at night for about ten years. Then he turned in his badge and went to work for Citigroup. His division funds large residential projects.'

'And he still has a job?'

'A job and a bonus.' Davy laughs. 'What could I say? It's not like it's the real world.'

Morelli comes in a few minutes later. He smiles and greets his detectives. 'Say goodbye to me, children. Three months from now, I'm gone.' He doesn't have to specify where to. Morelli's been angling for a position at the Chief of Detectives' office for years. 'Still, for the present, duty calls. Davy, Lenny ... in my office.'

'This case, it's gone through the fuckin' roof,' he tells us from the far side of his desk. 'And Baum? Well, nobody's askin' me to tank the investigation, not yet, but certain bosses want to keep his name away from the press.'

I'm remembering my conversation with Steve Park, remembering with no regrets. Still, I don't know what to say until Davy says it for me. As always, he has my back.

'Boss, you want Max Baum to stay in the background, you better speak with Hauptman's lawyer. I guarantee Howie Mankel's lookin' for a scapegoat and the only scapegoat on the horizon is Max Baum. I mean, somebody poisoned Joyce, right? So if it wasn't Charles, it had to be Max. But check this out.'

Davy covers Morelli's desk with the photos of Lola Baum and the bathroom where she died. 'Don't worry,' he tells Morelli, 'my fingerprints aren't on these. I got them from a friend of a friend, strictly unofficial. But you gotta admit, they're very interesting.'

210

Morelli stares down at the photos for maybe ten seconds, then says, 'Who investigated the suicide?'

'Manhattan North Homicide.'

'Pavone's outfit?'

'The very same.'

'Looks like they got sloppy here.'

Morelli spins his chair to the right and gazes fondly at a plaque on the wall, a commendation for conspicuous valor. He takes his time, which is only to be expected. Either decision, to investigate or call us off, has the potential to blow up in his face.

'Correct me if I'm wrong,' he says without taking his eyes off the plaque. 'Didn't you tell me the victim's body was cremated and the ashes dumped?'

'At sea, two years ago,' I admit. 'But if you remember, I also mentioned a digital surveillance camera by the garage, which would have been the only way a non-resident could gain access to the Ashley. Davy and I paid a visit to the company that manages the building, Freeman Associates, just a few hours ago. We were hoping they'd volunteer the DVD, but they refused. Serve us with a subpoena is what George Finkel said. Serve us and we'll eventually comply.'

Morelli raises a hand. 'The husband, Max, he was in Europe, right? He couldn't have killed his wife.'

'True, boss. We're lookin' at the chauffeur, Leonid Berevski. The guy did time for a serious assault.'

'And he would have done a lot more time,' Davy adds, 'if Max Baum didn't foot the bill for a high-end lawyer. But, look, if we get our hands on the surveillance video, it'll either show Berevski's face or it won't. And I think, as regards the media, we can do an end-around.'

Music to Morelli's ears. He leans forward to lay his hands on his desk. 'How so?' he asks.

'I know an ADA who'll draw up a subpoena for us, nice and quiet. If we serve it without officially reopening the case and the video shows nothing out of order, we put the whole thing to bed. No harm, no foul. On the other hand, if we find Leonid's mug on the DVD, we evaluate and decide our next move. Bear in mind, Lola's suicide took place in the early morning hours, around three or four o'clock. Leonid's presence, while his boss was in London, can't be explained away.'

Morelli's eyes return to the photos on his desk. For a moment, he stares directly at Lola Baum, at her butchered arms and floating hair.

'Right,' he finally says. 'Go to it.'

There are no trick-or-treaters on Charles Hauptman's block. There's no room for them. The street is choked with news vans sitting at the curb and haphazardly parked patrol cars. Television and print reporters block the sidewalks – forty or fifty at the very least. They've formed a semicircle on Charles's lawn where Charles and his attorney, Howie Mankel, are holding a press conference beneath a bank of lights. I'm hoping that Mankel's introducing his Max Baum

212

defense, but I don't approach the mob. Davy and I are here to canvass Hauptman's neighbors. Fortunately, most are standing outside their homes, enjoying the show.

Funny thing about the craft of detecting. Sometimes you go months without a break, sometimes you never catch a break, sometimes you get lucky the first time out. The couple we initially approach, Mr and Mrs Pontone, flash helpful smiles when he display our shields.

Davy introduces himself, then asks, 'Can we speak with you for a few minutes? About Charles?'

'Sure,' Mr Pontone replies.

'We support our local police,' Mrs Pontone adds.

Support your local police is a political catch-phrase that died out back in the 1990s when crime rates began to drop. But the Pontones appear to be well into their seventies, so maybe they're living in the past. Whatever the case, we follow them into their wood-frame colonial home, through a foyer and into a living room choked with oversized furniture.

'Take a seat,' Mr Pontone says, gesturing to a loveseat resting beneath a large window. 'My name's Alfonse, by the way. And this is Rosanna.'

I'm sitting off to one side, leaning back. By agreement, Davy will conduct the interview. My job is to take the occasional note.

Davy straightens his tie and unbuttons his jacket. He's leaning slightly forward, his hands resting on his knees. 'First thing, lemme thank

213

you for speakin' to us. I know your time is valuable.'

Rosanna flashes a rueful smile. 'Not so valuable as you might think. These days, all we have is time.'

'Be that as it may, I'll try to take up as little of it as possible. First thing, do you know Charles Hauptman well? And did you know Joyce?'

'Oh, yes. We've been living on the block even longer than Charles and Joyce. And of course, we invite Charles to dinner from time to time.' She pauses to glance through the window behind me at the gang of reporters across the street. 'Or we did before all this. Tell me, officer...'

'Detective. My partner and I are detectives.'

'Then tell me, detective, do you really think Charles did what they say he did? He was so devoted to Joyce, even before she had her stroke. It doesn't seem possible.'

'My wife's not exaggerating,' her husband adds. 'I saw Charles right after Joyce's stroke. He looked ready for the grave himself.'

Davy shrugs. 'What you're telling me, it's been confirmed by everyone I've spoken to. I mean without exception. Charles Hauptman loved his wife and devoted himself to her care. Case closed.'

'Then why was he arrested?' Rosanna asks, her tone exploring the boundary between honest curiosity and righteous indignation. 'How could he have killed her?'

'The best way I can put it, Charles was a victim of his own love. He couldn't bear to watch Joyce suffer.'

The Pontones, both of them, nod agreement. And why not? Davy's explanation confirms a rock-hard belief in their neighbor's devotion without damaging their law-and-order attitudes. But Davy's a master at manipulating good citizens, whereas I have more patience with murderers than eye-witnesses. Quickly, smoothly, he explains that he's only here to gather background information, then guides the Pontones into a free-form account of their relationship with Charles. He doesn't correct them when they digress, as they often do. Davy's not really interested in what they have to say because we've heard it all before, which makes his patience all the more remarkable. It's only when Alfonse and Rosanna run out of words that he reaches into his pocket for a photograph of Max Baum.

'Do you know this man?' he asks.

'Sure,' Alfonse replies. 'That's Max, Joyce's father. A miserable son-of-a-bitch. When Charles introduced us, he barely said hello. We were beneath him.'

'And he made sure we knew how he felt,' Rosanna adds.

'Did he visit Joyce often?' Davy asks.

'Every couple of weeks, at least.' Rosanna Pontone's braided gray hair is tied behind her head. Plump without being fat, she's wearing a simple yellow dress and sensible, flat-heeled shoes. The net effect is all jolly grandmother, a façade, apparently, because her pursed and narrowed eyes reveal a disgust that runs to the core of her being. When she speaks, she virtually spits out the words.

'I think Max was having an affair with that nurse. Right under Joyce's nose.'

'Which nurse would that be?'

'The Russian. I don't remember her name. She works on Sundays, the whole day.'

Alfonse breaks in. 'I've become an amateur gardener since I retired. Nothing heavy, of course. I hire a landscaper to mow the lawn and do the heavy pruning. But I like to get outside on Sundays after Mass when the weather's nice. To weed the flowerbeds, trim the shrubbery and the hedges, like that.'

'And you've seen Max visit on Sundays?'

'Oh, much more than that,' Rosanna explains. 'Charles has dinner at his brother's house on Sundays. Most of the time, Max Baum showed up after Charles already left.'

'Are you sure?'

The Pontones look at each other before nodding. 'The Mercedes in the driveway and the chauffeur,' Alfonse explains, 'you couldn't miss 'em.'

Twenty-Three

We're on our way back to Coney Island and the Berevski residence, fighting unexpectedly heavy traffic on the Belt Parkway. I'm feeling good, and I know that Davy is, too. Cops generally claim to hate being lied to, but exposed lies are often the most effective weapons in our collective arsenal. Confirmed by other neighbors, Anna's lie will be especially useful. Now I can get on my high horse, self-righteous as a born-again preacher in a gay bordello.

I gave you a chance. I didn't arrest you, though I might have, and I didn't call your probation officer. But how did you reward my generosity? You lied in my face. Give me a good reason why I shouldn't charge you right this minute? One good reason why I shouldn't put you into the system and let Immigration do what it should have done the first time you pretended to be a nurse?

These questions will not be put to Anna immediately, however. First she'll be removed from the comfort of her apartment and placed in a room eight foot by six, placed behind a small table with her back to a cinder-block wall.

'You know what I think?' Davy asks.

'No.'

'If Max killed his daughter, Anna had to be involved. Now she has to protect him to protect herself.'

Davy glances to his left, at a strip of the Atlantic Ocean between two apartment buildings. The ocean is quiet, the surf shielded by raised dunes. At the horizon, a freighter crosses the trail of silver light cast by a nearly full moon.

'Ask yourself this,' Davy finally says, 'would Max Baum know how to use a feeding tube? I don't. You don't. He had to have Anna's help.'

In fact, I'm familiar with feeding tubes and how they work from watching aides tend my Aunt Margaret. But I don't pop Davy's bubble. Nor do I jinx myself by announcing that our biggest advantage may lie in Anna's fear of being deported. What will she do when faced with the ultimate decision, cooperate with us or go back to Ukraine? I don't know, but I intend to find out.

A few hundred yards ahead, Davy guides our unmarked Chevy around a stalled van in the center lane. From there, it's only ten minutes until we're standing in front of Anna's apartment house. We don't announce ourselves by calling ahead, or trying to use the defective intercom. We wait until a resident shows up with a key, then flash our shields and follow him inside. Anna Berevski doesn't know we're coming until she opens the door to find us in the hallway.

'You're under arrest, Anna.' I take her arm with my right hand, reach for my handcuffs with my left.

'Can I please to get my coat?' she asks.

'Where you're going, you won't need a coat.'

I spin her around, cuff her hands behind her back, finally march her toward the elevator. I want Anna helpless. I want her heart to sink in her chest. I want her to abandon hope.

Davy punches the button and we watch the numbers in the little window increase as the elevator rises. When it stops a floor below us, I turn toward Davy just as Anna's brother, Leonid, bursts through the door at the end of the hall.

In an instant, my rational mind switches off, gone as if it never existed. I see Corinne Mariposa flying out of that bathroom, see the tongues of flame issuing from the barrel of her gun each time she pulls the trigger. My ears fill with the sound of gunfire, of six guns firing at once, loud as the trumpets of Armageddon, loud enough to stir the dead. Instinctively, I reach for my own gun, but I'm not quick enough, not even close. Davy's automatic is already drawn, already pointing. Then Anna's scream echoes in the confined space and I come back to myself. Davy, too, apparently. Though his hand quivers, he doesn't pull the trigger.

Leonid stops in his tracks. There are two cops standing thirty feet away. One has already drawn his gun, while the other is reaching for a gun. Leonid is armed only with his inner rage, a poor defense against bullets projected at supersonic speed.

'Where do you take her?' he demands.

'To the Sixtieth Precinct.' This is a lie. We're taking Anna to our headquarters, where no lawyer hired by Max or Leonid is likely to find her. 'Your sister will be allowed to make a phone call when she gets there.'

The elevator door opens and I shove Anna inside. 'You wanna put that gun away,' I suggest to Davy.

He looks at me for a moment, then slides his automatic into the shoulder rig he's been wearing since he earned his gold shield.

'Yeah, let's go,' he says.

Greg Lato and Eve Durand are still in the squad room when we arrive. They pay no attention to us, standard operating procedure since they have no idea what kind of a game we're running on the suspect. If we need their help, we'll ask for it. I march Anna to interview room number one, put her inside, finally remove the handcuffs.

'Please, I wish to make phone call now,' she announces.

I close the door and lock it without responding. 'Anyone for Chinese?' I ask my fellow detectives. My question provokes a short debate, which I lose. I have to settle for pizza and garlic knots, delivered a half-hour later.

Morelli comes out of his office to grab a slice for himself. He only nods when I describe the evening's developments. Davy is unusually quiet. I expect that he's reconsidering his return to active duty. There's nothing to be done, though, and he picks at his dinner. Myself, I'm on Davy's side. I'm thinking that maybe I should have gone out on leave when I had the chance. Still, my appetite is unaffected and I'm looking forward to my confrontation with Anna Berevski.

Dinner consumed, Davy and I gather at the one-way mirror to observe our suspect. Anna's sitting with her elbows on the little table. Her chin rests on her palms and the look on her face is so despairing I'm instantly cheered. Nevertheless, when I open the door, Anna's grimace is defiant. 'You are violating my rights. When I am to make phone call?'

'Forget it. You're not making any phone calls and you're not leaving until I say so. It's just me and you now.'

'I am need to use bathroom,' she announces.

'Wrong, Anna, what you need to do is stop the fucking lies. I've got four neighbors sayin' Max came to the house when Charles was at his brother's. Four, Anna, and they're tellin' me that he came often. What were you thinking when you bullshitted me? Were you thinking I would not check, that I was a complete asshole?'

My manner appropriately outraged, I go on to give my little speech, the one about offering a second chance, about her throwing my generosity in my face. Anna doesn't attempt to refute my accusations. Her spirits appear to sink with every word.

'You have a very simple choice to make,' I conclude. 'Tell me the truth or let Uncle Sam become your travel agent. There are no other options.'

I pause, but she doesn't reply. 'Take her to the bathroom,' I tell Davy. 'We wouldn't want the lady to have an accident.'

* * *

Anna takes her time, but I don't press the issue. I want her to carefully evaluate her situation. Sure enough, when she finally emerges, her expression is resolute. She's made a decision. Whether to tell me the truth or advance another lie remains to be discovered.

'I am ready,' she announces as she passes my desk. 'Can I please to have cigarette?'

Smoking is forbidden in public buildings in New York, but I make an exception, as do most detectives. By asking for a smoke, Anna has acknowledged my power over her, as she did when she asked to use the bathroom. I'm the bestower of favors, the captain of her fate. I don't have any cigarettes, of course, and I have to beg a few from Greg Lato, who still hasn't broken the habit. But that's not the hard part. The hard part is watching Anna light up without lighting up myself.

Anna draws the first hit deep into her lungs. Her eyes close for a moment, then open wide as she breathes out.

'How much do you smoke?' I ask.

'One pack each day. I have tried to give this up, but...'

'In that case, you've got something to look forward to. The way it's lookin', you're gonna get another chance to kick the habit. There's no smoking in city jails.'

'You have made up mind already?'

'I've arrived at a point where sympathy is no longer a factor in my decision-making. You want to remain free, you gotta sweeten the pot. You

222

have to give me something more valuable than the pleasure of seeing you punished for the lies you told me.'

I fold my arms across my chest. There's a commotion going on in the squad room, a complaining voice at high volume and even higher pitch. *Why you pickin' on me? I ain't done nothin', but you be all up in my face. I know my gottdamn rights. I'm gonna sue your white ass. When I get through with...*

A sharp grunt ends the tirade. One of my fellow detectives has had enough.

'I am lover with Max,' Anna announces, 'from long time ago.'

Anna's stiff hair is too black, her lipstick too red. Her belly protrudes as though she is in the early stages of pregnancy and her ass is so flat it's barely noticeable beneath her jeans. True, she's younger than Max by at least three decades. But Max, even on the balls of his ass, is rich enough to attract a trophy wife – or lover – far more beautiful and sophisticated than Anna Berevski. And then there's the question of why she and Max chose to meet in his daughter's home when they live in a city with fifty thousand hotel rooms.

'So, where did you get it on?' I ask.

'Get it on?'

'The fucking, Anna. Where did you do the fucking?'

'This is very rude.'

'So is lyin' to cops. Now quit stalling. Did you fuck right in Joyce's room? Did you wait until she fell asleep? Or did you want her awake? You know, for the kink effect.'

'Please...' Anna's skin is very pale. When she blushes, her entire face reddens, cheeks, forehead and chin. Her ears are glowing. 'For Max...'

She takes a drag on her cigarette, then begins to weep. I lean back in my chair, unconcerned. The question's been put. She has to answer.

'Max, he was old. He had ... difficulties.'

'Why didn't he use Viagra?'

'He uses this to get erection, but...'

'But what?'

'But he cannot have orgasm. He wants ... special things.'

I don't want to know and Davy doesn't want to know. I can tell by the expression on his face. But I can't let Anna off the hook. I want to break her down and describing the sordid details will surely contribute to that process.

We go at it for another half-hour, Anna speaking in a monotone, me prodding her along, sentence by sentence. The theme that emerges is ugly, though not sinister. Their sexual play took place in a guest bedroom at the end of the hall. It involved diapers, powder, ointment and starched white uniforms.

'OK, I get it,' I finally tell Anna, 'at least from Max's point of view. He's an old man and he's gotta take his pleasures however he can. But what about you? What's your angle?'

Initially, Anna claims that Max threatened to call her probation officer if she didn't cooperate. But I'm not buying the story and I browbeat her until she finally admits that Max paid for her services.

'How much?'

'How much?'

'How much did he pay you?'

'Two hundred dollars.' Not exactly high-end, but there's nothing high-end about Anna. 'I have told you truth, detective,' Anna adds. 'I have told you for what Max comes to house.'

'So?'

'So I can to leave, yes?'

'So you can to leave, no.' I can't stand it any more. I snatch one of the loose cigarettes off the table and light up. Maybe Anna senses my need because she remains silent while my head spins around for a moment. 'See, Anna, my partner and I, we're not really interested in Max's per-versions. We're homicide detectives conducting an investigation into the death of Joyce Haupt-man.'

'I know nothing of this.'

'Nothing?'

'Please...'

I get up, Davy rising alongside me. 'You lied to me before. How do I know you're not lying now? You remember what I told you? You wanna remain free, you gotta sweeten the pot? And something you might wanna think about. Knowing nothing means you have nothing to trade.'

I follow Davy into the squad room, careful to lock the door behind me. Morelli's standing by his door. He's staring at the cigarette in my hand. I head for the john, there to toss my smoke into a urinal after a final puff. A cigarette as a reward for cooperation is acceptable, but smoking detectives are a definite breach of protocol. Davy follows along, but I wave him off. The city's spending cuts have included the mainten- ance crews assigned to clean the precincts. The room smells of urine and the sinks are filmed with soap scum. A cockroach perched on the rim of a sink dives for cover as I head back to my desk.

'You think she's tellin' the truth?' Davy asks.

'Yeah, but so what? Max and Anna being lovers? That just increases the likelihood that they're also co-conspirators.'

Davy responds by fetching two mugs of coffee. He sets one on my desk and sips at the other. Finally, he asks a series of questions.

'What if the obvious is true? What if Charles Hauptman killed his wife? What if we're blow- ing smoke here?'

'If Charles is guilty, he'll go down. Our job is to investigate and I'm not ready to eliminate Max. Not when I think he had his wife killed. Not when I think he was motivated by his wife's fortune, the fortune his daughter inherited, the fortune that will drop into his lap if Charles is convicted.'

Davy shakes his head. 'You're not gettin' this. If Max didn't kill Joyce, or if he did and Anna doesn't know about it, she has no way out. She can't help you.'

'Then she's going down, simple as that. I mean, how else will I know for sure that she's not runnin' a bluff on me? Keep in mind, there's a strong likelihood that she'd rather get busted for nursing without a license than conspiring to murder her client.'

For the next fifteen minutes, while Anna stews, we busy ourselves with our coffee. I'm remembering something Davy told me over drinks a year ago. Cops are American untouchables. We get paid to do the jobs others won't do. We dirty ourselves so that civilians can stay clean. Most cops hold to a cliché about policing. In their view, cops are the thin blue line between order and chaos. But that's not strictly true, at least according to my partner. Society will always find a way to impose order, through family, clan and tribe, through warlords, through vigilante mobs if necessary. The difference is that, absent a police force, ordinary citizens would have to do the ugly things we now do for them. They'd have to get their hands dirty when they'd rather pretend that policing is a noble profession.

I don't care whether or not Anna plied her trade without a license. And I don't care about her games with Max, even though she got paid. Nevertheless, I'm willing to send her to jail and have her eventually deported because it furthers my investigation. What horrors will she face if she's sent home? When Davy and I return, she's not reluctant to spell them out.

Anna tells me that she was admitted to the United States as a political refugee, that she's a Russian, not a Ukrainian, that she was imprisoned in Russia for a decade, that she was raped by the guards at each of the several gulags where

227

she did time, that she was beaten and starved and forced to sign one bogus confession after another. Each of these horrors will be repeated if she returns. She can't go back.

I might ask her why she chose to jeopardize her refugee status by committing crimes if she has so much to fear in the old country. But I don't bother. Instead, I attempt to convince her that even if she had something to do with Joyce's death, she won't be raped or tortured in an American prison. I also hint that she might resurrect her blackmail defense. She might claim that Max threatened to have her deported if she didn't help him. Maybe, if her story and her testimony are convincing enough, she can avoid jail altogether.

But it's no good. Anna holds fast, admitting only that Max was occasionally alone with Joyce while she straightened up the guest bedroom, while she was in the bathroom, while she rustled up a meal in the kitchen.

'Sex,' she tells me, 'is making Max hungry.'

I keep at her for several hours more, then report to Morelli. I tell him I can't break her. He's obviously relieved. Max is a political problem, whereas Charles is a social problem.

'You did your best,' he declares with a grandiose wave of his hand. 'Now either book her, or cut her loose. Your choice.'

But Davy's more opinionated. He repeats his basic argument. Deportation is wildly out of proportion to Anna's crime. Then he adds, 'Suppose Max is innocent, suppose Anna has nothing to tell, suppose she has no way out. Do you really wanna send her back to Russia?'

My answer is direct. I cross the squad room
and place Anna Berevski under formal arrest.
'You change your mind, decide to cooperate?' I
tell her. 'Don't hesitate to call me.'

Twenty-Four

I arrive home a little after three o'clock, an early
edition of the *Daily News* tucked beneath my
arm. Over a hastily constructed tuna-fish sandwich, I read a pair of stories. The first, by Steve
Park, begins under a page-one headline: THE
BAUM CONNECTION. I take my time with Park's
article, pausing to admire his writing skills and
his restraint. Park's story includes the basics on
the Baum family fortune, Lola Baum's suicide
and the estate she left to her daughter. But he
doesn't attempt to connect Max to Joyce Hauptman's murder, doesn't mention the Americana
Fireworks Company or the use of realgar in the
manufacture of fireworks. That's for later, along
with anything else he can dig up to keep the
story alive. Over the years, I've come to respect
print journalists, the good ones at least. They're
as treacherous as cops and have at least as many
confidential informants.

The second story, written by a reporter named
Harriet Trotter, appears on page three. Besides a
short, unrevealing paragraph on the Hauptman

press conference, Trotter's piece cites interviews with Shirley Borders and Theresa Santiago, as well as several of Charles Hauptman's neighbors. The theme of the piece is devotion, as in how devoted Charles was to his wife.

According to Nurse Borders, 'Charles could easily have afforded twenty-four-hour nursing, but he wanted to care for Joyce himself. And he never complained about anything.'

Though not privy to the details of Joyce's care, the neighbors testified to his devotion prior to Joyce's stroke. One woman, three times divorced according to the reporter, declared of Charles, 'They don't make them like that any more.'

I go to bed an hour later, but sleep is a long time coming. My conscience is tickling at my awareness, demanding that I justify Berevski's arrest. This is not a place I want to go and I put the dragon to rest with a pair of convincing rationalizations. First, I put the blame squarely on Anna. She might have told me the truth, no matter how embarrassing, but her lies only confirmed a general sense that she couldn't be trusted. Anna's spent time in a Russian prison, posed as a nurse, engaged in acts of prostitution and lied repeatedly. Why should I believe that she wasn't involved in Joyce's death?

Beyond that, while I'm pretty sure that Anna will eventually be deported, the eventual part might be years away. Anna's not here illegally. That means she'll have to be convicted of the licensing violations – crimes for which she'll do, at most, a few months in a minimum-security prison – before deportation proceedings can begin. And even if those proceedings go badly, she's entitled to bail and her appeals could occupy the better part of a decade, especially if they're supported by Max's bankroll, not to mention his influence.

I sleep until noon, then shower, shave and wolf down a light breakfast before Davy shows up at one o'clock. We're driving to the Americana Fireworks Company's main plant in Farmingdale, a town fifty minutes away on Long Island. The day is crisp and I'm wearing a topcoat over my suit. Davy's wearing a battered trench coat though there's not a cloud in the sky. He's not in a good mood.

'We're painting ourselves into a corner,' he announces. 'There's no win here, not for us. Did you listen to the news this morning?'

'Didn't have time.'

'Berevski's arrest and her connection to Max Baum was the big story. I tell you, Lenny, the whole damn country's payin' attention.'

'Davy, please, we're doin' what we're paid to do. We're investigating. As for Nurse Berevski, her arrest was for a violation unrelated to the murder of Joyce Hauptman. This is a story with no legs.'

But Davy isn't satisfied. He folds his arms across his chest and shakes his head. 'We never should have followed Hauptman to the Gardens. We should've let the whole thing lie.'

'Now you sound like my mother.'

'No.' Davy reaches out to slap the dashboard, then finally gets to what's really bothering him.

231

'I feel like I'm workin' for Hauptman's lawyer, what's his name...'

'Howie Mankel.'

'Yeah, Howie the Prick. You just know he's gonna blow smoke by puttin' the blame on Max. And I'm helpin' him make the case. You, too, Lenny. You're helpin' the defense.'

We're driving through light traffic on the Northern State Parkway's sunken roadbed. The landscaped margins to either side rise to a low brick wall and it feels as if we're passing through a cut between two hills. Though the air smells mainly of exhaust, a gusting wind scatters red leaves from a cluster of maple trees across the roadway.

'There's no going back,' I finally tell my partner. 'We followed Charles to the Bronx Botanical Gardens, collected his wife's remains, picked up his garbage, searched his house and put his ass in jail. The way it is now, we can close the investigation and let him swing or continue to investigate Max Baum, who most likely had his wife murdered.'

But Davy's not satisfied. 'Another crime we'll never prove,' he says.

Our visit to Americana is brief. Though we arrive unannounced, a public-relations flak greets us cordially. Her name is Ashley McDougal and she answers our three most pertinent questions without hesitation. Yes, Americana uses realgar in its manufacturing. No, Americana's realgar is not kept under lock and key. Yes, Americana's new boss, Max Baum, accompanied by his chauffeur, visited the plant in late September.

About the rest – where Max went, what he saw – Ashley's responses are vague. But I'm satisfied with the effort, as I explain to Davy on the ride home.

'We've locked down access to the means. Americana stocks realgar and Max visited the plant. Who's to say that Leonid didn't slip away at some point? Or that Max didn't return?'

'Damned if I know.'

And that's all I'm getting out of David Lowenstein. We drive to the One-Twelve in silence, climb the stairs to the squad room in silence, take seats at our desks in silence. I'm thinking this is why I never got married when Morelli's door opens.

'You hear?' he asks.

'Hear what?'

Morelli shakes his head in disgust. 'Don't you jerks read the papers or watch television? Are you entirely fucking ignorant? There was a riot last night, in the housing area where Anna Berevski was being held. She's dead.'

Forget what I couldn't have known when I arrested Nurse Berevski. Like the Dominicans and Puerto Ricans in Anna's dormitory had been nurturing mutual grievances for more than a month. Like those grievances would boil over on the night Anna was taken into custody. Like persons unknown, for reasons unknown, would push a homemade shank into Anna's throat. Like she'd bleed out before order was restored, the

233

only fatality.

Forget all of that. For just a second, I feel like I killed her myself.

'I blame Corrections,' Morelli says. 'They don't classify their prisoners on Rikers Island. You could be arrested for jumpin' a subway turnstile and end up sleepin' next to a psychopath.' He pauses to clear his throat. 'What I'm sayin', Lenny, it's not your fault. In your place, I woulda done the same thing.'

'How about you, Davy? Would you have done the same thing?'

The look in Davy's green eyes is dismissive. 'People get killed every day in New York. They get run over crossin' the street. They get shot in drive-by shootings. Whoever pushed the knife into Berevski's throat is responsible, not you. And by the way, I never had any objection to Berevski doin' a few months for impersonating a nurse. My problem was with her gettin' deported.'

'Well, she won't be deported now.'

'And Corinne Mariposa won't be going to jail any time soon.'

'Which means what?'

'Which means these are events you just have to live with.'

Morelli retreats to his office. 'You want the night off, Lenny, it's fine by me,' he calls over his shoulder.

I'm trying to think of something to say when Greg Lato leads a suspect into the squad room, a short Latino pressing a wad of paper towels to a cut on the top of his head. Greg's partner, Eve

234

Durand, follows a moment later.

'In a desperate attempt to escape arrest,' Greg explains, 'Miguel tried to hop a schoolyard fence. And he would've made a clean getaway, too, because climbin' fences is an activity I abandoned on my thirtieth birthday. But then he caught a shoelace in one of those little spikes at the top and came down on his head.'

'Fuck you, *pendejo*. You hit me with a rock.'

'That was me,' Eve Durand says.

'Then fuck you, too, you *chingada* bitch.'

Normally, this sort of talk would inspire a heated response, but Eve and Greg merely chuckle as they lead their suspect to an interrogation room. Eve turns to Davy and me just before closing the door.

'His buddies witnessed the whole thing,' she tells us. 'The poor bastard's not gonna be able to show his face on the street for a month, even if he makes bail.' She flashes a kind smile, then says, 'Tough luck about your witness.'

Davy opens the middle drawer on his desk. He takes out a pencil and begins to chew on one end. 'She's right,' he says, 'about the last part. Without Berevski, we'll never make a case against Max Baum.'

'There's still his wife. Did you do anything about a subpoena for that surveillance tape?'

'My guy's workin' arraignments in night court. I'm meeting him at a Vietnamese restaurant in the back of the courthouse.' He glances at his watch. 'Which reminds me, that's an hour from now and I've got to get downtown. You gonna be all right?'

'Yeah, sure. But I think I'll take advantage of Morelli's generosity. Maybe I'll get lucky. Maybe Marie's off tonight. Maybe she's sitting at the bar in Dooley's. Maybe she's casting lustful glances at the door, hoping against hope.'

But I don't go to Dooley's, and I don't go home either. I drive along Queens Boulevard, make the left on to Hillside Avenue, then another left at 197th Street. Although I have no right to approach him now that he's represented by counsel, I'm heading for Charles Hauptman's home. I think Charles will speak to me and there's a question I want to ask him.

When Charles opens the door, he's wearing a Yankees sweatshirt over a pair of worn corduroys. He freezes for a second at the sight of me, but then steps aside, not quite smiling. A moment later, I'm again seated across from Otto Baum's portrait. A television tuned to a PBS documentary plays on what I originally took for an antique sideboard. As it turns out, after Charles presses a few buttons on the remote, the television's screen drops into the cabinet.

'You heard?' I slip a cigarette out of the pack on the coffee table and light up. 'About Anna?'

'Yes, I heard,' he says. 'You want a drink?'

'Sure, if you'll join me.'

'I've been joining you all night.' He blinks and grins. 'I've been joining you for days.'

Charles disappears into the kitchen, returning a moment later with a bottle of Absolut and two highball glasses, no ice, no mixer. He pours a couple of inches of vodka into one of the glasses

236

and puts it on the table in front of me. Then he fills his own glass almost to the brim.

'Number two,' he announces.

'Number two what?'

'Casualties. Deputy Gold was the first. She got off lucky, detective. She only lost her job. Anna lost her life.'

I take a hit on my smoke, but leave my drink untouched. 'Look, Charles, you told me you were innocent and you wanted me to continue investigating.'

'And have you?'

'Yes, but I keep running into brick walls.'

'Did you try Dr Meyer?'

'I interviewed him. He told me he was too exhausted to leave home on the night your wife died.'

'Did he tell you that his clinic wouldn't exist if not for a grant from the Baum Foundation?' Charles pauses to light a cigarette. 'Max is big on charity, as he should be considering he receives more than a dollar in tax benefits for every dollar he gives. He's been financing Meyer's operation for ten years.'

In fact, Dr Meyer chose not to mention his dependence on Max Baum. And Max never mentioned his charitable contributions. But Meyer's clinic depending on grant money for survival isn't out of the ordinary. The overwhelming majority of Meyer's patients – the ones who have insurance of any kind – are on Medicaid, where reimbursement rates are so low that most doctors won't treat them.

'OK, Charles, lemme see if I've got this right.

After Joyce dies, Max Baum contacts Dr Meyer before you do, then somehow convinces him to stay home. Max does this because he knows there won't be an autopsy if Meyer signs the death certificate. And Max needs an autopsy because he poisoned his daughter and wants to blame you so he can inherit her money.'

'I know it sounds unlikely...'

'Ya know, when you're right, you're right. And what makes the story even more unlikely, not to mention totally unbelievable, is that your father-in-law reached out to prevent the very autopsy he tried so hard to bring about. If not for his connections, the autopsy ordered by Singh would have gone forward and you would've been arrested long before you actually were.'

I finally sip at my vodka, only to realize that it was poured from a bottle kept in the freezer. It's ice cold, flavored with lemon and delicious. I'm tempted to chug the whole thing, but I don't. I want an answer to my question, a rational answer, if there's one out there.

Charles looks even more depleted than the last time I saw him. Maybe, now that he's had a taste of prison life, the rigors of a jury trial are weighing on his mind. Maybe he's imagining a jury foreman standing up to announce a verdict. In New York, the minimum sentence for second-degree murder is fifteen to life.

'It's been one long nightmare since Joyce's stroke,' he tells me. 'You know, I called 911 ten seconds after she fell, but it took them twelve minutes to arrive. Twelve minutes when Joyce wasn't breathing. Twelve minutes, when the maximum time the brain can go without oxygen is four minutes. But they defibrillated her anyway. Do you understand? They knew she'd be neurologically damaged but they got her heart beating anyway. And me, when Joyce started breathing again, I was so grateful I wanted to kiss them. But I didn't know, did I? I didn't understand the part about brain cells dying after four minutes without oxygen. And I didn't know that the first cells to die are the ones that make humans human.'

I shut him up by slapping the arm of the chair. 'I don't want to hear it, Charles. No more boo-hoo, look how miserable I am. No more suffering St Charles. If you don't answer my question, I'm going back to my desk to write up a report that eliminates Max Baum as a suspect.'

'I didn't kill my wife, detective. I couldn't.'

'Then who did? Max? But how would he do it, Charles? Joyce was given arsenic over a period of weeks. Max didn't have the opportunity.'

I already know the answer to this question, but I ask anyway. Charles answers without hesitation and I get the distinct feeling that he's been waiting for a chance to make just this point.

'But he did. Max often visited Joyce on Sunday afternoons when I was having dinner with my brother and his family.' Charles looks up and to the right, a gesture quite familiar to me. Humans, when they try to remember some past event, commonly look up and to the left. When they're trying to decide what to say next, they look up and to the right.

Charles finally smiles before continuing. 'Max

can be very abrasive, as I'm sure you discovered. But he knows it, too, and he didn't
have any objection when I asked him to visit
on Sunday afternoons while I was out of the
house.'

'If he's so abrasive, how could you work for
him?'

'I'm an accountant. I specialize in charitable
foundations and non-profits. The Baum Foundation is my employer and I rarely have contact
with Max on business matters. My manager at
Baum is Marty Green, the CFO.'

I take a final pull on my smoke, then grind the
butt into an ashtray. 'OK, let's go back to my
original question. Why did Max prevent the
autopsy if he wanted to frame you?'

Charles pours himself another drink. 'There is
the possibility that one of the nurses...'

'Poisoned her patient? With realgar?'

'You can't dismiss the possibility.'

'Yes, I can. And a jury will, too.' I know I
should lean back, cross my legs and let my suspect dangle. But I'm angry and growing angrier.
Deputy Gold resigning in disgrace? Anna
Berevski dead? Charles just doesn't get it. 'Last
chance,' I tell him. 'If you want me to keep investigating, you have to give me a good reason
why Max prevented the autopsy from going
forward. Otherwise, I'm gonna tell the jury I'm
certain Max wasn't involved.'

Charles stands up and walks over to the
fireplace. Motionless, he stares at a pile of ashes
on a wrought-iron grate. Otto Baum's portrait
graces the wall just above his head. The contrast

240

between the two is overwhelming. Otto's blue eyes project a serene confidence. They're the eyes of a man who never questioned his own judgments, a man who was always right. Charles couldn't be more different. Bald and stooped, the thick pouches beneath his eyes are dirt-brown. His skin is sallow and marked by clusters of tiny blackheads and his corduroy trousers are shapeless. Terry Hauptman was right when he called his brother soft. Charles is a geek's geek, a victim's victim, hapless and harmless. The jury will love him.

'Do you remember my telling you that I asked Dr Meyer to stop treating Joyce's infections?' he asks without turning around.

'Yeah, you told me he refused.'

'True enough, but I could have fired him and found someone more cooperative.'

'So?'

'So, I didn't kill my wife. So, I'm innocent.'

Twenty-Five

I'm at my mother's, in her ultra-neat kitchen, having lunch while we discuss my Aunt Margaret. Mom's a compulsive housekeeper, a trait that's rubbed off, to a certain extent, on her son. I like my apartment orderly – my life, too, come to think of it – but there's a big difference here. I pay someone else to do the work. Not Mom. She's elevated housekeeping to an art form and each of her days brings forth its required tasks. Wednesday, for example, is kitchen and bathroom day, so I'm not surprised by the immaculate floor and baseboards. The glass in the room's sole window is clean enough, inside and out, to be invisible.

We're having egg salad spiked with bacon, cilantro and kernels of grilled corn. The egg salad is piled on slices of jalapeno-cheese bread Mom buys from a Mexican bakery a few blocks away.

'You having second thoughts?' I ask when Mom finally takes a seat.

My Aunt Margaret's time on earth is running out, that much is obvious to all. But the pace has been slow because Aunt Margaret failed to leave an advance directive and Uncle Jack has to prove that she would have preferred death to her current existence. In practical terms, that means securing notarized statements from family and friends to whom she expressed a wish not to be maintained on life support. Mom completed her statement within a day. Mine came along a few days later. That should have been enough, to my way of thinking, but the review board at the hospice demanded additional statements from non-relatives. The last of these was hand-delivered yesterday.

'I don't know, Lenny. Whenever I think about Margaret gone ... I just can't put it aside, how close we were. At Blessed Virgin, everybody knew, all the other kids, if you messed with one of us, you had to deal with both of us. We were a team, the O'Neill sisters. I can still remember the time we beat up John Casey in the lunchroom. Father Bonanno made us pray so many rosaries our fingers were raw from counting the beads.'

I'm immediately reminded of Anna and Leonid Berevski, brother and sister. Leonid's out there somewhere, nurturing his grief, another victim, another unintended consequence. Mom picks up her sandwich, then changes her mind and returns it to the plate.

'But here's the thing, Lenny, and there's no gettin' away from it. If I was in that bed, I'd want somebody to pull the plug. The way Maggie is now, with the bedsores and infections, it's like she's decaying while she's still alive.'

Given my mother's penchant for abrupt transitions, and her uncanny ability to find the sore point, her next question doesn't catch me by surprise. 'Are you sure that Charles Hauptman actually killed his wife?' she asks.

'You want certainty, Mom, ask a priest. As for St Charles, there's enough evidence to arrest him and bring him to trial. More than enough.'

'That's not an answer.' She blinks twice, then shifts her focus. 'He was devoted to her, right?'

'That's the consensus.'

'And he took care of her? He did everything the nurses did, just like the reporters are sayin'?'

'To the best of my knowledge, he did.'

'For five years?'

'Five long years.'

'Lenny, I gotta tell ya, if I was on the jury, I wouldn't find him guilty.'

'That's what you think now, Mom, but the judge will tell you, and forcefully, that you're obligated to follow the law. That means if you should decide, beyond reasonable doubt, that Charles poisoned Joyce and the poison caused her death, you have to convict him. In fact, before the trial even begins, during jury selection, the judge is likely to ask if you can put your sympathies aside and base your verdict on a determination of the facts. If you say no, you won't get to serve. That's good for the prosecution, by the way. Jurors who swear to put aside all human emotion are more likely to be law-and-order types.'

I watch my mother carry our dishes to the sink, watch her rinse them carefully before loading them into the dishwasher. 'How can a judge do that?' she finally asks. 'Is there some law that says jurors have to follow other laws exactly?'

'No, there isn't. A jury can acquit for any reason, or for no reason. That's called jury nullification. In the past, it was mostly used down South, to acquit white men accused of killing black men.'

Mom's standing in front of the kitchen's only window. The window is open a few inches at the bottom and its sheer curtains, embroidered with tea roses clinging to a serpentine vine, extend toward my mother's back as though seeking purchase.

'So, what are you sayin', Lenny? He's gonna be convicted? Which I think is a travesty of justice.'

'I'm not saying that at all. In fact, after speaking to Charles last night, I'm predicting an acquittal.'

'How?'

When I finally speak, the bitter edge to my tone comes as no surprise. 'Do you remember the championship fight between Muhammad Ali and George Foreman? The Rumble in the Jungle? Me and Dad watched it on closed circuit at the Fresh Meadows Theatre.'

'Yeah, sure. That's the one that took place in Africa. Or was it Manila?'

'You were right the first time. The Manila fight was between Ali and Joe Frazier. The one I'm talkin' about was staged in Zaire.' I slide my chair back and cross my legs. I'm thinking I really need a smoke. 'Anyway, aside from being one of the greatest upsets in boxing history, the bout is famous for Ali's defensive strategy. If you recall, the ring ropes were relatively loose that night, loose enough for Ali to avoid most of Foreman's punches by leaning back. Foreman, unfortunately, was slow to realize what was happening. He eventually ran out of gas and Ali knocked him cold. Afterward, Ali told the media that fighting with his back to the ropes was part of some plan he concocted in training camp. He even gave his strategy a name. He called it the Rope-A-Dope. Myself, I'm not convinced. I think Ali was improvising. But I don't question what George Foreman said in an interview twenty years later.

"'Ali used the ropes,' he admitted, 'and I was the dope.'"

Leonid makes his move ten hours later, at eleven o'clock. Davy and I are returning from an encounter with one of our snitches, Jaime Pulveda. We're investigating a drug-related homicide that occurred six months before, in May. We know that Pulveda is a devious punk who routinely fabricates information, but we're hoping he's telling the truth this time. The man he's named, Fabrizio Cummaro, is a violent career criminal. We've been trying to take him off the street for a couple of years now.

All the parking spaces in front of the precinct are taken when I pass by. I'm reduced to circling the block for ten minutes before a space opens up on a side street lined with stubby red-brick apartment houses. I shut down the engine and step into a light mist halfway between fog and rain. The gloom is pervasive and I'm walking with my head turned down. Not Davy. His eyes are shielded by the brim of his customary fedora and he's looking straight ahead. It doesn't help him, though. When Leonid opens up from fifty feet away as we turn the corner, Davy is the first to be hit.

My hands go to the buttons of my coat, a matter of pure instinct, because my thoughts are whirling through my brain like clouds around the eye of a hurricane. I'm as aware of the door-man having a smoke a hundred yards behind Leonid, and of a dog-walker on the other side of the street, as I am of the automatic in Leonid's hand. I note the flickering bulb in an amber streetlight, a low-flying airliner, a tricked-out van turning into the block, woofers thumping. I hear a voice crying, 'Davy, Davy,' a voice so far away that I fail to recognize it as my own. A bullet slams into my thigh, but I don't fall or even stumble, and I feel no pain at all as I retreat around the corner where I'm shielded by the brick wall of an apartment building. I watch my fingers unbutton the jacket of my suit and I feel my right hand snake around to the holstered Glock behind my hip as though hand and fingers belong to someone else.

Then I yank the gun free and my confusion disappears, instantly replaced with a rage that blots out every other consideration. The blood running down my leg? So fucking what? Davy on the ground? So fucking what? Killing Leonid is the only thing that matters and I'm imagining him unarmed, on his back, staring up at the barrel of my Glock when I pull the trigger. I want to kill him and I want him to know he's

247

dying. I want my face to be the last thing he sees before he's carried off to hell.

I don't get my wish, not entirely. I turn the corner to find Leonid twenty feet away. His automatic is pointed at Davy, who's rolled onto his stomach, but the barrel turns up when I show my face. I'm holding my Glock out, bracing my wrist with my left hand, and I'm remembering my firearms instructor at the Academy. Outcome is not determined by the number of rounds fired. Outcome is determined by the number of rounds that find their intended target.

The lesson is reinforced when a bullet slams into my shoulder. The impact spins me to the left, and my left hand drops to my side, useless. But I don't care. I drop the sights of my weapon to Leonid's broad chest and begin to pull the trigger. I'm not counting the number of rounds I fire, but I'm spacing them out as I take a fraction of a second to re-sight after each shot. Kill him, kill him, kill him, kill him, kill him.

Somewhere along the line, Berevski drops his gun, but I continue to shoot until he topples over backward. The crunch of his head slamming against the concrete is so completely satisfying that I want to pick him up and drop him again. I hobble forward, my left arm dangling, my right shoe filled with blood. The blood is warm and slippery and I'm beginning to hurt, but I want to make sure Berevski's dead. I find him un-conscious, his chest flat and unmoving, but I'm taking no chances. I drop the sights of my Glock to the center of his forehead. I'm just about to pull the trigger when I feel Davy's hand on my elbow.

'Don't do it, Lenny.' He drops to one knee, shielding Leonid with his shoulders, and puts his fingers to Leonid's throat. 'Don't be a fool.'

Though well intentioned, Davy's advice is unnecessary. My head is already spinning, my balance gone. But I'm cheered, nevertheless, when Davy looks up at me and says, 'He's already dead.'

Twenty-Six

Painkillers. That's what my doctor calls the little white tablets I'm given every four hours. But from the beginning, I think of them as Pain Killers. Two words, not one. And there's plenty of pain to kill. As it turns out, Leonid was a good shot. The .50 caliber Desert Eagle handgun he attacked me with holds only seven rounds. That he hit me twice and Davy once before expending his ammunition is a tribute to the instruction he received in the Russian military. Or maybe not. Leonid's past refuses to be dissected. He was a former Russian special-forces operative. He worked exclusively for a Ukrainian oligarch named Galevsky, himself the victim of a hit man. He was a black-market arms dealer who supplied weapons to the Chechen resistance. He was a former KGB enforcer from a faction that opposed Vladimir Putin. The story changes every other day.

From my point of view, of course, it hardly matters.

Davy gets off easy. The light body armor he wore beneath his shirt was the difference between a broken rib and the loss of his lower ribcage. The doctors taped him up, held him overnight, released him the following morning.

My story is different. Leonid's 300-grain hollow-point bullet smashed every bone in my left shoulder. The exit wound in my thigh was roughly the size of a baseball.

The leg wound, they tell me, will eventually heal. I may or may not have a limp, but if I do, it won't be severe. Not the shoulder. The shoulder doesn't work and though my elbow and wrist are unaffected, my left arm, in its blue-cotton sling, is useless. Any attempt to move my shoulder – for example, when the nurses demand that I get out of bed, or when an unbearably cheerful therapist teaches me to use a crutch – is followed by an onslaught of searing pain that leaves me sweating and nauseated.

Unless, of course, I've killed the pain with painkillers.

Painkillers are misnamed. They don't actually kill pain. They just make you so high that you don't give a shit. As if the pain belongs to someone else, someone you don't really care about.

I remain in New York Hospital on Booth Memorial Drive for ten days. Mom visits, relatives visit, Marie Burke visits once but doesn't return. Davy continues to visit after his discharge.

250

'We're heroes,' he claims, 'I may write a book.'

Meanwhile, the little TV above my bed runs the story (and every conceivable variant) non-stop. With Max Baum, shielded by a posse of five criminal-defense lawyers, the last villain standing.

I'm in a private room, a hero's perk, apparently. Commissioner Kelly visited on the first night, as did Mayor Billionsberg. Archbishop Dolan swept into my room on the second day, at the head of an entourage larger than the Mayor's.

But I don't care about any of that. I'm waiting for Steve Park and I make sure I'm good and stoned when he arrives three days after the shootout.

'Thanks for callin' me,' Park says. 'I'm serious, man. This is fucking big. My agent's negotiating a book deal with three publishers. He's got 'em bidding against each other.'

I stare at his pretty face for a moment, at his creamy skin, the oddly rounded eyes that suddenly narrow at the corners. His lips are full, though not out of proportion, and his black-on-black curls roll across his scalp, every hair in place. I try to imagine what he sees when he looks down at me. Everything has changed for me and there's no going back and I'm wondering if it shows.

But Park's eyes reveal nothing, not until I tell him that I was investigating the suicide of Max Baum's wife before Davy and I encountered Leonid, that I now consider Lola's death a likely homicide. Then his eyes become feverish and I know I can squeeze him. I can ask for money, or to be named a consultant should the book deal come through. I don't, though. I don't ask for anything.

'From what I understand,' I tell him, 'the case is now in the hands of a homicide detective named Eve Durand.'

I know I could have died. The bullet that passed through my leg might have torn the femoral artery, in which case I would have bled out before help arrived. The bullet that smashed my shoulder might have impacted my throat, in which case I would have been virtually decapitated. So there's no getting around the fact that I'm lucky to be alive. And I feel lucky, at least until a pair of Fire Departments paramedics load me onto a gurney and wheel me out of the hospital on the day of my discharge.

Every bump, every turn, every lift – the pain in my shoulder and leg is as unrelenting as it is astonishing. No amount of painkillers short of a life-threatening overdose is likely to make a difference and I know it. But I'm not being offered painkillers. I'm expected to suck it up and I do, throughout the long ride from Flushing, in central Queens, to Long Island City on the East River. Then we finally park and I realize that my apartment is two flights up and there's no way I can make it on one leg, one arm and a crutch. I have to be folded into a wheelchair kept just for this purpose, folded into the chair, carried up the steps and deposited, howling, in my bed. By that time, the pain is all I have. It surrounds me, a cocoon walling off the outside world. Even when my mother stands at the side of the bed, holding a glass of water in one hand and a pair of little white tablets in the other, a long moment passes before I get the message.

As I wait for the painkillers to take effect, I think of Leonid and the hate I felt, and still feel, for him. I think of Max, too, my rage undiminished, and of Charles Hauptman, that model of devotion, the husband every woman desires.

Relieved of all responsibility, I drift. Davy comes almost every day, Mom, too. A home health aide shops and cleans the apartment, but Mom reserves the cooking to herself. I become a master at manipulating my elbow, wrist and hand without moving my shoulder as much as a millimeter. My physical therapist has a predictable take on this strategy. She wants me to use the joint. But Inez only comes by three days a week and she leaves after a couple of hours. The rest of the time, I drift.

Davy and my mom clash from time to time, his free-wheeling cynicism an affront to her Catholic-driven respect for authority. She becomes particularly outraged when he calls our mayor, Mike Bloomberg, 'Mayor Billionsberg'.

'Have some respect,' she demands.

'Gimme a break, Sarah, the guy spent fifty million dollars gettin' re-elected before he even had an opponent.' Davy winks at me. 'The best little mayoralty that money can buy.'

I ignore the tension, self-absorbed as a feeding

insect.

Over time, I begin to heal. By the end of the third week, I can hobble around with the aid of a cane. By the end of the fifth, I put the cane next to the crutch in a hall closet. I'm hoping my shoulder will follow along and I'm naturally disappointed when Dr Arnier Berthold, my orthopedic surgeon, tells me that I need more surgery. Berthold's examining my X-rays and he doesn't bother to look up when he delivers the bad news. Nor is any more patient when he attends me the day after the surgery.

'Your glenoid, that's the end of the scapula, and the head of your humerus, that's the long bone in the arm, are basically destroyed. I've done the best I can to keep the joint in place, but if you hope to regain any significant function, you'll need shoulder-replacement surgery.'

This time, with the help of Davy and Mom, I'm able to leave the hospital on my own two feet. The pain is terrific, but I don't really mind. I've got a fistful of painkiller prescriptions, dated a month apart. I'm good to go.

Eve Durand shows up on December 7, Pearl Harbor Day. Eve's a motherly type, a black woman from a Caribbean family. She has a sure touch in the box, especially with frightened suspects and witnesses, especially when delivering bad news, which is what she has for me.

'So, how you doin', Lenny?' she asks. 'You makin' out all right?'

In fact, I gulped down a hundred-milligram tab of Demerol thirty minutes before Eve rang the

254

bell and I'm feeling pretty good. But I don't raise the subject of painkillers, or my growing addiction to them. Already, I know enough to hide it from the kids.

'I had a visit last week,' I tell her, 'from an inspector named Mahler, like the composer. Mahler's from the Puzzle Palace, a flunky, pure and simple. He was firm with me, though.'

'What did he say?'

'He gave me a choice. First, I can retire on a line-of-duty pension, which is what he strongly advised me to do.' A line-of-duty pension is no small thing. In addition to lifetime medical and dental coverage, I'll get three-quarters of my current pay, about sixty grand, also for life. And that's whether or not I pursue another career. 'Option number two, I return to duty in some administrative capacity, say with the property clerk's office. But I can't go back to Homicide, my investigating days are over. As far as the job is concerned, I'm a cripple.'

'I'm sorry, Lenny. I truly am.' Eve's round face relaxes for a moment and her eyes become evaluating. Something has changed between us. 'Anyway, I want to bring you up to date on the investigation.'

With me and Davy on the sidelines, Morelli dumped both homicide investigations, Joyce's and Lola's, in Eve Durand's ample lap. I wasn't there, but I'm pretty sure Eve didn't complain. She never complains.

'I personally examined Charles Hauptman's phone and credit-card records,' she tells me, 'and I had another geek pick apart the hard drive on his computer. There's no indication that Hauptman ever purchased realgar. No calls to individuals or stores that sell the crystal. No computer searches for realgar. No computer search for any poisons, or visits to commit-the-perfect-murder websites. No incriminating evidence of any kind.'

'When's the trial?'

'It's scheduled for April 3rd. But there's something else. I had a forensic accountant examine all the Probate Court filings relative to Max's administration of his wife's estate. There were no irregularities. The payouts were either for taxes or Joyce's care. Max didn't even take the fee he's entitled to as Lola's executor.'

I'm in a small, non-denominational chapel at my Aunt Margaret's hospice. The big day has come and the room is packed with friends and relatives who haven't visited Aunt Margaret in years. Uncle Jack is present. He's sitting right next to me. My mother's on my other side. She and Jack are reconciled, at least in theory, but Jack chose not to sit next to her anyway. I'm thinking that's because Mom is crying, but then Jack starts to cry, too.

'This is too much for me,' he admits. 'I know it has to happen – I don't have any doubts, not one – but it's still too much for me.'

A few minutes later, I accompany my mother and Uncle Jack into Aunt Margaret's room. They're letting the family in, a couple of people at a time, and we're the first. Aunt Margaret is lying in her bed, as peaceful as I've ever seen her. And for good reason. A clear plastic patch on her right forearm bears an imprint: Fentanyl 12mcg/hr. A synthetic opiate, Fentanyl patches deliver a continual dose of painkilling medication for seventy-two hours. I know this because I wore a patch for the first two days following my second surgery. When then nurse pulled it off and I was consigned to oral medications, I nearly cried.

But I'm not crying now. I'm drifting, as Aunt Margaret is drifting, the both of us toward oblivion. I watch Uncle Jack take her hand, watch my mother bend to kiss her sister goodbye, watch Uncle Jack drop to one knee, sobbing now. The vent continues to hiss every few seconds, the last machine standing. The feeding pump has been turned off, the IV no longer drips. One of the hospice's counselors, Mrs Prejean, stands with her back against a wall. She carries a box of tissues, holding them out in front, an offering, I decide, to the god of sorrow. Her mouth moves, but she doesn't speak.

We have another look at Aunt Margaret twenty minutes after they pull the vent. This time, Uncle Jack puts his arm around my mother, leading her into the room. The staff has arranged Aunt Margaret carefully, uncurling her arms and legs, closing her eyes, pulling her blanket up to her chin. I watch Mom run her fingertips across Aunt Margaret's forehead, watch her kiss her sister's eyelids.

'Goodbye, Maggie,' she whispers. 'Goodbye, goodbye.'

* * *

I flush my painkillers down the toilet that night, and for the next three days I'm barely able to function. I do manage to attend Aunt Margaret's wake and the funeral, but when I come home, I collapse.

A week after the funeral, I join a low-rent gym, PowerPartners, on Vernon Boulevard. Half its members are from the projects near the 59th Street Bridge and many of them are veterans of New York's prison weight yards. They know who I am, of course, but they're more interested in my disability than my profession. They see that I'm fighting through the pain and they respect the effort.

And the pain is terrific, not in my shoulder, but in my supposedly healed leg. Half my thigh is scar tissue and tight as a bridge cable. But I'm not discouraged. In fact, now that I'm no longer drifting, I welcome the pain. Which is not to say that I'm foolish enough to work my left shoulder. No, I've got that arm in a sling because, thanks to my recent surgery, my shoulder dislocates if I let it hang.

I take it easy at first. Charles Hauptman's trial has been postponed until May 1st and I have a month to prepare. And I do prepare. Assistant District Attorney Patricia Eng calls me into her office no fewer than six times for just that purpose. I can't blame her. The media, Steve Park leading the way, have continued to vilify Max Baum. Heartless in his personal relationships, ruthless in his business relationships. As far as the *New York Post* is concerned, Max Baum dispatched Leonid to kill me. Case closed.

Charles, by contrast, only grows more saintly.

'What I think,' Patricia tells me, 'is we have to find a way to tear him down. If we don't, the jury's gonna convict on the lesser charge, at best.'

The lesser charge is attempted murder. A fall-back in case the state fails to prove that arsenic poisoning was the cause of Joyce's death, or the jurors can't bring themselves to convict a saint of murder.

I have to feel sorry for Patricia Eng. At the time of Hauptman's arrest, the case appeared to be a prosecutor's dream come true, a big-ticket slam dunk. Not any more. Only a week before our meeting, Charles was offered a deal. In return for a guilty plea to attempted murder, he'd receive the minimum sentence of two years. Instead of the fifteen-to-life minimum he'll face if he goes to trial and strikes out. He refused.

Every few minutes, Patricia tells me not to be nervous. But I'm not worried about testifying. I've testified many times in the past and the case against Charles is straightforward. I did this, I did that, I did the other thing. Howie Mankel will surely contest the many admissions Charles made, but the issue of what I can, or can't, tell the jury will be decided at a hearing before the trial begins. The outcome doesn't concern me, either. The outcome of the hearing or the trial. I'm content to know that if Charles is acquitted, he'll have me to thank.

The seasons have come and gone, fall and winter. Davy and I are in my living room, watching a Yankees–Orioles baseball game with the Yanks on the losing end of a twelve-to-one blowout. Joe Girardi, the Yankees' manager, has a rookie pitcher on the mound, a kid named Jonathan Albaladejo, who's getting killed. This is a rite of passage rookies are commonly forced to endure. With the game already lost, Girardi has no incentive to use his veterans. Better to save their arms for another day. Better to sacrifice the rookie.

'I turned in my papers,' Davy tells me after finishing a second beer. 'My shield, too.'

Me, I'm still hanging on. I can't see myself toiling in the Property Clerk's Long Island City warehouse, even though it's not far from my home. But I can't see myself without a gun and shield, either. What would I do? Where would I go?

Davy answers both questions an inning later when Girardi finally takes pity on his rookie pitcher, replacing him with José Veras.

'I'm gonna open an office. No divorce work, no skip tracing. I'm gonna work strictly for defense lawyers.' Davy's sitting in a rocking chair I bought from Ethan Allan a few years ago. He turns it slightly, so that he's more or less facing me. 'What I was thinking, Lenny, is that we could go partners. Between your pension and mine, we can afford a decent office and take a few years to build up the business.'

When I don't answer right away, he adds, 'It beats sittin' around the house, Lenny. Sittin' around, that's the worst.'

I can't dispute his assertion and I don't try. But

I won't be sitting around, waiting for some un-specified but inevitable end. There's a trial three days away and it appears that I'll have to testify twice. Hauptman's attorney, Howie Mankel, has added me and Eve Durand to the defense's witness list.

'Correct me if I'm wrong, but don't you hate defense lawyers?' I ask. 'Don't you generally refer to them as vermin, scumbags or shitheads?'

I watch Davy squirm in his seat. Either of us could probably get a job working in the security division of some giant corporation. New York is the Promised Land for giant corporations. But I suspect that Davy wants to be his own boss. Him and me, both.

'Right now,' I tell him, 'I've got other things on my mind. For one, there's the trial. For an-other, I'm lookin' at shoulder-replacement sur-gery and months of physical therapy afterward. But I'll think it over. And thanks, Davy. Thanks for asking.'

I turn back to the game. The Yankees have closed the gap and the score is now 12–6. With two outs in the eighth inning, Derek Jeter's on third, Johnny Damon on first, Mark Teixeira at the plate. So far, a month into the season, Teix-eira's been a total bust and he does nothing to here to justify his twenty-million-dollar salary. With the count one ball and two strikes, he flails at a slider in the dirt and strikes out. The Orioles' pitcher hops off the mound and pumps his fist. The inning is over, the rally killed.

'There's something else,' Davy tells me. 'Something I got from Eve when I handed in my papers this afternoon. She was gonna come over herself, but her kid's sick and she had to get home.'

Davy gets off the couch and fetches his jacket. He takes a single piece of folded paper from an inside pocket, hesitates for just a second, then passes it over. I unfold the page and stare down at a computer printout of a still photograph.

'The photo was taken by the parking-garage camera at the Ashley on the night Lola Baum died,' Davy explains.

'At what time?'

'Two thirty-three in the morning.'

Framed in the driver's side window of a car, Leonid Berevski stares up at me. He's leaning forward, one arm extended through the window, staring directly into the camera, his glare as hard as ever.

'What's Morelli say?' I ask.

'According to Eve?'

'Yeah, according to Eve.'

'The Chiefs are whispering in Morelli's ear. They want the whole thing to go away, Charles, Max, Joyce and Lola. The job's gettin' killed.'

'So that's it?'

'Face it, Lenny. If Max sent Leonid to kill Lola ... Well, Leonid is dead, so there's no way to prove it. And by the way, Eve says she went through Leonid's personal effects with a fine-tooth comb, Anna's too. She found nothing to indicate that Max sent Leonid after you or Lola, and nothing to indicate that Anna was involved in Joyce Hauptman's poisoning. Nothing, Lenny, nothing at all.'

Twenty-Seven

As far as the general public is concerned, I'm a mixed bag. On the one hand, I bravely fought and killed Leonid Berevski, who, all agree, was a monster. But I'm also the cold and callous detective who trailed the grieving St Charles to the Botanical Gardens before collecting samples of what was left of his wife's body.

My fellow cops have no such conflict and I'm picked up on the morning of Charles Hauptman's trial by a sergeant from Borough Command. I'm a hero on the job because I stood my ground, though severely wounded, and killed the man about to kill my partner. For cops, it doesn't get more heroic than that.

'What you did?' Sergeant Chestnut declares. 'Nobody's forgettin', Lenny. You ever need a favor, all you gotta do is ask.'

I'm tempted to say, 'Thanks, can I have my arm back?' But I don't want to burst Sammy Chestnut's heartfelt bubble and I hold my peace.

When we finally pull up, the plaza fronting the Queens County Courthouse in Kew Gardens is packed. Show time, with the whole city watching. Again, my peers show me respect. A phalanx of court officers and uniformed cops leads me from the curb to a conference room in the

263

district attorney's suite of offices. The mob of howling reporters and photographers never gets within fifteen feet.

Inside the conference room, I find coffee brewing on a sideboard, a plate of donuts next to the coffee pot, a little pile of folded napkins next to the plate. No more waiting in the hallway, hoping against hope that a maintenance crew cleaned the public bathrooms on the night before. No more hanging out with the assorted mutts and mopes and skells who haunt New York's courthouses.

Heroism, apparently, has its privileges. And me, Lenny Shaw, I can see that gravy train rolling down the tracks. I'm thinking about writing a book.

Charles Hauptman's day in court begins with a series of pre-trial hearings. I testify at two of these, a Mapp hearing and a Miranda hearing to determine the admissibility of the physical evidence and the damaging admissions Charles made in the course of our interviews. Howie Mankel, naturally, wants everything tossed. At the Miranda hearing, he contends that I should have informed Charles of his right to silence before I questioned him on that first night. That's because Amar Singh, the ME's death investigator, believed that a crime had been committed and Charles was the only logical suspect.

Mankel's fallback position, that I should certainly have warned Charles before my second interview on the night I collected his trash, is

264

more compelling. By then, I'd trailed Charles through the rain to the Bronx Botanical Gardens and collected bone fragments from a muddy field. Would I have gone to all that trouble if I didn't consider Charles a suspect? Mankel doesn't think so.

Relative to movie trials, real trials are conducted in slow motion and I'm on the stand from ten o'clock in the morning until past three o'clock. By early afternoon, though I down several ibuprofens during the lunch break, I'm hurting so bad that Judge Mead interrupts the proceedings. Mead's well into her sixties, a no-nonsense jurist with a reputation for fairness.

'Detective?' Thin enough to be shapeless beneath her black robes, Mead's skin is the color of the floor-to-ceiling oak panels that line the room. 'Are you all right?'

'All right?'

'Well, you're perspiring and it's quite cool in the room.'

At home, I'm able to slump back on the couch so that my sling rests on my stomach. But the wooden chair I now sit on lacks even a cushion and the full weight of my arm drags on my shoulder. Pain is the inevitable result.

'If we delay the trial until I stop hurting,' I tell Judge Mead, 'we'll be here until the Second Coming. I'm ready to go.'

Mead stares at me for a moment, her gaze compassionate. Then she nods and orders Mankel to proceed.

Mankel needs no encouragement. His words come swiftly and his tone is crisp. He's a tall

265

man, in his fifties, broad in the chest and shoulders, with a resonant voice that easily fills the courtroom, the largest in the building. Mankel's hair has retreated at the temples, leaving him with a widow's peak, a spear point that he thrusts at me as he asks his questions.

'Detective, you say you were upset when you learned that Joyce Hauptman had been cremated and her remains were about to be scattered.'

'Yes, that's true.'

'In fact, you were so upset that you followed Charles Hauptman through Queens, over the Triborough Bridge, all the way to the Bronx Botanical Gardens, your mission to collect a sample of those remains for chemical analysis. That's right, isn't it?'

'Yes, it is.'

'And this happened within hours of a shooting incident that involved the death of a woman named Corinne Mariposa, an incident that had you up half the night answering questions and writing reports?'

'Correct.'

'Correct? Good, so far we're in agreement as to the facts.' He pauses to look down at his notes, then smiles a we're-all-in-this-together smile. 'Would it be fair to say that you were extremely determined to collect those remains, given all you went through.'

'It was then or never. I wasn't going to get another chance.'

'That's not the question I asked.'

'I did my job.'

'Despite Charles Hauptman not being a

suspect? You went to all that trouble?'

'One step at a time, Mr Mankel. You can't have a suspect until you have a crime. At that point, I couldn't know that Joyce Hauptman's death was a homicide.'

The answers come easily, thanks to Patty Eng's meticulous preparation, and I focus most of my attention on Charles, who refuses to meet my eyes. Charles is nicely dressed for his day in court. His dark brown suit – I note the common touch with appreciation – hugs his shoulders and chest, as does his fitted yellow shirt. His perfectly knotted yellow tie is a touch darker than his shirt and decorated with rows of tiny green fleurs-de-lis.

I wonder who dressed Charles, Howie Mankel or Max Baum. Whoever, they've made him presentable. Without doubt, he'll photograph well. But even though his eyes are lowered, it's obvious to me that the man's devastated. And I understand why he doesn't want to look at the crippled cop testifying against him. The only issue is whether he knows that I know. Somewhere down the line, I intend to get an answer.

I'm not in the courtroom for Mankel's and Eng's final arguments, but given Judge Mead's law-and-order reputation, I don't give Howie Mankel much of a chance. Eng, on the other hand, worries that Mead will bend on the admissibility of the bone fragments, there being no precedent in New York law on this issue. Her worries are needless for two reasons. First, my grisly actions on the day I trailed Charles from central Queens to the Bronx were leaked to the media in late November, along with the fact that the bone I recovered tested positive for arsenic. Second, the bone evidence didn't play a vital part in my securing a search warrant. The arsenic levels in Joyce's hair and feeding tube were more than sufficient to establish probable cause.

But Eng worries about everything, a fact of life she makes clear during the lunch break. 'If Mead tosses the bone fragments, Mankel's gonna contend that the bone fragments led to the trash collection, which led to the search warrant. Toss out the bone, toss out everything that came after.'

Judge Mead does not exclude the bone fragments. Her ruling is more nuanced. First, she compares Joyce Hauptman's scattered remains to the discovery of a body in a public place. The right of every American to be free of illegal searches and seizures does not apply. Eng's triumphant reaction – she throws Howie Mankel a significant look – is short-lived. A moment later, Mead rules on my various interviews with Charles. The first interview is in, the second, when I collected the trash, is out.

'Detective Shaw's actions on the prior day, in following the defendant and collecting fragments of the deceased's bones, indicate a level of suspicion that justified informing the defendant of his rights prior to the interview.'

Score one for Howie Mankel and Charles Hauptman? I was sure the media would run with that slant, but the sad truth was that Charles made no admissions, damaging or otherwise, in the course of that second interview. By then, I already knew, from his statements as well as those of the nurses and his brother, that Charles wanted his wife dead. And I will so inform a jury when it comes time for me to testify before them.

Twenty-Eight

Judge Loretta Mead is charged, among other things, with empanelling an unbiased jury. But I doubt even she believes this can be done. Virtually every facet of the story has been thoroughly explored by the media. Worse yet, sides have been drawn. As with Terri Schiavo, a large majority of eligible jurors believe the state had no business interfering in what was essentially a family matter. But there are those law-and-order types who cling to the belief that we're a nation of laws and that all laws must be obeyed. It's the principle that counts, a principle that leaves no room for compassion. On a third front, the pro-life crowd, admittedly small in New York, is nevertheless vocal. According to their pundits, the man who ended Joyce Hauptman's life, be it Charles or Max, should pass the rest of his life in a prison cell. As he would undoubtedly spend eternity in hell.

In a perfect world, Judge Mead would eliminate both extremes, but she's hampered in that effort by a simple fact, a fact confirmed by one jury study after another. Potential jurors often lie. They lie to avoid jury duty and they lie to get on juries, especially when it comes to show trials. The former claim that they are, in fact, biased, and should therefore be excluded. The latter, of course, make the opposite claim.

Judge Mead does her best. I know this because the process takes all of Tuesday and Wednesday. I'm on call throughout, but I spend most of my time in the gym. I've got a workout buddy now, Gustavio Guadalupe. Sicilian by birth, Gus doesn't much care for cops, as his cynical observations make apparent. But we have something in common. Gus has a club foot. We're both gimps.

I've become much stronger since I joined PowerPartners, my legs especially. This time the docs were right. My injured leg, though usually stiff when I awake in the morning, loosens up as I go through the day. I've reached the point where I can work a stationary bike for an hour with no ill consequences.

I'm working the bike hard on Tuesday afternoon, while Judge Mead and the attorneys wrangle with jury selection. Gus is right beside me and he brings up the Hauptman case for the first time. Despite his orthopedic shoe, Gus pedals faster than me, and against greater resistance.

'Ya know what I think?' he asks.

'What's that?'

'I think you shoulda minded your own business. I think everybody woulda been better off. What was she anyway? I'm talkin' about the

270

wife. Look at her condition, lyin' in that bed, year after year. It's like the husband killed someone who was dead already.'

Mom delivers a similar message over dinner on Wednesday night. By now, I've heard from Patty Eng, who told me I'd be on the stand by late Thursday morning, early afternoon the latest. Patty wanted to know if I was nervous. I wasn't, and I'm not.

'You're familiar with that thing about good intentions?' Mom asks.

'You mean about them paving the road to hell?'

'Yeah, right. Charles might've started off with good intentions. I mean, I can't quarrel with him wantin' to end his wife's suffering when I just did the same for my sister. But look what happened afterward. Not just you, Lenny. There's Anna Berevski and the woman, Gold, from the ME's office. She's gonna have to testify that she caved in to political influence. And even Leonid, may his soul rot in hell. If Joyce hadn't been poisoned, Leonid would probably be alive.'

And, she might have added, I wouldn't be crippled.

Sergeant Chestnut picks me up at nine thirty on Thursday morning and I'm safely ensconced in the DA's conference room when Patty Eng delivers her opening statement. I'm not alone this time. Officer John Carter, the first responder on the night Joyce died, and Amar Singh, are present, too. Having set a precedent with me, Eng has apparently decided to spare all her witnesses

271

the indignity of waiting in the hall.

Carter will be the first witness to testify for the prosecution. He's been on the stand before, but not in a show trial with every word subject to analysis. He seems nervous, though his testimony will be straightforward. Joyce died at home with no doctor in attendance. Informing the Office of the Medical Examiner was standard operating procedure.

Amar Singh's position is more controversial. When Singh demanded an autopsy, Carter notified his supervisor, who called in the heavy artillery. That would be me, homicide detective Lenny Shaw.

There's really nothing much that Howie Mankel can do with the specifics of Amar's testimony. After all, the death investigator was right. Joyce Hauptman was poisoned. But when the time comes, Mankel doesn't really challenge Amar's judgment. He's content to portray Singh as a heartless bureaucrat who injected himself into someone else's tragedy. And Singh rises to the bait, growing more and more defensive until his testimony finally degenerates into a series of sullen exchanges.

Then it's my turn.

Prodded by Ms Eng, I reel off a string of well-rehearsed answers to her well-rehearsed questions. Along the way, various items recovered pursuant to the search warrant are entered into evidence: the file and feeding tube and Charles's fat pants, Joyce's hairbrush, the nurses' notes, a sprinkling of red crystals. There's nothing grisly about any of this, but the exhibits appear to have a cumulative impact. By the time I finish, most of the jurors are closely scrutinizing the defendant.

I'm also scrutinizing Charles, and he's returning my gaze from time to time. I think he knows where I'm coming from. I think he knows that I've crossed a line and his trial is on the other side of it.

From the physical evidence, Eng turns to the various interviews I conducted with Charles, before and after I read him his rights, and to the surrounding events. I tell the jurors that Charles freely admitted a wish to end his wife's suffering and that he took steps to accomplish that end. I tell them he asked her doctor not to treat her infections and that he contacted hospices in a vain attempt to end nutritional support. I tell them I wasn't upset when Joyce's autopsy was called off because the objection was on religious grounds. Religious Jews don't cremate their dead and I assumed the body would be available for an autopsy, should an autopsy become necessary. I tell the jury I was stunned when I found out, less than twenty-four hours later, that Joyce had been cremated and her ashes were to be scattered a day after that. I tell them I was forced to make a snap judgment. I could trail Charles to the Botanical Gardens and collect fragments of his wife's remains or I could walk away from the case. I chose to investigate.

For the most part, I face the jury when I deliver my answers, as all cops are trained to do. Thus, I'm aware of a collective distaste when I describe my trip to the Botanical Gardens. Most lean away. A few glare openly.

I try to look contrite, a poor cop pushed into corner by circumstances beyond his control. But I'm not fooling anyone, including Patty Eng, who turns this corner without slowing down.

'Now, Charles Hauptman told you, at your first meeting, that he wanted to end his wife's suffering. Is that right?'

'Yes, it is.'

'Did he offer any other motive besides compassion for wishing his wife dead?'

'No, he didn't.'

'Detective Shaw, did there come a time when you conducted an interview with Charles Hauptman's brother, Terence Hauptman?'

My testimony, that Charles had twenty million reasons for wanting Joyce dead, and that he concealed this motive, has its intended impact. St Charles has finally been humanized.

Eng busies herself with her notes, giving the jury a well-calculated moment to absorb my testimony, then brings me forward to October 17th, when the search warrant was executed. That was the night when Charles admitted, after having been read his rights, that he knew all about realgar.

'He told me that realgar was another name for arsenic sulfide and that realgar is a crystal and collectible. He told me that realgar can be easily purchased from websites like eBay.'

'Did there come a time when you attempted to verify this claim, that realgar can be purchased on eBay?'

I look through my notes, then shift so that I'm

facing the jurors. 'Yes, on October 16, I visited the offices of Dr Herzog at the medical examiner's office. Dr Herzog is a toxicology expert. She went online, to the eBay website.'

'And what did you find.'

Again, I glance at my notes before raising my eyes. 'I discovered fifty-three offers for realgar. The cheapest was selling for a dollar ninety-nine.'

'No more questions,' Patty Eng declares.

Judge Mead glances at her watch. It's approaching four o'clock. 'Mr Mankel,' she asks, 'would you like to begin your cross-examination in the morning?'

'No need, your Honor. I have only a few questions for the witness at this time. However, as I intend to re-call him when I present the case for the defense, I ask that he be made available.'

'So ordered.'

Mankel walks to a podium about fifteen feet from where I'm sitting. His manner is almost kindly. 'Detective Shaw,' he asks, 'you testified that you and your partner, Detective Lowenstein, followed Charles Hauptman, his brother, Terence, and his father-in-law, Maxwell Baum, to the Bronx Botanical Gardens. Is that correct?'

'Yes, we did.'

'And was your partner wearing a trench coat and a broad-brimmed hat?'

'Yes, he was.'

'And were you wearing an overcoat and carrying an umbrella?'

'I was.'

'No more questions.'

275

Twenty-Nine

Because I'm to testify again, this time on behalf of the defendant, I'm excluded from the court-room prior to re-taking the stand. The fear is that I might tailor my testimony to that of other witnesses if I was to hear that testimony first-hand. This worry is groundless since Patty Eng has taken great care to ensure that her witnesses are on the same page. I already know what the others are going to say. Beyond that, I have an informant who remains in attendance throughout the trial. That would be my buddy, reporter Steve Park, to whom I speak nightly. I've become one of those well-placed sources in the NYPD that Park loves to cite.

With my testimony complete, Patty Eng turns to an issue sure to be raised by the defense. Was Joyce Hauptman's death the result of arsenic poisoning? Or did she die of natural causes?

A high-normal level of arsenic in human hair is three parts per million. The tested level in six different samples of Joyce's hair was 90ppm at the roots and near normal at the ends. While this proves she was fed large doses of arsenic over time, it doesn't prove that her death was caused by arsenic. To make that particular determination with certainty, a forensic pathologist – like

Dr Harold Konig, who testifies for the prosecution – would have needed to examine Joyce's internal organs, her liver and kidneys especially. This, of course, never happened, which is another reason why the defendant is charged with both murder and attempted murder. Given the 90ppm level, someone tried to kill Joyce Hauptman.

I've seen Konig in action before. In his mid-fifties, he's a tall man, broadly built, with a grandfatherly manner that plays well. His full head of hair is gray and a bit disheveled, as his thick mustache always seems to need a slight trimming. Konig smiles a lot, his blue eyes twinkling with delight.

Prompted by a free-form question, Konig begins his testimony with an explanation of how cause of death is determined. Sometimes, he tells the jury, the evidence presented by an examination of the deceased's internal organs is clear and unambiguous. At other times, even after close examination, an immediate cause of death does not present itself. In that case, both the cause and the manner of death have to be pieced together from all the available evidence, including the surrounding circumstances.

In Joyce Hauptman's case, he tells the jury, his job was made easier by the excellent nursing care she enjoyed. The nurses' own testimony, given prior to Konig's appearance, along with the notes they kept, proves his point. Joyce's temperature was taken, and her heart and lungs examined with a stethoscope, on every shift. At no point did her fever rise above 100.5 degrees, while her heart and lung functions were absolutely normal. Thus, her unconfirmed infection was not the cause of her death.

Might she have died of a heart attack or another stroke, or even some completely unsuspected malady, perhaps a brain tumor? Yes, but death would have had to be instantaneous because she displayed none of the symptoms associated with these maladies. Instead, she'd slowly weakened over a period of two weeks, exhibiting symptoms traditionally associated with arsenic poisoning. Exactly what you'd expect from an individual with an arsenic level of 90ppm in her hair.

Howie Mankel launches a slashing cross-examination when his turn comes, but Konig remains unflappable. Yes, he admits, *undetermined* is a classification often used to describe cause of death when autopsies fail to expose a clear indicator. And yes, he originally classified Joyce Hauptman's cause of death undetermined. But facts are facts and he was forced to reconsider as they accumulated. Joyce Hauptman did die, and the arsenic level in her hair was thirty times the normal level at the time of her death, and she exhibited symptoms of arsenic poisoning, and there were no other indicators observed, either by the nurses or Death Investigator Singh. Beyond any reasonable doubt, arsenic, deliberately administered, caused Joyce Hauptman's death.

'Konig was good, but Mankel has his own expert waiting in the wings,' Park tells me over dinner on Sunday evening. 'The real issue is whether the jury wants to convict Charles of murder.' He pauses long enough to spear an asparagus tip sautéed in butter and garlic. 'I've been covering the criminal-justice system for a long time, Lenny. When it comes to murder, I think most jurors are looking for an excuse to convict. That old saw about a presumption of innocence? It's legal fiction. Once a jury hears from the grieving family and views the crime-scene photos ... Take this to the bank, Lenny. They'd convict the judge if there was no one else available.'

'But not this time?' Davy prompts.

'No, not in this case. I mean, I'm not in the jurors' minds, but I've been watching them closely and they look bored to me. Like they're saying, "OK, tell me something I don't know."'

I've invited Davy along because I've decided to accept his offer. We're eventually to become partners in Lowenstein, Shaw, Private Investigators. Steve Park will be a good contact for Lowenstein, Shaw, a source for us, as we're now a source for him.

Over dinner, I describe the testimony I expect Howie Mankel to elicit when he calls me back to the witness stand. I keep my prophesying light, stressing the many ironies, as Charles Hauptman once stressed the ironies in his own life. Only at the very end, as we finish tiny cups of espresso, do I bring up Max Baum.

'That business I asked you to check out, did you get to it?' I ask Steve.

'You mean about Max's fortune?'

279

'Yeah.'

Park's sitting on my left, his expression curious. Am I still investigating Max Baum? Park would love to know, but I'm not volunteering and he doesn't ask.

'I met with a friend of mine at *Forbes*,' he tells me, 'and with a contact I have at *Fortune*. They're telling the same story. Even though Max read the handwriting on the wall and was moving away from real estate when the market collapsed, he took a major hit because he had projects already in the ground. But if he was close to being wiped out, a deal he made five years ago – with no less than the Indonesian Land Minister's brother-in-law – rode to his rescue. Even as we speak, Max's minions are logging the Indonesian rainforest. He's cutting down the trees and shipping them off to China and the money's rolling in. My guy at *Forbes* estimates Max's personal fortune to be three-quarters of a billion dollars. Not the richest man in America, but he won't be going hungry any time soon.'

Howie Mankel makes his two-part strategy clear when he delivers his opening argument. He tells the jurors that Joyce Hauptman's death was not caused by arsenic poisoning, not beyond a reasonable doubt. But even if it was, the evidence against Charles Hauptman is no more compelling than the evidence against his father-in-law, the dastardly Max Baum. He reminds the jurors that the defense has nothing to prove, that proof is the prosecution's responsibility.

Nevertheless, ever generous, he will show that his client's indictment was a rush to judgment that would have been better delayed. What's more, he will use the prosecution's star witness to make his case.

That would be me.

I'm hoping to go first. No such luck. Mankel calls Dr Abel Callaway to the stand. A graduate of Harvard Medical School, the forty-year-old Callaway, in addition to being medical examiner for the city of Philadelphia, hires himself out from time to time. He admits this when Mankel asks if he's being paid to testify.

'Yes, certainly,' he tells the jurors. 'But I'm also paid when I testify for the prosecution, as I have many hundreds of times. Paid with tax dollars supplied by citizens like you.'

Callaway is Konig's polar opposite. He's clean shaven and his pin-striped business suit hugs his shoulders and chest. His speech is clipped and rapid, projecting a confidence that isn't lost on the jurors.

Calloway's testimony is predictable. No concentration of arsenic in hair or bone, he claims, is definitive when it comes to determining cause of death. Standard protocol demands an examination of the internal organs. To illustrate this point, he introduces the somewhat lurid story of a murderess named Audrey Marie Hilley. Hilley took out insurance policies on her husband, mother and daughter, then fed them lethal doses of arsenic. She was caught when the hair of her daughter, Carol, was examined in an Alabama hospital. The arsenic levels in Carol's hair were

281

as much as a hundred times normal levels. But not only wasn't she dead, Carol lived to testify against her mother. And when she finally died, some time later, her death was caused by cancer, not arsenic poisoning.

'How much arsenic does it take to kill someone? There's no clear answer to this question. One has to ask how much arsenic was administered at any given time, and over how long a period of time, then factor in the varying ability of individuals to tolerate the poison. The dose that kills me, might not kill you. That's why we examine the internal organs.'

Calloway's followed to the stand by Joyce Hauptman's two surviving nurses, Shirley Borders and Theresa Santiago. Shirley goes first, but their testimony is essentially redundant. Mankel has them repeat the testimony they gave when called by the prosecution. Yes, Charles did express a wish to end his wife's suffering. Yes, Charles approached Dr Meyer about not treating Joyce's many infections.

Mankel nods agreement with each response before coming to the point. 'Now, Nurse Borders,' he asks, thrusting a hand into his pocket, 'did you ever see Charles do anything, anything at all, to actually *harm* his wife?'

'No, absolutely not.'

'And how would you describe the care he gave her?'

Shirley Borders is Charles Hauptman's biggest supporter. Her response is naturally expansive and Mankel allows her free reign. The portrait of

Charles that emerges might have been made by a Vatican cardinal advocating the canonization of Mother Teresa. Nurse Santiago is less effusive, but nevertheless admits that Charles did everything for Joyce that she did, including changing diapers and urinary catheters. There was no task he refused, no duty he passed on to the nurses, and he never complained or took a day off, even when he was ill.

I hear none of this testimony. I'm in the conference room when the nurses testify, waiting my turn. Eve Durand, who's to follow me, is here, too. I have to feel sorry for Eve. Eve's still a cop, still devoted to the job, and she loathes the prospect of testifying for the defense. Nevertheless, she echoes Mankel's essential argument when she admits that she continued to investigate Max Baum after she inherited the case. Why would she do that if she was certain of Charles Hauptman's guilt?

Eve's grown to hate Max. She considers him, in her own parlance, an AFM, an Asshole of the First Magnitude. Charles, on the other hand ... Like everyone else, Eve has nothing bad to say about Charles.

When I'm finally called to the stand, Charles is sitting at the defense table with his hands folded, his eyes cast down on a yellow pad covered with doodles. If sainthood is characterized by suffering, Charles looks saintly indeed. When he finally glances my way, his eyes are almost lifeless.

'Let me remind you, detective,' Judge Meads admonishes, 'that you're still under oath.'

I acknowledge the reminder with a nod and a curt, 'I understand.' In fact, I fully intend to tell the truth, the whole truth and nothing but the truth. God, however, has nothing to do with it.

Mankel wastes no time. 'Detective, were you actively investigating a man named Maxwell Baum at the time Charles Hauptman was arrested.'

'Yes, I was.'

'And did you continue to investigate Maxwell Baum after Charles Hauptman was arrested?'

'Yes.'

'And were you still investigating Mr Baum when you were wounded by a man named Leonid Berevski and placed on sick leave?'

'I was.'

I don't begrudge Mankel – or Charles, for that matter – these admissions. And I'm not surprised when Howie Mankel, his main point established, drags me through the investigation of Max Baum, step by weary step. We begin with the Terry Hauptman interview, when I learned of Joyce Baum's inheritance and Max Baum's efforts to control it. Though Charles would inherit if Joyce died of natural causes, he'd surrender all right to the money if he was convicted of her murder. That would leave Max, Joyce's closest living relative, to pick up the twenty million pieces.

'Did there come a time, detective, when you interviewed Dr Rania Herzog?'

'Yes.'

'Can you tell us when and where that interview occurred?'

'On October 16th, at the Office of the Medical Examiner on First Avenue.'

'On that occasion, did you learn that arsenic sulfide is also called realgar?'

'Yes.'

'And did you discover that realgar is used in the manufacture of fireworks?'

'Yes, I did.'

There's a big no-no in the detecting business. Once you make an arrest, you never investigate another suspect. That road leads to where I'm sitting right now. The question raised by my actions, a question already put to Eve Durand, a question for which there no good answer, is very simple: why would I investigate Max Baum if I was certain of Charles Hauptman's guilt?

Means, motive and opportunity. Max Baum had all three – as Mankel will surely claim when he sums up – and my own investigation proves it. I went online to research Max and discovered that he owned the Americana Fireworks Company. I then visited the factory, where I uncovered two facts. Realgar, stored in an unlocked bin, was routinely used to add the color red to skyrockets and Max Baum toured the operation a month before Joyce died. A few days later, I uncovered multiple eye-witnesses who told me that Max Hauptman commonly visited his daughter on Sunday afternoons, when Charles was out of the house. Nurse Anna Berevski eventually confirmed these visits and admitted to having an affair with Max.

The means, the opportunity and twenty million motives.

It's closing in on five o'clock when Howie Mankel winds it up. Mankel wants the jury to go home with the right impression and he's timed this final disclosure for the end of the day. Despite the late hour, he looks fresh and eager.

'Detective, I want to take you back to the night of November 2nd. Do you remember that night.'

'Yes.' November 2nd is the night Leonid shot me.

'Will you please describe the encounter you had with a man named Leonid Berevski? In your own words?'

As I said, the courtroom is packed. There are journalists in attendance from as far away as Japan, including three artists bent over their sketchbooks. Strung out along a bench at the back of the room, six women, their arms linked, wear identical pink sweatshirts imprinted with identical legends: *all life is precious*. I drop my eyes to my shoes, as though I'm gathering my thoughts. When I raise them, I look directly at Charles.

'There's not much to tell. Me and my partner, David Lowenstein, were on our way back to the house after a routine interview. When we turned the corner, a block away, Leonid Berevski was waiting for us. He didn't say a word. He just opened fire. Davy was hit first. He went down to the sidewalk and I was hit a moment later, in the leg. I couldn't return fire because my coat and jacket were buttoned and my weapon was underneath them. The last thing I expected was an ambush. So I retreated around the corner, until I was out of sight, and finally got to my gun. When I came back, I found Berevski leaning over my partner. He turned on me and began to fire. I was hit in the shoulder as I returned fire. Leonid went down and that was the end of it.'

The gallery is hanging on my every word, including Judge Mead. I feel like I'm Wyatt Earp describing the gunfight at the OK Corral: *The bullets was a-rainin' down like hail.* But the truth is more complex. I remember the details – this happened, then this, then this – mainly because I've been over them so many times. But I have no memory of my reasoning, or of any emotion besides anger. Nor do I care. Leonid's dead and what I really want, what I'll never have, is my arm back.

Mankel's gentle tone acknowledges the extent of my sacrifice. 'Detective, will you please explain the relationship between Leonid Berevski, the man who attacked you, and Maxwell Baum, the man you were investigating?'

'Leonid Berevski was Max Baum's chauffeur.'

'No further questions.'

Thirty

Patty Eng makes a feeble attempt to rehabilitate me on the following morning. She asks if my investigation of Max Baum turned up any direct evidence of his guilt. It didn't and I say so. She then asks me if I believe Charles Hauptman to be guilty of the crime with which he's charged. My reply is evasive, but no one notices.

'I believe that Joyce Hauptman's death resulted from arsenic poisoning.' I stare directly at Charles, who looks up, his expression serious. He's not afraid, though, at least as far as I can tell. 'And I believe that her husband, Charles Hauptman, is responsible.'

Patty Eng dismisses me a moment later and I take a seat in the courtroom. My testimony over, I'm allowed to witness the proceedings.

As I squeeze onto a bench, careful to avoid bumping my arm, Howie Mankel calls Detective Eve Durand. Eve is openly belligerent, but she can't wriggle out from under a pair of essential truths. First, Charles Hauptman's computer was thoroughly examined, as were his financial records, for any attempt to buy realgar, or research the use of poisons. Needless to say, the results were negative. Second, Eve continued to investigate Max Baum after I was shot and the case dumped in her lap. Of course, most of her efforts were directed at connecting Baum to the death of his wife, not his daughter. But that little fact goes unmentioned because Judge Mead has ruled out testimony relating to Lola's death. Score one for Patty Eng, who argued long and loud to exclude all mention of Lola Baum, the jury pool already being sufficiently influenced by the negative publicity surrounding Max.

On another crucial point, however, Patty was badly beaten. Months before the trial began, when Howie Mankel added Deputy Director Jennifer Gold and Maxwell Baum to his witness list, subpoenas were issued for both. Unfortunately, neither professed a desire to hang themselves on the witness stand. If called, their attorneys informed the court, they would invoke their right to remain silent. They'd take the Fifth.

At a contentious pre-trial hearing, Mankel insisted that the jury be allowed to witness their refusals, while Eng argued that the jury would view Max Baum's refusal to testify as an admission of guilt. Mead eventually struck a compromise, one that pleased the defense a lot more than it did Patty Eng. Mead announced that Max and Deputy Gold would not be required to appear. She, Judge Mead, would tell the jury why.

And so Mead does, after Eve is dismissed, with a packed courtroom watching and the jurors sitting on the edge of their seats. 'The right to remain silent is given to every citizen,' she admonishes, 'and you will not construe the invocation of that right to be an admission of guilt.'

Thanks for sharing.

Mead announces the mid-morning break and the jury files out. A few minutes later, I emerge from the courthouse to find a bright yellow sun floating in an azure sky, a picture-book day. Across the street, in a little park, an early-May breeze stirs the budding branches of a few stunted trees. I glance at a coffee wagon parked at the curb. The line is already fifteen deep.

Steve Park comes up behind me. He taps me on the shoulder and says, 'Let's take a walk.'

I follow him east along the sidewalk fronting Queen Boulevard for two blocks before he slows down. Along the way, he tells me that the jury didn't like what Mankel did to me. To them, I was a sympathetic figure, a wounded warrior. Still, my testimony had the intended effect. Max Baum has emerged as a perfectly viable suspect.

'I've seen a lot of lawyers blow smoke, Lenny, but this time Mankel's got it right. Charles or Max? Max or Charles? I go back and forth. And mind you, I do think Joyce was murdered. Her death wasn't some coincidence. But who actually killed her...? I think the jury's gonna decide on the basis of Charles's testimony.'

All along, Mankel's been toying with the press, hinting that his client would take the stand without actually saying so. This tactic is commonplace because it forces the prosecutor to prepare a cross-examination whether or not the defendant eventually appears. Usually, it's a bluff.

'You know something I don't know?' I ask.

'Yeah, I got it from one of Mankel's paralegals. They've been preparing Charles for weeks. He'll begin his testimony this afternoon.'

We walk on for another block, to a delicatessen on the far side of the Boulevard, a hole in the wall run by a pair of Arabs. I know they're Arabs because there's a relief map of Yemen behind the cash register. Steve and I order coffee and buttered rolls. As we wait for our coffee to be poured, he moves into my line of vision.

'I got a story I'm working on,' he says, 'and I was wondering if you'd like to comment.'

My antennae rise, but I manage a smile. Park's a committed journalist. He'll use anybody, anytime, anywhere. 'Let's hear it.'

'Two things. First, I called the medical examiner's office this morning. They're releasing Anna Berevski's body.' He pauses to gauge my reaction, then adds, 'Only there's no one out there to receive it.'

I pay for the coffee and the rolls and we carry them into the sunlight. The day is brisk, though not unpleasant. The worst days of winter are behind us.

'Anything else?' I ask Steve.

'What, no comment? The woman's gonna be buried in a pauper's grave.'

'Call it the wages of sin.'

Park starts to speak, then stops, his mouth closing with a little click. He stares at me for a moment, then says, 'All right, lemme ask you something else. I've got a connection inside Homeland Security. She's telling me that the Berevskis aren't Ukrainians or Russians. They're Uzbek separatists who spent years in a gulag after a failed coup. How they got here, to the good old USA, he doesn't know. The Ukrainian documents they carried appear to be legitimate, but so what? Every bureaucrat in the Ukrainian government's for sale. Oh, and by the way, Leonid and Anna aren't brother and sister. They're father and daughter.'

Charles looks somehow different. He's sitting next to his lawyer, as usual, and I'm directly behind him, only a few rows back. But it's not until Judge Mead enters the courtroom and we rise to our feet that I figure it out. In contrast with his appearance this morning, Charles's hair is now rumpled and the jacket of his plain brown suit looks as though it passed the noon break in a laundry bag. By contrast, Howie Mankel's as sharp as ever. There's not a wrinkle in his pearl-gray three-piece suit.

'The defense calls Charles Hauptman.'
I watch Charles take the oath, thinking that it was me who put Max's name before the public when I alerted Steve Park. Thinking I alerted Steve because I'd come to hate Max, like the general public now hates him.

Despite the hangdog attitude, Charles is very good. I know he's been well prepared, but the rehearsal time isn't apparent and his responses appear spontaneous. Initially, he turns to face the jury after each question, but then he stops looking away. His manner is somewhat hesitating, the attitude of a man still reflecting on events, still comparing the costs to the benefits.

Mankel starts Charles off with Joyce's stroke,

then leads him through his decision to confine his wife to a nursing home, and his subsequent decision to bring her home. This is old news to me, a story Charles has been telling for a long time. His wife's care at the nursing home was substandard and it broke his heart to witness the neglect. Surely, if she came home, if he assumed responsibility for her care, she'd do better. For a time, as he considered the logistics, he'd hesitated. He'd have to alter his life dramatically should he go forward, somehow finding time both to make a living and to nurse Joyce. He didn't know if he had the stomach for the job, or the stamina.

'It's ironic,' he tells the jury, 'and funny, in a way. Joyce was always the responsible one. I was the goof who couldn't find his car keys, or be trusted to run an errand without taking along a written list of what to buy. Joyce even paid the bills at the end of the month. Then, out of nowhere, I was forced to take responsibility, for the household and for all of Joyce's medical supplies. Until I got organized, there were times when I didn't know whether I was coming or going.'

The jury eats it up and Charles continues in this vein throughout the afternoon. Far from naturally courageous, he portrays himself as an ordinary citizen, a reluctant caregiver who had responsibility thrust upon him, and who rose to the occasion because there were no better options. By the time Judge Mead calls a halt to the proceedings, not only the jury but even the most cynical reporters are enthralled. And they're right, as I finally admit. There's no doubt that Charles faced his wife's ordeal with courage, not to mention fortitude, as there's no doubt that Joyce received far better care in her own home than she received in the nursing home from which her husband plucked her.

I sleep well that night, and wake to a chorus of television pundits whose assessment of Charles Hauptman echoes my own. By nine o'clock, I'm back in the courtroom, sitting next to Steve Park. Judge Mead is still in her chambers, as the jurors are back in the jury room. The courtroom buzzes with conversation. Thus far, Mankel has confined his client's testimony to the years preceding Joyce's death. Now it's time to face a number of more unpleasant facts. There's a lot of evidence against Charles, from the quick cremation of his wife's body, to his familiarity with realgar, to the traces of arsenic sulfide on the file in his basement. Funny thing about evidence. It doesn't go away, even if the jury likes you.

Howie Mankel starts by placing Joyce Hauptman's will into evidence. He asks Charles if he recognizes the document, then asks him to read a one-sentence paragraph on the fourth page. Charles settles a pair of reading glasses on the bridge of his nose before complying.

"'It is my wish that, subsequent to my death, my body be cremated, and my ashes scattered in the Bronx Botanical Gardens.'"

Charles removes the glasses before turning to the jury. 'In the Jewish religion, cremation is forbidden,' he explains. 'But we weren't very

294

religious, not in that way, and Joyce wanted to head off any family objections. That's why she put her wishes in writing.'

Mankel's tone, as he questions his client, is studiously gentle, a quality echoed by his client's responses. Charles explains that if his aim was to destroy evidence, he would never have invited the nurses to accompany him to the Gardens. What's more, he knew he was being followed by two men, one in a trench coat, the other carrying an umbrella. If he'd had anything to fear, he could have turned around and driven home. But he didn't. He continued on, unafraid, because he was – and is – an innocent man. He didn't kill his wife.

There's a concept in law, one commonly employed by detectives in the course of an investigation: evidence of a guilty mind. Any attempt to destroy, or dispose of, evidence, like Joyce's cremation and the trash Charles hauled to the curb, is evidence of a guilty mind. But even casual lies, about a suspect's whereabouts, or a false alibi, are viewed in the same light. Charles has turned this concept on its head. His actions, he claims, are evidence of an innocent mind.

For example, Charles freely admitted that he wanted to end his wife's suffering. And it was Charles who told me, without my asking, that realgar was collectible and that he'd once owned a collection of crystals. If he'd actually poisoned Joyce, he would certainly have hidden this from me, hoping I wouldn't find out.

Charles applies the same principle to the trash

laid out by the curb. Would a murderer have placed incriminating evidence by the curb fourteen hours before it was scheduled for pickup? Would a guilty man have stood by, unprotesting, when a cop turned up to confiscate that trash? Would a guilty man, a murderer, have discarded incriminating evidence, like the hairbrush and the feeding tube, in the first place?

'I didn't object when Detective Shaw confiscated the trash bags,' Charles insists, 'because I didn't kill my wife. In fact, I was glad. The detective was suspicious, that much was painfully obvious, and I remember thinking that I wouldn't hear from him again. Let him examine anything he wants to examine.'

But I hadn't, much to his surprise, gone away. No, less than a week later he opened his door to find me on his doorstep, search warrant in hand.

At this point, Mankel places a videotape into evidence. The tape was made by a Crime Scene Unit cop on the night we searched the defendant's house. The traces of realgar revealed by the tape, on the file and the workbench and in Joyce's sickroom, are bright red and extremely conspicuous. They would not have been missed if any attempt was made to sanitize the crime scene.

'Mr Hauptman, do you enter your basement regularly?'

'No, I don't.'

'You don't have any hobbies, woodworking, for example, or a model railroad, that take you into the basement?'

'No.'

'What about your laundry? Is your laundry room in the basement?'

'No, it's in a small room off the garage.'

'All right, now before your wife passed, when was the last time you were in the basement? To the best of your knowledge.'

'Shortly after New Year's when I took down the Christmas decorations. We kept the decorations in the basement.'

'And that would be ten months earlier?'

'Yes, just after Christmas.' Charles is looking directly into the eyes of juror number six, a bespectacled black lady wearing a hat the color of imperial jade. 'I always decorated Joyce's room during the Christmas season. Joyce loved Christmas.'

Every comedy act, no matter how good, needs a finish, a seal-the-deal move guaranteed to leave 'em rolling in the aisles. Still, I'm the only one in the courtroom who finds Charles hilarious when he walks into the courtroom wearing his size-forty fat pants. The trousers are big enough to contain another person, the legs voluminous. Charles could not have worn them when he prepared the realgar in the basement, or when he fed it to his wife, or at any other time. Therefore the little red crystals found in the trousers' cuffs are evidence of innocence, not, as the prosecutor claimed, of guilt.

Charles stands before the jury, mouth compressed, eyes serious. He's hooked his thumb behind the button at the top of his trousers and extended the waistband as far it will go. The jurors stare, pop-eyed, as do the onlookers in the gallery, including Steve Park, who nudges me with his elbow.

'God,' he whispers, 'I love this game.'

I shift my arms slightly. I'm thinking I used to love the game, too. Before I was sidelined by injuries.

Thirty-One

Patty Eng does her best. She batters Charles for three hours, but she can't move him. He freely admits what he's already admitted. He wanted to end his wife's suffering – no one could watch that suffering, day after day, and not want it over – and he took steps to bring that end about. He was familiar with realgar, too, both as a poison and a collectible red crystal, and he was alone with his wife for six hours every day, routinely pushing medications, nutrition and fluids through her feeding tube. And while the trousers hanging in the closet were too big, they were definitely his trousers, as the file in the basement was his file.

As Eng proceeds, an unasked question hangs in the air. If not Charles Hauptman, who? I'm thinking that Patty wants Charles to name Max Baum. She's hoping to paint Charles as a desperate man willing to point the finger of guilt at anyone, even his father-in-law. If so, St Charles doesn't rise to the bait. He doesn't know how the realgar got into Joyce's hair and bone, any more than he knows how it got into the basement, and he's not willing to speculate. He didn't murder his wife, though. He loved Joyce too much for that.

'Let me see if I understand you,' Patty snarls. 'Are you telling this court that you loved your wife too much to kill her?'

'Yes, I did.'

'But you were willing to let someone else kill her, right? Say by withdrawing fluids so she'd die of thirst.'

'Yes, that's exactly right. I was that much of a coward.'

'So you did think about killing her? You thought about putting an end to your wife's suffering ... with your own two hands?'

'Yes,' Charles repeats, 'that's exactly right. I thought about killing Joyce, but I was too much of a coward to do it.'

Patty's standing at a podium fifteen feet away from the witness. She's leaning out, head thrust forward. I think she'd like nothing better than to get right in the defendant's face, but that can't happen in a New York courtroom. Prosecutors and defense lawyers have to ask permission to approach a witness. But I don't think Charles would be intimidated, even if he and Patty went nose to nose. Charles put on his sad-sack demeanor before he walked into the courtroom on the first day of the trial and he's not about to switch roles. His doleful expression remains firmly in place, right up until the moment Patty dismisses him with a sarcastic, 'No more questions.'

Charles takes a moment before crossing the room to regain his place behind the defense table. Already standing, Howie Mankel waits until his client is seated. Then he tugs at his jacket, unsmiling.

'The defense,' he tells the judge, the jury, the spectators and Patty Eng, 'rests.'

I don't come back the next morning to hear final arguments. I've been listening to news reports since early in the morning and I can't find anyone – not even Judy Veremos, commonly called Judy Venomous because of her rabid law-and-order stance – who predicts a conviction.

I head off to the laundromat at eight o'clock. Along the way, I pick up two newspapers at a candy store, the *Times* and the *Daily News*.

There are two articles about Max Baum in the *News*. The first includes a photograph taken yesterday on the island of Tobago. Max is lounging on a beach chair, surrounded by a bevy of twenty-somethings, male and female. The headline reads: 5-STAR HIDEOUT FOR MAX BAUM.

The second article, by Steve Park, contains a detailed account of Max's Indonesian timber operation. The only thing it lacks is a photo of Max killing Bambi's mother.

I'm feeling pretty good. I'm thinking that part one is over, the part where the state, acting as a surrogate for its citizens, individually and collectively, seeks justice. The paperwork on my retirement has been completed. Every two weeks, for the rest of my life, I'm to receive a twenty-five-hundred dollar check from the NYPD's pension fund. The check's supposed to compensate me for my loss. It doesn't come close.

Final arguments will take place in Judge Mead's courtroom today. A mere formality, as far as I'm concerned. The jury was halfway prepared to acquit Charles before the trial started, even if the state proved his guilt beyond a reasonable doubt. Which it definitely has not. Patty's only hope is that some anti-abortion fanatic lied about his or her affiliations to get on the jury. But even then, the most the state can expect is a hung jury and another futile trial.

Steve Park calls me at one o'clock, after Mankel completes his summation. 'Your testimony was the main attraction,' he tells me.

'That I continued to investigate Max Baum?'

'Yeah, but even more about how Charles cooperated. Mankel read some of your testimony word-for-word.'

'What'd I say?'

'You described the night you picked up Hauptman's trash, how Charles was completely nonchalant. He just didn't act like a guilty man.'

Park's got more to say, but I cut him off. Enough is enough.

'How long until they come back with a verdict? What's your best guess?' Patty Eng will deliver her closing argument this afternoon and Judge Mead will charge the jury tomorrow morning.

'A few hours, at least.'

'That long?'

'The foreman's a civil engineer. I have him figured for a real tight-ass. He'll demand that they review the evidence, piece by piece, before they vote. But, look, there's a pool. Ten bucks, if you wanna get a bet down. I picked three hours and twenty-eight minutes.'

'Fine, put me in for ... fifty-two minutes.'

'Done.'

In fact, the jury is out for a grand total of fifty-five minutes, just long enough for me to lose my bet. Most likely, the tight-ass foreman took a quick poll and the vote ran twelve–zero for acquittal.

The defendant's reaction, according to the media, is subdued, both when the verdict is read, and when Charles, still wearing his wrinkled brown suit, gives a short statement on the court-house steps a few minutes later. He first offers thanks to the jury for carefully considering the evidence, then expresses his sympathy for the collateral damage. Davy gets a mention, Anna and Leonid, too, but Charles reserves most of his sympathy for yours truly.

'I'm deeply sorry for the injuries suffered by Detective Shaw. We had a number of conversations and I believe him to be a decent man and a dedicated police officer.'

A few hours later, I'm in Dooley's, admiring a set of cut-glass mugs bearing the graven images of the Budweiser Clydesdale horses. Davy's next to me. He's passed the afternoon in a fruitless search for affordable office space. We want

302

to be close to the action, but can't hope to pay the rents on Queens Boulevard.

'You apply for your PI license?' he asks me.

'Not yet.'

'Are you going to?' He goes on before I can answer. 'Because I don't like the way you're looking.'

I don't know how I'm looking, but I'm feeling fine. Earlier in the afternoon, after Charles and the jury and media went home, I drove to the DA's office and spoke to Patty Eng and her boss, Roy Carmody.

'There's no case against Max Baum,' Carmody told me. 'Put it out of your mind. That digital photograph? It proves exactly nothing. It proves nothing and Leonid Berevski's dead.'

'And as for Joyce Hauptman,' Patty adds, 'absent a confession, we'll never know who killed her.'

Patience may be a virtue, but there are times when circumstances force your hand. A day after the verdict comes in, I journey to the Hospital for Special Surgery in Manhattan. There, in an examining room with a window overlooking the East River, Dr Arnier Berthold advises me against unrealistic expectations. French by birth, his English is flawless, if slightly accented.

'In most cases, shoulder replacement is done when the joint has been worn away by years of use. We see this in many athletes. In these cases, however, the bones are intact. They can be re-shaped to accept an artificial socket. In your case, I'm afraid, the bones were smashed. One

303

cannot plane bone that isn't there. The soft tissues were severely damaged as well, the rotator cuff and the biceps tendon especially.'

Doctors can be intimidating, but I've been examined by so many doctors over the past few months that I've lost my fear. I walk to a window, turning my back on Dr Berthold, and gaze at a barge moving north on the river.

'So what are you telling me, doctor? That I should forget about replacing my shoulder and go for the amputation?'

Berthold's soft laugh flows around me and through the window. 'No, that is not what I am telling you. Surgery will reduce your pain significantly and prevent your shoulder from separating, so you will no longer be dependent on that sling. But it's unlikely that you will regain full use of your arm.'

'How unlikely?'

'Very unlikely, detective.'

'Mister.'

'Pardon?'

'I'm not a cop any more. So it's Mr Shaw, not Detective Shaw.'

My mom is there for me, Davy, too, and I'm definitely a hero at Dooley's. I haven't had to buy my own drinks for some time. But I'm feeling the full effects of an error in judgment. No marriage, no family? Deliberate choices, made after considerable thought, to compensate for the pressures of a cop life. But I'm no longer a cop, and I have no family, no wife or children, to compensate me for the loss of that life.

304

'I've decided to bury Anna Berevski,' I tell my mother on the Sunday morning after the trial. 'Otherwise, they're gonna put her in a cardboard box and bury her on Hart's Island.' I pause, but get no immediate response. 'I had her body picked up yesterday. She's over at Mondello's.'

Mondello's funeral parlor has been run by the Mondello family for three generations, with the fourth generation already in high school. Mom nods approvingly. Mondello's buried my father.

'Why are you doing this?' she asks.

'Because it's my fault that she's dead.'

'No, it's not. You were doing your job.'

'Gimme a break. I put Anna Berevski in jail because I wanted her to rat on Max Baum. An unlicensed nurse? If I wasn't out to squeeze her, the very most I would have done is give her probation officer a heads-up. Anna wasn't exactly public enemy number one.'

Mom stares at me for a moment, then shrugs. 'So how much is this burial gonna set you back?'

'Nine grand.'

'Lenny, that's a hell of a lotta guilt. Me, I would've settled for a novena at Blessed Sacrament.'

I consider hiring a priest to conduct a service at the funeral home, but decide against it. The Berevskis might have been Christians, Jews, Muslims or atheists.

Mom is with me, Davy, too, as I follow the hearse out to Cherry Wood Cemetery on Long Island. Cherry Wood is an older cemetery, famous for a grove of cherry trees crowded along a slight rise. In full bloom, the trees are beautiful, no doubt, but they seem overly festive in a cemetery. Weeping willows would be more appropriate. Weeping willows and a lonesome pine.

Despite what I told Mom, I don't feel all that much guilt. Burying Anna is a necessary step, a step that has to be taken after a tragedy, like Charles getting rid of his wife's medical supplies. Closure's not a word cops use. We know that experience is cumulative and you carry the past forward. That's why you take care of the little details. You don't want the past to become a permanent present. You want to put the past in the past, no obligations left unfilled.

Thirty-Two

I turn the corner at eleven thirty and walk halfway up the block to the Hauptman mini-mansion with its slate roof and fluted chimneys. The skies are overcast, the moon and stars lost to sight. I'm wearing a waterproof topcoat, though it's not yet raining, and a hat with a three-inch brim. My eyes move with each step I take, searching the windows of the surrounding homes for silhouettes. On the lower floors, most of the windows are dark, as you'd expect on a Thursday night. But many of the second-floor windows are lit. I'm hoping the good citizens are already in bed, perhaps watching Conan O'Brien or David Letterman, or having sex, or gabbing away on cellphones, or text messaging, or playing super-violent video games. There's no reason for anyone to be looking out through a window at this time of night, what with all the distractions available, and I find nothing to excite my instinct for self-preservation. Still, I take a last look, sweeping the windows on either side of the street before I turn on to the field-stone walkway leading to Charles Hauptman's double doors.

Charles answers within seconds of my ringing his bell and I have to figure he was sitting in his nearby living room, in the dark. We stare at each other for a moment, neither speaking. I'm prepared to force my way inside, but then Charles steps back.

'I'm not entirely surprised to see you, detective,' he says.

'Call me Lenny. I'm not a cop anymore.'

'Yes, I was told that you resigned.'

'Then you were told wrong. The job doesn't want crippled cops. The resignation part was for the media. Like everything else about this case.'

Charles responds with an affirming grimace, then leads me into the living room and turns on a lamp. There's a glass next to the lamp, half-filled with whisky, probably Scotch, but no pack of cigarettes. I unbutton my coat and take my customary seat across from Otto Baum. I've been imagining this moment since I concluded that no jury would convict St Charles and I'm anxious to get started.

Ever polite, Charles asks, 'Would you like a drink?'

I shake my head. 'You told the press you were sorry about the collateral damage. Was that true?'

'Collateral damage?'

'The Berevskis, Davy, Deputy Gold, Lenny Shaw...?'

'Oh, I see. Well, I don't think I'd use the term collateral damage.'

'But you're still sorry?'

'Yes, of course.'

'Good, now I want you to put your regrets in writing. Your regrets for Anna and Leonid – they were father and daughter, by the way. Your regrets for Deputy Director Gold – there's talk they'll she'll be indicted for abusing her office. Your regrets for Davy Lowenstein and Lenny Shaw – homicide detectives no longer. I want you to commit your regrets to paper.'

Charles considers my request, his eyes dropping momentarily to his lap. Then he looks up. 'I'm not admitting responsibility. If that's what you came for, you're wasting your time. I didn't kill my wife.'

I nod admiringly. The defiance in his eyes and his voice contrasts nicely with the hangdog expression he wore in court. I think back to our first meeting, to the mini-expressions I detected. Charles isn't a bad guy and I believe that he accepts personal responsibility for the consequences of his actions, unintended though they were. Nevertheless, he wants to survive. He

308

is not suicidal and he's prepared to resist.

Unfortunately for Charles and his show of defiance, he's playing an unfamiliar game on an unfamiliar field. I rise to my feet, withdraw the untraceable .38 revolver tucked beneath the waistband of my trousers and place its barrel in the center of his forehead.

'Write an apology for all the pain you've caused or I'll kill you. I'll kill you and leave the gun in your hand and hope the medical examiner decides that you couldn't live with your pain.'

I mean exactly what I say. Shooting Charles is not my preferred ending, but I'm willing to settle if I can't do better. Charles swallows twice, the reflex seeming overly theatrical. Fixed on the barrel of the gun, his eyes are noticeably crossed.

'Please...'

'No, Charles, not please. It's yes or no.'

'All right.' His hand flutters up to his waist, a gesture he quickly aborts. 'Don't shoot me.'

I drop back on to my chair, but hold the gun where Charles can see it. My intention is to move him along quickly. 'Get some paper.'

'What do you...'

'Get some fucking paper and a fucking pen and start writing.'

Charles slowly rises. For a moment, he stares down at me, unmoving. Now that I haven't killed him, he's maybe thinking I don't have the balls to pull the trigger. I end that fantasy when I draw back the .38's hammer and the ratchet gives off a sharp click that focuses his attention on the consequences of a mistake in judgment.

Without a word, he turns and marches off to a secretary resting against the southern wall of the living room. The secretary is massive, a towering hulk from some bygone era, its wood nearly black with age. Charles opens one of the lower drawers and removes a box of stationery and a fountain pen.

'What do you want me to write?'

'A mea culpa, Charles, but not for Joyce. Despite the fact that you can't be tried again, I won't ask you to incriminate yourself. I know you didn't kill your wife.'

The last bit catches Charles's attention. He looks at me for a minute, then settles a piece of stationery on the coffee table and begins to write. I let the .38's hammer down and take my finger off the trigger. No need for accidents.

Charles completes a first draft in less than five minutes. Obviously pleased with himself, he drops the page in front of me. I scan the document and shake my head. As I expected, Charles has written a very terse apology. I'm sorry for this, for that, for the other thing.

'Try again. This time with feeling. Remember, you're St Charles, fountain of compassion, patron of caregivers everywhere.'

'Is the sarcasm necessary?'

'Start writing, Charles.'

His second try is much improved, but I'm still not satisfied and I make him start over. I'm patient, though, and I don't interrupt when his third effort covers three pages and takes more than a half-hour to complete.

My life has been one of regret since it became clear to me that my wife was poisoned. I did not administer the poison, but I hold myself responsible for the tragedies that followed. I know I'm being irrational, but I can't help myself.

Despite the little denial, Charles has given me exactly what I want. His apology continues on for three pages, naming all the right names, expressing the deepest of deep regrets. More than likely, this is what he truly believes.

'I think I'll take that drink now,' I tell him.

The tension released, at least for the moment, Charles hops to his feet and trots off to the kitchen. I should follow him, just to make sure he doesn't phone 911. Instead, I remove a vial from my coat pocket, pry off the cap and pour the contents, a fine blue powder, into the drink he left standing on the end table. I give the drink a quick stir, then wipe my pinky on the inside of my coat.

I'm leaning back in the chair when Charles reappears a moment later. I accept the glass he offers, wait for him to sit down, then offer a toast.

'To crime and punishment.'

'I'll drink to that, or just about anything else.' Charles raises his glass to his mouth and drains it. 'What now?' he asks.

The 100mg of Valium I slipped into Charles's drink is ten times the normal dose for an adult. The drug will need forty minutes to fully take effect, but Charles will fall asleep long before then. Valium being a potent muscle relaxant, he'll go limp, as well, and his respiration will slow, but he won't die. That's the nice thing about Valium. Unlike opiates and barbiturates, Valium is rarely toxic even in quantities far higher than the one I fed to Charles.

We sit without speaking for some time. I don't check my watch, so I can't be sure exactly how long. I don't know what Charles is thinking, either. But me, I'm almost thankful. I'm a new man now, certain to walk along unfamiliar paths, paths I would never have taken but for Charles Hauptman and Leonid Berevski.

I'm the first to speak, but not because I'm unable to contain myself. I want to make my case while Charles is still alert.

'I finally answered that question,' I tell him. 'The one I asked you last time we met.'

'How about refreshing my memory after I refresh my drink?'

'Forget the drink.'

Charles stares at me. He's finished the job I gave him. Why can't we be pals again?

'Fine, Lenny, what's the question?'

'I asked you why your father-in-law would reach in to prevent the autopsy if he wanted to frame you. Do you remember?'

'I do remember, now that you've repeated it.'

'You told me that you didn't know, but that was a lie.'

Charles attempts a smile. 'I never argue with a man carrying a gun.'

'Smart move.' I sip at my drink, a single-malt Scotch that tastes of smoke and peat, then set the glass on the table. 'See, I'm a little guy, a poorly educated cop from a working-class family. I never thought of myself that way until I caught this case, but it's one of those truths I can't avoid now. A twenty-million-dollar inheritance? I was dazzled, Charles, and I just couldn't see past that bundle of loot. That goes for my partner as well. I remember the two of us, me and Davy, calculating the income twenty million could generate. Even at four per cent, twenty mill would return eight hundred thousand a year. Charles, that's ten times my base salary. I wouldn't even know how to spend that kind of money.'

'Nor would I, although I suppose I'll have to learn.'

'Now you understand where I'm coming from. I assumed poisoning Joyce was about you and Max battling over her estate. Either you killed Joyce for the money, or Max framed you, also for the money.' I tap my forehead with the .38's cylinder. 'What a fucking dummy I was. What an idiot. Money was never Max's motive, yours either, when you conspired to kill Joyce. No, the motive you and your father-in-law shared was actually noble. You wanted to end Joyce's suffering.' I lean forward, smiling now. 'You see what I'm getting at? Once you take the money out, Max's reason for preventing the autopsy becomes obvious. He hoped to end the investigation before it got started. He was protecting his son-in-law.'

'Your logic's impeccable, Lenny, but I'm not confirming your conclusions.'

'OK, but let's start right there, with the money

off the table. Now, you told the jury that you would have taken matters into your own hands if you hadn't lacked the courage to kill your wife. I accept that, Charles. I think you lacked the balls to do what you believed should be done. But not Max. Max had balls enough for both of you. And why not? He'd already gotten away with one murder.'

I remove a photograph from the inside pocket of my coat, the one taken on the night Lola Baum died. I hold it up, revealing Leonid's face, then put it back.

'Where was that taken?' Charles asks.

'The photo was snapped by the garage camera at the Ashley just about the time Lola Baum expired in her bathtub.' I wave away his response. 'Don't worry. I'm not here about a murder that took place years ago. A murder the state doesn't intend to prosecute. And like I said, I don't expect you to confess. I'm using Lola to illustrate the subtlety of Max's thinking. Lola's murder included a number of touches that derailed the initial investigation before it got started. Your wife's murder, or at least the after-math, was equally subtle.'

'How do I know you're telling the truth? How do I know where or when that picture was taken?'

'You're missing the point. I'm talking about subtlety. Like going ahead with scattering the remains, even though you knew you were being followed. Like putting out the trash fourteen hours before pick-up. Like admitting that you had a crystal collection and wanted to end

Joyce's suffering and that you tried to persuade Dr Meyer to stop treating her infections. Like putting realgar in the cuffs of your fat pants and leaving traces of realgar in the basement and Joyce's room. Like using me, a cop, to put all those proofs of innocence before a jury, including the fact that I continued to investigate your father-in-law after you were arrested. Charles, you played me for a sucker and I'm man enough to admit the tactic was beautifully executed. When you wore your fat pants in that courtroom, I wanted to give you a standing ovation.'

I pause for a moment, out of breath. Charles, apparently, has nothing to say, though his eyelids flutter.

'I think, initially, your plan was simple. Dr Meyer would sign the death certificate and no investigation would take place. And that's exactly how it would have gone down if Meyer hadn't been too exhausted to leave his house. But he never showed up and the death investigator summoned in his place, Amar Singh, smelled a rat. That's when I was called in. Tell me, Charles, what did you think when you saw me in the Gardens?'

Charles yawns, covering his mouth with the back of his hand. Then he pulls himself together and smiles. 'That you wouldn't give up. That you wouldn't – or couldn't – admit defeat.'

'Did you know that arsenic is deposited in bone?'

'I know it now.'

'I think you knew it then. Like you knew you had a big problem with the hair in Joyce's brush and with her feeding tube. I suspect your first instinct was to destroy the evidence. That would've been mine. Flush the hair down the drain, burn the feeding tube. But what if the police took the drain apart and found a few stray hairs? Or if traces of plastic were discovered in the ashes? Or if there were particles of realgar you overlooked? Or if you waited for the sanitation truck to come down the block and I happened to be staking out the house when you ran out? That would be evidence of a guilty mind, Charles, and...'

I'm wasting my breath. Charles is already asleep, though it's only been fifteen minutes since he finished his drink and the Valium I slipped into it. Too bad. I want to speak to him about consequences and how noble motives don't cancel them out. I want to tell him about what happens when the state fails in its obligation to seek justice. I want to explain that grievances, and the festering anger that accompanies them, don't vanish because a jury fails to convict. Now I'll never have the chance.

I slip into a pair of latex gloves, the kind Charles routinely donned when he cared for Joyce, then turn off the lamp and settle back to wait. I'm not going to move until the Valium takes full effect. The wait doesn't bother me all that much. I finish my drink, taking my time, and watch Charles until he becomes entirely immobile. He doesn't stop breathing, though, which is just as well.

When I'm finally satisfied, I rise and walk around the coffee table to the couch where

Charles waits. I lift an arm, let it drop. I might as well be dealing with a stuffed animal. Time to get moving.

I make my way to a guest room with a full bath at the rear of the house, rooms I first discovered when the house was searched. The shade across the only window in the bathroom is drawn and the room is very dark. Only the silvery figures on the wallpaper, mermaids and dolphins, glow faintly. I give it a minute, waiting for my eyes to adjust, then fill the tub before returning to Charles in the living room. I'm thinking I could leave now. I'm thinking that I'm about to cross a line that can't be re-crossed. I look down at my arm in the sling, remembering Dr Berthold's warning about unrealistic expectations, remembering how Charles and Max played me for a fool, remembering my visit to the witness stand and the testimony I was forced to give. I wonder which had the greater effect, the injury or the disrespect. But it comes to the same thing. Charles and Max fucked me over and they're not getting away with it. The hatred I felt when I confronted Leonid, when I killed him, hasn't been consigned to the region of my unconscious that deals with past events. It's merely grown colder.

I drop to my knees and grab the front of Charles's shirt with my good hand. This is what I've been training for, but I know it won't be easy. If I make a mistake, if I should, for instance, drop Charles and break some piece of furniture, I'll have to abandon ship. I yank Charles off the couch, far enough for his head to drop across my right shoulder. Then I inch him forward, until his head hangs almost to my waist, and encircle his upper thighs with my one good arm. This is called a fireman's carry and it's the easiest way to support an unconscious human being. Or it will be if I can get to my feet. I take a moment to find my balance, bringing Charles closer to my neck. In the best of worlds, I'd have a left arm and I'd use it to add a little thrust. As it is, I'm completely dependent on my legs.

Well, that's why I spent all those hours in the gym, working my bad leg. It's why I dumped the little pain pills and stopped drifting. It's why I don't hate Leonid Berevski, or even blame him for shooting me. Leonid did time, in Russia and in the USA. He knew exactly why Lenny Shaw arrested his daughter, as he knew he couldn't go to the state for justice.

I smile as I imagine an attempt to reason with Leonid Berevski: *I never meant for your daughter to die. How could I have known there'd be a jailhouse riot? The consequences were unintended!*

Charles and Max didn't intend the deaths of Leonid or Anna, or the political destruction of Deputy Gold, or Davy's broken rib or my ruined arm. But I don't give a shit, any more than Leonid gave a shit. I rise in one smooth motion. Either I'm stronger than I thought or Charles is lighter. The short walk to the bathroom at the rear of the house presents no problems and I find myself standing at the foot of the bathtub less than a minute later.

I squat down, almost losing my balance in the process. I can't drop Charles. If water splashes over the edge of the tub and I track it through the house, investigators will know that Charles had company. Beyond that, any sign of physical injury will arouse the suspicions of the death investigator who examines the scene or the pathologist who performs the autopsy.

I hook the back of Charles's knees over the edge of the tub, then lower him slowly, my hand wrapped in the top of his shirt, until he slides beneath the water. It's not until his head becomes submerged that I notice that his eyes are open.

Doctors like to use Valium or one of its many clones to relax patients undergoing procedures like colonoscopy. That's because patients on Valium are able to respond to questions and follow directions. But the dose I fed Charles is far higher than any used for medical reasons. My guess is that his eyes are open because he's lost the strength to hold them shut, like the eyes of the dead are commonly open.

A minute goes by without Charles drawing a breath. I need him to breathe because I want the autopsy to reveal water in his lungs, a guarantee that he was alive when he got into the tub. I'm almost rooting for him to breathe. C'mon, Charles, give it the old college try. Finally, a stream of bubbles pours from his nose. They rise to the surface and burst, emitting a series of little pops before the surface of the water calms again.

I turn to leave the room, feeling more or less what I felt when I testified, which is a whole lot of nothing. The sequence of events that brought me to this moment runs back to the beginning of time. Lenny Shaw's just along for the ride. But then Charles moves his right hand.

I watch his hand rise almost to the surface, watch it glide across his chest. I tell myself that I'm observing an unconscious struggle, or as much of a struggle as man immobilized by 100mg of Valium can muster. But, damn, it sure looks like he's waving goodbye.

Back in the living room, I crumple the first two drafts of Charles Hauptman's apology and toss them on the floor. The third I leave face up on the table. Then I take a second vial from my pocket, lever the cap off with my thumb and scatter six blue Valium tablets on the end table next to Charles's empty glass. Finally, I carry my own glass into the kitchen, where I rinse it out and slip it into my pocket. Shortly after I get home, I intend to dispose of the glass, along with all of the clothes I'm wearing. The Office of the Medical Examiner claims its new lab has the capacity to retrieve DNA from a finger-print.

I run into one final piece of luck. I discover three sets of house keys in the single drawer of a small table next to the door. I use one of them to lock the door behind me on my way out. I'm not really worried about someone noticing that the keys are missing. No plan, no matter how elaborate, is without risks. For example, if somebody spots me now, I'll have a lot of explaining to do. Thus my instinct, driven by an unexpected surge of adrenaline, is to get out of Dodge as fast as my little feet can carry me. I don't run, though. I saunter, instead, parading down the sidewalk as if I owned it.

Thirty-Three

I'm sitting in my car on East 78th Street, just west of Park Avenue and the Ashley. I'm keeping an eye on the front and garage entrances to the building. Five grueling months have passed and today is the first anniversary of Joyce Hauptman's death. But that's strictly a matter of coincidence. This isn't the first time I parked alongside this particular fire hydrant and it won't be the last.

A week after Charles Hauptman's death, I entered the Hospital for Special Surgery where I had my shoulder replaced. The surgery went, according to Dr Berthold, 'as well as can be expected given the damage to your shoulder'. The rehabilitation has also gone 'as well as can be expected', this time according to my physical therapist Inez Aguillera, who still meets with me from time to time. Inez has the instincts of a malignant narcissist, her smile widening in direct proportion to the pain she inflicts.

Still, I can't be too hard on Inez. The workouts she pushed on me have had positive results. I haven't needed a sling for months and my shoulder, when I'm not working out, is only painful enough to remind me not to push too hard. I can use my wrists and elbows freely, and little jobs, like buttoning a shirt, are no longer a problem. But the muscles in my arm were atrophied after months in a sling and I haven't come close to regaining my full strength. Nor have I recovered full mobility. I can touch my left hand to my chin, but not to the top of my head. I can touch the right side of my chest, but not my right shoulder.

Davy and I have set up shop. The delay, as it turned out, was fortunate. The real-estate crisis in New York is still ongoing. With vacant office space running into the millions of square feet, commercial rents have come way down. Not only are we located on Queens Boulevard, in a building famous for its law firms, we have separate offices and a small reception area. Perhaps, if we work really hard, we'll be able to afford a receptionist one day.

Not that we're entirely without business. Most criminal-defense lawyers in New York spent their formative years in the district attorney's office, prosecuting the same criminal types they now defend, but for a lot less money. Davy and I have been around for a long time. As cops, we worked with these lawyers when they were new to the job. Those ties and my fading celebrity resulted in productive interviews with several firms. We're not getting rich, but rich was never the point.

I can't say the work is fun, or even challenging. It's much like police work, a matter of burning shoe leather and running your mouth, except there's no payoff at the end. We don't handcuff the bad guy and lead him to jail. We report back to a lawyer, our client, instead. Last week, I spent three nights trying to confirm an alibi offered by an accused armed robber named Ahmed Rasavari. According to Rasavari, he and a pal were in a Manhattan nightclub when the crime occurred. The pal, unfortunately, has spent six of the last ten years in prison and will not make an impressive witness.

I did my job. I spoke to the bartenders, the bouncers and a dozen patrons who were in the bar on the night in question. I showed Ahmed's picture to each of them, the pal's picture as well, and I reviewed footage taken by three different security cameras. If defendant and pal were in the club, they must have been invisible.

Our client, Morris Gordon, took the news philosophically. Like all criminal-defense lawyers, the last thing he expects from his own clients is the truth.

'I'm gonna teach this prick a lesson,' he told me. 'I'm gonna personally write an invoice that covers every minute you spent at that club and I'm gonna personally present it to him. I'm gonna teach him that bullshitting me comes with a price. He doesn't wanna pay up, he can find another lawyer.'

It's one o'clock in the afternoon and the city is covered by a dense fog. The sidewalks are busy, as usual, but the city's frenetic energy is obscured by the mist. Water drips from the street signs and the traffic lights and the Ashley's long green canopy. There's a black man, a panhandler, beneath the canopy. His clothes are filthy and he's leaning on a rusted shopping cart heaped with his possessions.

As I watch, the doorman, my old pal, Ben, emerges. I can't hear what he says, but the black man's response is loud enough to be heard in Brooklyn.

'This here is a public sidewalk. You and all these Park Avenue bitches got no more right to the sidewalk than me. Now fuck off, fore I lose my temper.'

Ben's no fool. He's supposed to keep the front clear of trash, human or otherwise, but there's no arguing with this man. Plus, Ben's the older and the smaller of the two, and I suspect the less aggressive. He says something and drops a bill in the beggar's cup. The man looks down at the bill, then nods once and heads off into the mist, pushing his shopping cart before him. His gait is slow, almost shuffling, his rage of a moment before entirely manufactured. Or so I decide as I bite into a jelly donut.

Charles Hauptman's body was discovered at ten o'clock on the morning after his death. Steve Park called me within hours. He wanted to know if I had any comment. I didn't. Three days later, Steve called again.

'There was a note,' he told me.

'A suicide note?'

'No, more like an apology.'

'An apology? For what?'

'For you and your partner, for Leonid and his

daughter, even for Jennifer Gold. The note was handwritten.' Steve paused there, but I didn't respond. 'The way I heard it, there were two early drafts found on the floor.'

'OK.'

'Ya know, Lenny, you're being awful tight-lipped here.'

'Tight-lipped? More like I don't give a shit. Charles is behind me. My life as a cop, too. I've got surgery in my immediate future, and I'm talkin' three days from now. You ever have surgery, Steve? Me, I've been through it twice and I can tell ya, the prospect of having your shoulder sliced open concentrates the mind.'

Why do suspects talk to cops after they've been informed of their right to remain silent? One reason, among many, is that they want to know what the cops know. How much evidence do the cops have? Were there witnesses to the crime? A surveillance camera, fingerprints, DNA? As a general rule, the more willing a suspect to talk, the more likely that he or she is guilty.

I didn't make that mistake. I didn't phone my contacts, either on the job or in the ME's office, to check on the progress of the investigation. To do so would be evidence of a guilty mind and I didn't feel guilty. Like I told Steve, dead or alive, Charles Hauptman was in my rear-view mirror. Not Max Baum, though. Baum is in my headlights.

Park called me one last time after the medical examiner, despite the presence of Valium in Charles Hauptman's blood, ruled the manner of

325

his death a suicide. By then, I was well into rehab and I still had no comment to make. Davy presented a different problem. Given the parallels between Charles's and Lola's deaths, I expected him to ask a few probing questions. But his attitude was solicitous. I was his partner, in the past and the future, and I needed his post-surgical support. As for Charles, Davy made only a single comment.

'It couldn't have happened to a nicer guy.'

I've been seeing Marie Burke again. She came to visit me in the hospital and one thing led to another. I've met her kids, too, Irene and Teddy. Teddy's eleven years old, a star on his Little League baseball team, the Ridgewood Lumberyard Cougars. His nickname is T-Burke and he's a Mets fan. We've gone to a couple of games together, a bonding experience that set me back several hundred dollars.

Teddy needs a father bad enough to welcome a half-crippled ex-cop into his life. Not so Irene, who eyes me suspiciously whenever I show up. I'm not particularly surprised. A year after my father died, Mom had a brief fling with a widowed neighbor, Nick Moran. My ensuing resentment came as a shock. I could barely stand to be in the same room with the guy. Meanwhile, Nick was a decent man, not to mention financially independent, and he treated my mother well.

I was still dealing with my reaction when Nick disappeared, so Irene's little tantrums (she's all of seven years old) don't upset me. Also, in common with most cops, or even ex-cops, I've grown a thick skin. I don't expect people to like me. I don't need people to like me. That's why I don't suck up to Irene, why I don't try to bribe her with gifts. My attitude is simple: here I am, ready or not.

My relationship with Marie is more complicated. She's been living independently for a long time, almost as long as Lenny Shaw. Sharing doesn't come naturally to either of us. But the sex is good and we don't crowd each other. Nor do I display my need for a new anchor, not to mention a new identity. I'm no longer a cop – the tribal identity familiar to every cop is lost to me – but I'm not anything else, either.

I can't see the Ashley's garage door from where I sit. One floor down, the door is situated at the lower end of short, steep driveway. But I do recognize the black Mercedes that glides up the driveway. Max Baum is on the move.

As I've already said, I've managed to evade the suspicions of Steve Park, Davy and the NYPD. Not Max, though. Max knows better. When he leaves his apartment, he doesn't use the Ashley's front door. He exits through the garage, already in his car, his exact position shielded by the vehicle's darkened windows. And while there's no convenient garage at Baum Capitol Management, throughout the short walk, from the Mercedes to the townhouse, Max is carefully attended by his new chauffeur. The chauffeur isn't particularly big or threatening, just hyper-alert. His head never stops moving and he stays close enough to Max's person to be a jealous lover.

I watch the Mercedes turn east on the one-way street, glide the length of the block, finally turn right on Lexington Avenue. I don't follow. There's no point, as there's no real point to my being here. I'm not going to assassinate Max on the streets of New York. And I seriously doubt that he'd open his apartment door to me, even if I managed to bypass the doorman. A real opportunity won't come for months, not until next summer, when Max vacations at his East Hampton home on Long Island's Gold Coast. I discovered the home while visiting a blog devoted to Max. BaumJustice.net first went up in the midst of the hate-Max campaign foisted on the American people by Howie Mankel. Its many contributors are convinced that Max killed his wife as well as his daughter. They're vowing not to give up their crusade until Max is arrested, convicted and transported to some hell-hole of a prison, there to spend the remainder of his life.

The bloggers at BaumJustice have uncovered many things, some damning, most trivial. Among the damning facts, Baum Capitol Management is heavily invested in 'extractive' industries located throughout the world, including Sudan and Burma. Coal, oil, timber, iron, bauxite, tin ... the list goes on and on. I don't know how BaumJustice uncovered this information, or even if they've got their facts straight. I don't care, either. But the trivia did catch my attention, especially a list of Max's vacation homes. In addition to his apartment at the Ashley, estimated to be worth $20,000,000, Max owns property in Colorado, the Côte d'Azur on the French Riviera, London and East Hampton, Long Island.

I drove out to East Hampton, to Max's fifteen-room house, one afternoon when he wasn't there. Low and sprawling, Max's home is located on a spit of land jutting into the Atlantic Ocean. A beautiful spot, what with the rolling dunes and the swaying reeds and the booming surf. Private, too, a big plus for status-hungry millionaires. Not that Max is nouveau riche. While the house is fairly new, the property has been in the family for more than fifty years.

At 96th Street, I make my way east to the FDR Drive. I'm heading for the office where I've agreed to handle the phones while Davy searches for a defense witness with cold feet. Later on, I have a date with Teddy Burke. We're going to watch a baseball playoff game. The Mets didn't make it into the post-season, as usual, but Teddy's following the action anyway. He's rooting against the Mets' hated rivals, the Philadelphia Phillies.

I'm not a baseball fanatic and I don't care about the Phillies. But Teddy has school tomorrow and he'll be sent to bed as soon as the game ends. Assuming he doesn't fall asleep on the couch. After that, hopefully, Marie and I will make love for the first time in a week. I won't stay the night, though. We haven't yet reached that stage. Not that I'm particularly anxious to set up housekeeping. No, the way I see it, I've got all the time in the world.